The Miracle of Mrs. Claus

O. L. Gregory

D1472978

DEDICATION

For **Daniel** and **Julianna**,
Never lose the magic, no matter where your lives take you.
A little believing can carry you an exceptionally long way.

CONTENTS

1	North Pole Crisis	1
2	Preparations	9
3	Operation Save Santa	14
4	Santa Ensuite	18
5	Call Me Joy	25
6	A Little Something	34
7	What Are We Going to Do?	38
8	The Problem at Hand	43
9	She Just Can't Help Herself	50
10	Can They Really Do This?	66
11	The Truth, the Full Truth	79
12	Sure, You Can	85
13	Slow Going	92
14	Announcement	98
15	The Last Week Down South	106
16	Busy Week	120
17	What the Hell Was That?	129
18	Call It Off	135
19	Joy Sent Me	141
20	Benjamin From OT	147
21	Christmas Eve	158

22	Midnight in DC	166
23	Merry Christmas	172
24	The Gift	183
Epilogue	Two Years, Minus a Day and a Half, Later…	190

1 NORTH POLE CRISIS

Gasps of surprise and frowns of worry flitted around North Pole Village on a frosty November afternoon, when Santa, arriving back from a research trip, could not be spotted piloting the sleigh as it flew overhead in the twilight, towards the barn.

One by one, elves previously bustling along the pathways saw other elves pointing to the sky. Gazes lifted as they each forgot their tasks. Shocked, they had no idea what to make of the sight. The reindeer would never leave their driver behind. Four would have been left behind to stand guard, if Santa could not get into the sleigh, while the other four flew back for help.

Realization began to come over them. An empty sleigh and all eight reindeer could only mean one thing…

Elves, drawn from their homes by the sudden, stunned silence of the village, joined others as they started running for the barn, as the unmanned sleigh circled and came in for the final descent.

A little rougher of a landing than usual, the reindeer slowed and hit their mark, just as they'd been trained and trusted to do. Their part of the job over, they halted, waiting for the elves around them to take over.

Elves drew closer and peered over the sidewall of the sleigh to find Santa lying across the front bench seat, unconscious, with boxes full of electronic gaming technology sitting in the back.

In short order the director of health was summoned, a stretcher was carried out for transport, and water brought to the reindeer. Three elves then took off in search of Mrs. Claus.

"He's had a heart attack Mrs. C." Claude, the elf in charge of the Sniffles Ward, or the Elven Health Building, informed the waiting room full of worried souls.

"A heart attack?" Mrs. Claus asked. "How could he have had a heart attack? Doesn't the magic protect him anymore?"

"Only inside the North Pole. Every time he leaves, his human frailties grow that much closer to catching up with him."

"Oh," she fretted, looking down the hall towards the room her husband lay in, "and instead of once a year, he's been taking trips to learn more and more about computers and such, so our elves can learn to make them. But, still, he's here now. Can't the magic save him?"

Claude shook his head. "The magic can speed healing that would happen naturally, but it can't repair the damage done to his heart. He's going to need surgical intervention. As it is, I had to google which meds I needed to begin treatment with so I could stabilize him. I'm afraid he's beyond my medical knowledge of humans. He needs a skilled surgeon and the proper equipment."

Mrs. Claus wrung her hands. "Why couldn't this have happened before takeoff? We should have trained the reindeer to head for a hospital if Santa lost consciousness."

"You know it's for his own safety that the reindeer are trained to come ho⬛⬛⬛⬛⬛⬛r found him wouldn't have believed he wa⬛⬛⬛⬛⬛⬛ave stolen the technology, freed the rei⬛⬛⬛⬛⬛ an ambulance before fleeing the scene. An⬛⬛⬛⬛⬛g him wouldn't have known what to do wit⬛⬛⬛⬛his differences."

⬛⬛⬛r mind searched for the solution. "Is he sta⬛⬛⬛

⬛⬛ut to transport him, I'm afraid the sleigh jus⬛⬛⬛dical equipment on hand, because I fear his⬛⬛⬛ve a vehicle like that."

⬛⬛tant look down the hall and nodded. "You'd best get back to him and keep him as stable as you can, for as long as you can, while I go call in some favors."

Claude nodded. "Let me know where he's going as soon as you know. I'll track down the number so I can send scans and find out if I need to tweak meds for him."

Mrs. Claus nodded and forced herself to leave the building and head for their home. She knew once she laid eyes on her husband all logic in her mind would flee her and she wouldn't be able to make the arrangements she knew he now needed her to make.

Opening her front door and stepping inside, she pulled out her phone. For the first time she was grateful for her husband's insistence that they both be provided with secure cellphones, because she was about to make calls and send texts that would require it. She followed instructions that she'd long ago committed to memory. Opening her contacts list, she hit the emergency button, and it dialed 011-1-202-456-1414.

Thousands of miles south, in a riverside city, in a big white house, a telephone rang. An operator on duty picked up the line, "White House Switchboard."

"Hello," Mrs. Claus said, "I'm afraid I need the party line."

The operator sat up straighter, flummoxed over the possible need for such a request. "Clearance code, please?"

"MRC002."

The operator recognized the identity as she plugged the code into the computer. Permissions associated with the code popped up on her screen. "Yes, ma'am. You should receive a text invite to the party line within a few seconds. Accept the invite and type in what you need. Responses should begin quickly, depending on each member's local time of day. Should you not get what you need, call back in, and I will connect you with the President, directly."

"Thank you, dear."

"Good luck, Mrs. C."

Mrs. Claus disconnected the call, accepted the text invite, and typed her problem and needs into the chat.

Leaders from nearly every country around the world, who participated in the party line, received simultaneous texts. And leader by leader, responses began to come through.

She was offered bits and pieces of aid from a number of countries, but only a couple offered a complete plan to help from start to finish. She wanted to opt for a complete plan, in the hopes of a smoother experience as they transitioned from one phase of the rescue to the next. Weighing her options, she chose the Americans. Santa would be picked up by the military, flown to Walter Reed Medical Center, placed in the President's private suite – where she was welcome to stay by his side – and then be treated by one of the best cardiothoracic surgeons in the world.

Other countries with top-notch cardiothoracic surgeons immediately offered to have their people consult on the case, if needed. A few even offered to fly their best surgeon over to assist, if wanted by the US doctor.

The US President thanked them for their offers and promised to pass the messages to the surgeon who'd oversee the case. After booting Mrs. Claus from the party line, because they had met her needs, the President called her personally.

"Mrs. Claus," the President began, "how are you holding up, really?"

"I was in a little shock, but as long as I know help is coming, I'm fine. What I really need is the name and contact number for the surgeon, so that I may give it to our doctor here, and they can consult on pre-travel meds."

"My secretary will send that information to you momentarily. Were there any other injuries when the sleigh landed? Are the reindeer all right?"

"They're fine. They've been trained to handle unassisted landings."

"Is there a runway for the sleigh?"

"It's minimal. Not much distance is required. You're going to be better off sending in a helicopter."

"That's fine. We have some large helicopters at our disposal. You are, of course, welcome to accompany him in the chopper."

That gave her pause for a moment. "I think I'm going to come separately. With Christmas coming up so quickly, and my potential need for overseeing things here, from time to time, it will be better to have my own transportation. It'll be faster for me, as well."

"With all eight reindeer?"

"Oh, no. The smaller sleigh, with just two reindeer, will be sufficient for my needs. I will need assistance with their care and security, though."

"I'm sure the airmen at Andrews Air Force Base will get a kick out of having them around. If you could forward detailed care instructions for their unique breed, I'll be sure to pass it along."

"You'll receive that soon."

"Very good, anything else?"

"Not that I can think of at the moment."

"Good. Someone will contact you when we have an exact ETA for transport."

"Thank you."

"Good. Talk to you soon," and the President ended the call.

Mrs. Claus dialed Chip's number and detailed her travel plans with the elf in charge of the barn. She requested the list of care instructions for the President, said she'd be down in a bit, and asked him to send a couple of elves to her home, to collect the luggage.

She saw the email from the President's secretary, forwarded it, pocketed her phone, quickly finished packing, then made her way to the Sniffles Ward.

Upon arrival, the awaiting elves cleared a path for her, and she followed the parting until her husband came into sight. She sat on a stool by his bed and picked up his hand to hold, giving it a squeeze.

She turned slightly towards Claude, "He's going to the United States. Walter Reed Medical Center, Dr. Hershey."

"Hershey, as in the candy bar?" Claude asked, holding back a smile.

Mrs. Claus nodded.

"And he went into cardiology?"

The look of irritation she gave him clearly indicated her lack of mood for his banter. "Better that than endocrinology, I suppose. At any rate, I've already sent all his information to you via email. He's expecting your call."

"I'll go make the call now," Claude said, before turning to exit the room.

The doors to the room remained open, but the elves were respectful enough to remain quietly in the hall, affording Mrs. Claus a modicum of privacy with her husband.

She leaned down to his ear. "I called for the party line," she told him.

Santa's breathing seemed to draw more steadily at the sound of her voice.

"I wish it could have been on video-chat," she said. "I could feel a number of them tripping over themselves, to try and offer more help than another, in hopes of being chosen."

He cracked open an eyelid, to stare up at her, too weak to speak, but not so weak that she missed the mix of worry and adoration in his eyes.

"You're going to have to hang in there. Claude says you can't be moved without medical equipment nearby, so you must wait for human transportation, my love. Not to mention the length of the trip to get you down there. I'll follow down with the smaller sleigh—"

He squeezed her hand.

"I need the reindeer to get back and forth quickly. We don't know how long you're going to have to be in human care, and Christmas is coming. I need to be mobile in case I have to occasionally come back here to keep everything on track. I promise, I'll be at the hospital when you get there."

The worry in his gaze only increased when she mentioned the closeness of Christmas and needing to keep everything on track.

She squeezed his hand right back. "You're going to have to trust me to handle some things and trust the elves to do the job they've been doing for centuries. I will make sure all the preparations are taken care of. You just focus on making sure you're still around to do your part, when the time comes, you hear me?"

He gave her hand a quick squeeze of acknowledgement.

She nodded her head. "Good. Now that we have that settled, I'm going to slip away and go over to the barn. I have to make sure they're ready for our guests and that two of the reindeer are fed and prepared for another journey." She leaned over and kissed his forehead. "You don't move. I'll be back shortly."

He released her hand and gave a thumbs up, his eyes having already closed.

With a supreme amount of effort, she found the strength within to step away from his bed and leave his side.

Inside Walter Reed Medical Center, Dr. Jacob Hershey was having a bit of a day. His latest surgery had begun at seven that morning, and he'd run into complications. What was supposed to have been a four-hour surgery stretched to eight. His second surgery of the day had to be bumped to the next day. Phone calls went unanswered and messages unreturned. A friend had picked up lunch for him and put it in his office fridge, for later. He'd just sat down with his cobb salad when his cellphone rang.

Honestly, he'd wanted to ignore it. But the department head couldn't allow himself such luxury when he was no longer wrist-deep in someone's chest cavity.

Stubbornly, he forked the first bite into his mouth before pulling out his phone. He was still chomping down on lettuce when he saw the number on the phone. Chomping turned to vigorous chewing and hurried swallowing when recognition hit. He quickly cleared his throat, hit the button, and put the phone to his ear. "This is Dr. Jacob Hershey."

"Please hold for the President," the caller stated, promptly followed by the click of being placed on hold.

Jacob used the interim to close the lid on his lunch, use a napkin to wipe his mouth, and swish a mouthful of water around before swallowing.

"Dr. Hershey, how are you today?" the President's voice asked.

Jacob sat straighter in his chair. "Still saving stubborn lives, and you?"

"Still trying to save the world from itself."

A hint of a smile crossed over Jacob's mouth, "So, same old, same old."

The President gifted Jacob with a small chuckle. "Say, listen, I have a high-profile patient that I need to send your way."

"It isn't you, is it?"

"No, no. I'm fine."

"You can't blame me for wondering. You usually aren't the one I speak with directly. Is your Secretary of State on vacation?"

"No. Time is too short for me to update somebody else and staff it out. I need to secure your services and get you in contact with the limited care team the patient has."

"Can the patient not get to a hospital?"

"No. A clinic of sorts is the best they have."

"Is this a military member? Or a leader of a terrorist organization? Or someone out on vacation in the middle of nowhere?"

"No. Why?"

"Well, what high-profile patient are you sending me that can't get to proper medical attention?"

"Santa Claus."

That drew Jacob up short. "…I'm sorry, who?"

The President sighed in Jacob's ear. "The patient is Santa Claus."

Jacob suddenly became aware that this was a moment that was going to remain forever etched into his memory. "Is this a drill?"

"No."

"A prank?"

"Afraid not."

"I'm being watched on some sort of hidden camera, for a television show, right?"

"Dr. Hershey, I know this may be hard for you to believe, but you have drilled for this."

"Sir, with all due respect, because of this hospital's relationship with you, we've had to drill for nearly every conceivable possibility. That doesn't mean I expect the most fantastical and mythological of them all to happen."

"Okay, I'm just going to give it to you straight. And even if you still aren't ready to believe, I need you to pretend that it's real and play along. Ready?"

Jacob closed his eyes, let out a breath, and cleared his mind, "Go."

"The patient had a heart attack in mid-flight and lost consciousness. There's no way to tell how long he was out for. He was still alive upon arrival and was transported to a nearby clinic that only has meds to stabilize him for transport. They have no facilities capable of repairing the damage. You should be receiving an email with the known stats at the time of the call for medical assistance."

"May I switch you to speaker while I take a look at the stats?"

"As long as you are alone in a room with the door closed."

"Yes, Sir." Jacob hit the speaker button, opened his email notification, and began evaluating. "I'm encouraged that they have the proper meds."

"A handful of countries take turns updating the meds they have on hand just in case something like this ever happened. Now, can you tell from the information provided whether he can be saved?"

"Well... If we're still saying that this is Santa Claus, then your guess is as good as mine. He'd be several centuries old. I have no way of knowing what that heart tissue is like. But, if he's a normal human being, then yes. I'd say this is survivable with surgery. The quicker the surgery happens, the better. How long until we can get him here?"

"I can send in a rescue chopper from Alaska to go get him, fly him to Greenland, and put him on a plane to you."

"No. He doesn't have that kind of time. And frankly, diving deeper into this being a centuries old, mythological being, I would feel a bit out of my depth. I'd want to see him, prior to flight, and oversee his care on the flight. I need time to familiarize myself with any differences he may have in comparison to us. I might even be able to run a few tests in their air, if we're talking about a stocked medical chopper. But, again, you're pushing your luck on what a body can tolerate."

"We can't lose him. That cannot become our reputation for rescue missions. This is one mission of mercy that we must come through on."

"Then you either have to transport all needed equipment to this clinic to do the surgery, or you'd better figure out how he manages to travel so fast on Christmas Eve and replicate it."

The President's sigh was long. "Let me see what I can do."

Jacob looked at the phone in his hand, took it off speaker, and put it back to his ear. "You're serious, aren't you."

"Dr. Hershey," the President said, trying to choose his words, "Just get ready to fly."

The call ended and Jacob drew his phone away from his ear. All he could do was stare at the device, while his brain ran through one scenario after another.

2 PREPARATIONS

Mrs. Claus bustled through the village, stopping to talk to no one. Onlookers who'd kept their distance began to realize how serious the situation truly was, merely from the look on her face.

She entered the barn, drawing the full attention of the elves inside, as well as the reindeer. She came to stand in the center, and taking in a breath she declared, "The Americans are coming!"

"The smaller sleigh is all prepared, Mrs. Claus," Chip, the elf in charge of the barn told her. "Your bags have been loaded, as well. Which two reindeer were you thinking of taking?"

"Whichever ones are the least exhausted."

"I think they're all willing."

She let out a little sigh, "I'll go talk to them."

"Very well, Ma'am."

Mrs. Claus moved from the sleigh room to the stables. "How are my lovelies doing tonight?" she asked.

All eight reindeer looked up from their troughs and stepped toward her.

"I have a big job ahead of me, and I need some help. I need two of you to go with me. Santa is gravely sick. He's being taken to the United States, to Walter Reed, in Washington DC, where they have human doctors who can help him. I need two of you to fly me back and forth, as needed. Whichever two go, you'll both be staying at the American Air Force base nearby."

Prancer put her head down.

"That's fine, Prancer. I know you don't like being around so many large airplanes." She continued to address the other seven. "While I can insist the two of you are kept together at all times, I can't promise to see you every day. Santa will be my primary focus. He's very ill."

Blitzen side-stepped and looked to the others.

"I know, Blitzen, you like what you're familiar with and I'm telling you that there won't be anything familiar except for your partner. You can stay... What I don't know is how long this will go on for. But I can swap reindeer if anyone wants to, when I come up to check on things. So, if you want to stay and rest this time, maybe you can go next time."

Dasher and Dancer shared a look, and both took a step back.

Mrs. Claus nodded. "You two had the lead and had to navigate home on your own. It's very mentally taxing, I'm sure you both need sleep." She looked at the four, remaining reindeer. "Are any of you particularly antsy to hit the skies?"

Vixen walked up to her and carefully nudged her hand.

Mrs. Claus smiled. No one ever seemed to pick Vixen for anything, but she was the absolute sweetest animal to ever exist, which was why Vixen was her unspoken favorite. "You absolutely may come," she murmured. Then she looked over the remaining three. "Donner, you're still nursing that right, front hoof. You're staying. And Comet, you and Vixen don't always get along. I think Cupid would be the better partner for her."

Donner let out a sigh and went back to eating. Comet looked mildly insulted, and Cupid looked to be smiling.

Truth be told, Vixen and Cupid were the two who were never chosen when her husband was in charge. There was nothing wrong with them, mind you, it's just that their personalities were more her speed, and less his. For her, though, she couldn't think of a better pairing.

Mrs. Claus' phone beeped in her pocket with a text notification. She reached inside to retrieve it, finding the text to be from the US President.

'In an effort to expedite patient retrieval, the Coast Guard is requesting assistance with speed. In addition, the cardiothoracic surgeon would prefer to evaluate the patient personally, before extraction takes place, given the limited nature of care the patient has been able to receive.'

It took an extreme act of discipline for Mrs. Claus not to roll her eyes in agitation. She understood the what-and-why of the request, she just didn't know why he couldn't just say it plain. After all, she was familiar with every language of the world. Every slang reference, every colloquialism. She even understood the political need for propriety in international incidents, but no one was talking about a country here. This was simply the North Pole. If a country was ever naughty towards them, they were simply removed from the nice list. That action seemed to put a government back in its polite place, after they have to listen to their people complain about it for a year.

She had to shake off her annoyance. She wasn't upset over his political correctness. She was upset that he was asking her to put more distance between herself and Santa. She'd assumed that they'd send a chopper up from an Alaskan base. But to know they were coming from DC? She wasn't willing to let Santa go without skilled help for that many additional hours. She wanted to be mad at the doctor for his insistence on coming here. She wanted to bitterly think the worst of him, to believe he was just using his position to gain entrance to a place so few get to see. But then she had to push those thoughts away, she'd never be able to trust him otherwise. He simply wanted to check on the case and see for himself the kind of care his new patient had been receiving before coming to him. She told herself the man was simply being thorough, given the circumstances.

She took a deep, calming breath. *Hospital or Air Force Base?* she typed.

Hospital roof. The doctor is already there, gathering supplies.

Fifteen minutes.

They'll be ready.

Mrs. Claus pocketed her phone and turned back to Chip, "Let's get Vixen and Cupid hooked up to the sleigh. I have to go fetch the help."

Elves, standing on the sidelines since Santa's arrival, just waiting for the opportunity to do something – anything – that might be of some help, moved forward as Vixen and Cupid quickly moved into position.

Mrs. Claus felt as though she were holding her breath, until she finally took her seat in the sleigh and felt the weight of the reins laying across her hands.

"Now," Toot, the head of sleigh maintenance told her. "You have to remember that the magic is imbued in the sleigh. You'll have to pace yourself in time with their aircraft, which will be tricky with you in the lead. If you lose them in the Confetti Tunnel, and it closes behind you, there's no telling where they'll end up."

Mrs. Clause nodded.

Toot turned for the barn entrance, "We'll get the runway lit up for—"

The snap of leather rang out. "Dash away!" Mrs. Claus yelled.

Vixen and Cupid took off at a perfectly synchronized run, gathering speed as they pulled the sleigh through the doorway, onto the dark runway. The trio took to the sky, quickly disappearing from sight.

Dr. Jacob Hershey fairly buzzed down the hall as he made his way to gather surgical supplies. "Stephanie!" he called out, spotting her at the far end. "Got a few minutes? I need an extra set of hands."

Her gaze shifted to him, taking in his change in outfit and the fairly frazzled look in his eyes. She nodded, coming to a stop and waiting for him to get to her, before falling into step beside him. "You're wearing a flight suit. Is that military chopper that just landed here for you?"

"Yes. And I trust them to have general medical supplies, but I need cardiac surgical tools, if I have to crack him open before I can get him here."

"Okay, what about meds?"

"I already sent Danielle off to get them."

"Okay… is the person not in a medical facility? Are they landing you in the field?"

"It's an inadequate facility."

She lowered her voice, "Is it the President?"

"No. But I've already spoken to him twice in the last ten minutes."

"Who the hell is it?"

"Someone that I cannot lose." They'd reached the door to the surgical supply room. He reached out for the doorknob and paused long enough to look at her. "I cannot be the surgeon that loses him." He turned the knob and refocused on his task.

"Who the hell is he?" she asked, following him into the room. "If you're going to put him on my caseload after surgery, you may as well just tell me now."

Jared sighed hard before looking to meet her eyes. "Santa Claus."

Stephanie's head tiled, "Is that a codename?"

"I'm told, no."

So many emotions stirred within her. Disbelief for starters. Anxiety that it might be true. Giddiness over the idea of getting to treat him. Wonderment over who might accompany him here… And then dread settled in as her hand wrapped around and picked up a Finochietto retractor and then a Surtex. She looked over at Jacob with nothing but sympathy for the pressure he must be feeling.

Silently, she handed him the rib spreader and shears.

Mrs. Claus made quick work of opening the Confetti Tunnel and headed for Washington DC in record time. She didn't have a radio to contact local flight controllers, as the sleigh avoided typical flight paths. Besides, the sleigh typically moved through an area so fast it normally didn't register so much as a blip on radars. But in this moment, she was moving at a more normal pace, and she didn't want to be seen as a UFO this time. Once in DC skies, she activated the transponder, so she'd be identified properly on military radar, and proceeded to the hospital.

The Coast Guard rescue chopper and the entire team were waiting for her on the roof when she landed.

Dr. Hershey was wide-eyed and open-mouthed. In theory, he'd always known this was a possibility. The hospital did hold drills for such an occurrence. But to see her, to see a sleigh and two of the reindeer, right before his eyes… He was already forever changed. Life would never be the same after tonight.

Mrs. Claus pulled the sleigh up to the grouping, so she didn't have to waste time getting out of the sleigh to be heard. "Dr. Hershey," she said, "I'd prefer for you to ride with me. In case I lose the chopper in the Confetti Tunnel, I can get you to Santa before going back and fetching the military team."

"Lose them in the what?" he stammered.

"The Confetti Tunnel. It's a portal, almost like a worm hole. It's what allows Santa to travel as fast as he needs to on Christmas Eve. The elves like to call it the Confetti Tunnel because it shimmers a bit."

All he could do was nod.

"Excellent. Climb up and get settled," she told him, before turning to the Coast Guardsmen and pointing to the chopper. "How fast does this bird fly?"

3 OPERATION SAVE SANTA

"Turn on the beacon! Light the runway!" Elvin, the head of flight security, called out.

A beam of light shot straight up into the sky, as the edges of the runway lit up in the dark.

"It's a helicopter," Toot, head of sleigh maintenance, deadpanned.

"It's not like they know the area, and we don't have a helipad. The beacon light will guide them to our exact location and the runway will show them where they can land."

"Not if you don't drop the shield. The chopper will bounce right off, and they won't know why."

Elvin scanned the sky and then his control panel before cringing and moving for the lever at the edge of the panel and pulling it down. In his defense, the sleigh could fly right through it, and it had been years since they'd needed to drop the defense. Elvin went back to his position, overlooking the runway.

Toot just stared at him and waited.

Elvin could feel his stare and muttered, "Thank you."

Toot nodded, "You're welcome."

Within moments the elf sitting at the radar called out, "Two aircraft, inbound!"

Elves from all over the village were aware of the direness of the situation, and all came outside at the sound and lights of the chopper flying overhead, drowning out the familiar sound of the bells on the sleigh.

Mrs. Claus and the reindeer landed on the runway, coming to a halt in the barn, so Vixen and Cupid could drink and eat to refuel.

The chopper landed just outside, men disembarking as soon as the rails touched land.

"Come," Chip stepped forward to look at the doctor and directed, "I'll take you straight over to the Sniffles Ward."

Mrs. Claus leaned over to Dr. Hershey's ear and whispered, "The Elven Sick Ward."

Dr. Hershey nodded in stupefaction as he climbed out. On the walk over to the ward, his legs carried him along on autopilot, as he gawked at all the sights he was seeing.

They made it outside just as the rescue team was unloading the gurney they sought to transport Santa on. The head of the rescue team rushed to catch up with them, to eavesdrop and lead his group as they headed for the ward, while a couple of others set about with preparations for both the rescue setup inside the craft and the coming flight back to the states.

Every single Guardsmen maintained a professional, military façade. And yet, you could tell they were gawking through their peripherals.

"This is Claude," Mrs. Claus introduced as soon as they entered the Sniffles Ward. "You spoke to him on the phone. Claude, this is Dr. Hershey."

Claude, who'd come to the lobby to meet them nodded and extended his hand to the doctor, in what he knew to be a friendly American greeting. He shook the doctor's hand as he gave a nod to the Guardsman Rescue Swimmer.

Claude turned, to lead them down the hall. "He remains critical, but he is maintaining stability."

Dr. Hershey couldn't help the stupid grin that slashed across his face. *He'd just touched an elf! A real, live elf.*

"Here," the rescue swimmer said, handing a bag to Claude. "This should replace the meds you've used tonight, with some additional medications for future use, just in case."

Claude nodded his thanks as he accepted the package. The evening had proved very humbling for the elf. He was used to being the one giving assistance around here. He was seldom on the receiving end of it. He had to clear his throat to help him refocus on the crisis at hand.

As Claude rattled off the latest round of vitals, Dr. Hershey started coming out of his own sensory stupor. He began to feel more like himself again, his professional self. He was here for a very specific reason, to evaluate the patient for transport and oversee his care while in transit.

They entered the patient's room, where silence was broken only by the sounds of the medical equipment around them.

Dr. Hershey's eyes immediately went to the monitors for a quick sweep of stats. Then he moved to touch each IV bag, to make sure they were the meds they should be. It wasn't that he didn't trust Claude to have followed his instructions. It was that Claude had admitted to him that he was out of his depth with the case, and limited on available meds.

Dr. Hershey had served in third-world countries, and simply had the habit of double-checking the treatment underway, to see if he needed any particular med fetched from the supplies he'd brought. Finding that everything was as it should be, given the circumstances, he then turned his attention to the patient, to make sure he was accepting and responding to the treatment as expected.

As his gaze landed on the man on the gurney, Dr. Hershey's eyes began to unexpectedly well up with tears. He moved forward, his hand coming to rest on the patient's forearm.

The old man's blue eyes opened and made contact with the doctor's.

From somewhere, deep inside Dr. Hershey's mind, the remnants of the little boy he used to be bubbled to the forefront as he stared at a hero. "Santa," he whispered with reverence.

Santa mouthed something, but the oxygen mask, along with his weakness, made him impossible to hear.

Mrs. Claus stepped forward. "He said, Jacob Hershey, always on the nice list."

Dr. Hershey wiped tears from his eyes.

"What do you think, doc," the Guardsman asked. "We brought the chopper because of the lack of length on the runway. Can he handle the tunnel, so we can get him there faster, or do we go the human way and take it slow? And taking it slow requires landing in Greenland and transferring to a plane that can travel faster and farther."

Dr. Hershey cleared his throat, took one more look at the monitors and said, "If this were anyone else, I'd say the slow way. But time is not on our side, and his body is used to traveling the tunnel. So, tunnel it is."

The Guardsman nodded. "How soon do you want to move?"

Dr. Hershey looked back down to his patient. "Are you ready to fly?"

Santa lifted an unsteady hand and raised his thumb.

Dr. Hershey nodded and looked to the Guardsman, "Let's move."

The Guardsman moved to the opposite side of the bed and both men prepared for transfer. The Guardsman waved his team forward as he lowered the bed flat and Dr. Hershey unplugged machines. Then, nodding to one another, they rolled Santa toward the rescue swimmer. Dr. Hershey took the backboard from the Guardsman next to him and placed it on the bed, before they rolled Santa onto his back. The rescue swimmer counted down from three as men took their positions, then lifting Santa up from the bed and transferring him to the gurney the last Guardsman edged closer as the men placed him on it. Connections were changed as machinery was swapped out, so that the Sniffles Ward wouldn't be missing any of their limited equipment. Santa was rolled and the backboard was removed. The doctor and rescue swimmer raised the rails on either side of the gurney, and together the team began pushing to move the bed out of the room. Claude followed behind, carrying IV bags.

Mrs. Claus fell into step, creating the end of the procession, not knowing whether to cry because this was really happening, or to breathe a sigh of relief that they finally had Santa on his way to getting real, meaningful help.

Through the village pathways they went, elves lined up on either side, waiting to get a glimpse of Santa, to wish him well on his journey. All wondering if this would be the last time they would ever see him.

All wondering what would become of them if it was.

4 SANTA ENSUITE

They rolled Santa into the Presidential suite not more than a half-hour later. The OR was still being cleaned from the last surgery and would soon be prepped for Santa's.

"I've looked at all the scans Claude sent, Mrs. Claus," Dr. Hershey said, as two nurses bustled about, checking meds, taking vitals, and setting up machinery.

"Please tell me you're doing an angioplasty." She had a fondness for watching medical dramas and had just enough medical knowledge to ask pertinent questions and keep up with most of the jargon. She'd never had reason to use it before, but she was grateful for it now.

Dr. Hershey let out a small breath. "I can't. It's going to be a double bypass."

"Open-heart?"

"Yes, Ma'am."

"Is it really that bad?"

He gentled his expression, "I must look at all the factors. He can't get adequate medical care where you live—"

"But he doesn't age when he's at the North Pole! This happened on the ride back from a research trip. The reindeer knew how to get him home, so when he collapsed on the way, they continued to bring him home."

"Bringing him home to limited medical care is all the more reason to perform the surgery that I know will give him the best results. Ma'am, I'm trusted to care for the hearts of world leaders. I've won many awards. Cardiologists of other world leaders call to consult with me on cases. My experience, my gut instinct, is telling me that a double bypass is the way to go."

She looked at him in silence.

He silently looked back at her.

"Do you understand the ramifications of a twelve-week recovery time?" she asked.

"Better that than the ramifications of the stents not being enough to keep his blood flowing, and some child wakes up to find Santa dead in the living room, still holding the kid's stocking in his hand."

She glanced at the floor before looking back to him. "I was hoping you were going to tell me my knowledge of such things is old and that it no longer takes twelve weeks to recover from this."

"It's six to twelve."

"We only have five."

Dr. Hershey's features became sympathetic, but no less determined. "He's not going to be ready in five."

"Can't you do stents now, and then open-heart after the new year?"

"I'm sorry, did you want him to still be alive, come January?"

She let out a heavy sigh just as orderlies arrived.

"We're going to prep him for surgery now. Once I get him in there, it usually takes three to six hours to complete the procedure, depending on what I find once I get inside. Scans don't always tell the full story."

She stepped a little closer to him and lowered her voice, "His anatomy might be a little... off."

Dr. Hershey straightened as he took in the warning. "I did note a few subtle differences, but nothing too alarming."

"We'd only aged into our fifties before the magic of the North Pole came into our lives, but we've been around a... very long time, unaffected by modern human evolution. Just make sure you're prodding at what you want to be prodding at before you go poking."

He nodded. "All the more reason for me to open him up, so I can actually see it with my own eyes, to know I'm repairing the problem correctly."

She nodded, finally conceding the point.

Within moments the orderlies, trained to remain professional with a high-profile patient, had Santa whisked away, the doctor and nurses exiting with them, leaving her utterly alone.

Before the sudden silence could jumpstart her anxiety, she used a moment to take in her surroundings.

The room was sizeable, with an office area. One could hold small meetings here, if needed. The bathroom was spacious, with many more amenities and toiletry products than she was used to. There was a cot next to the patient bed, and a separate sleeping room for her where she could store her things.

There was also a small kitchenette area. Drinks and snacks filled the fridge and cabinet. She'd also been told that her meals would be complementary and were to arrive with Santa's.

As she looked around at the furnishings and décor, she noted that if not for all the medical equipment surrounding the patient bed, she'd have a hard time discerning the difference between the hospital suite and a very nice hotel room.

There was a brief knock on the opened door, before a young woman entered the room. "Mrs. Claus?"

"Yes, dear," she answered.

"I just wanted to take a moment to introduce myself. I'm Stephanie Bellini. I'm on the VIP team and will be your husband's physical therapist."

"VIP team?"

"Yes. Our Very Important Patient team. We're chosen for our skills and our discretion."

"And is it a requirement for you to be here at this hour of the evening, instead of with your family?"

Stephanie smiled. "At times, yes. But I was putting in time, catching up on paperwork, so I said I'd come up and introduce myself. I would have introduced myself directly to your husband, but I was told he wasn't particularly coherent and that his surgery would last hours. So, I opted to introduce myself to you."

"Perfectly reasonable. And how involved in his care will you be Ms. Bellini?"

"Stephanie, please. Let's have a seat," she said, gesturing to the chairs at the meeting table.

Mrs. Claus moved to sit in a chair and watched as the therapist took hers.

Stephanie laid some pamphlets on the table in front of herself. "Can I assume you read English, as well as speak it?"

"Yes."

"How familiar with the concept of physical therapy are you?"

"We have some use for it, for the elves. Once, I took a tumble and required some therapy for my shoulder. The head of our Sniffles Ward – our health building – consulted the internet for the exercises and stretches I would need. He gave them to his assistant, and she guided me through them. And I do watch television shows. So, I am not without reference."

"And that therapy proved beneficial to you?"

"Yes."

"Excellent. I have pamphlets here that explain our philosophy of physical therapy and the specific types that we'll be using for Mr. Claus' recovery."

"Is this something that can be done at the North Pole?"

Stephanie sighed. "I don't think we'd be comfortable with that. Your elves, they aren't trained in cardiac recovery. It's important that we set Mr. Claus up for the best possible outcome."

20

"And for how long will he need physical therapy?"

"It varies from patient to patient. But, generally, the window is three to four weeks. We'd then probably set him up with an at-home routine, if we can get the patient to agree to do it."

"So, not only can he not take his trip in five weeks, but you're also telling me he can't even be at the North Pole for the final preparations?"

Stephanie gave her a sympathetic half-smile. "It's possible that he'll be there for the last week or two, but he won't be able to really do much to help. And, frankly, the stress of preparations may be too great for him to tolerate."

Mrs. Claus buried her face in her hands, the totality of the situation falling upon her shoulders for the first time since hearing that her husband was ill.

Stephanie grimaced. "I know, it's a lot to take in."

"I'm sorry," Mrs. Claus said, looking up. "It's just that I was so focused on what I needed to do tonight, to get him to proper help, that I wasn't thinking about much of anything past getting him here. I thought he'd get a couple stents and rest at home for a couple of weeks. And I'm just now beginning to understand that his situation is more complicated than I thought it was."

"Neither of you have ever needed medical care before?"

"We don't age while at the North Pole. Diseases can't progress, if they even develop at all. Injuries occur but tend to be fixable or treatable at the Sniffles Ward."

"Diseases can't progress, but injuries can heal?"

"We don't age, yet we live every moment that passes. The magic may be old, but that doesn't mean we understand all of its mechanisms."

"And the elves have fixed all your other injuries?"

"Once, Santa tripped over a curious dog, while making his deliveries. The dog was fine, but Santa knew he was hurt. He suffered through the pain until his deliveries were done, before finding an ER. They x-rayed his arm, found it to be broken, and they casted it. Other than that, yes, they have. Even the reindeer, with only one exception, have always been treated at home without a problem."

"Well, you're welcome to attend any or all sessions. We'll be working with him every day while he's here. And we'll need you to stay in the area so that I can work with him two to three times a week, until he graduates. And it won't just be me. He'll see an occupational therapist and receive some other services, as well. If it will help your medical assistant back home, you can send her digital copies of those pamphlets. I'll even direct her to a few books that will help her better understand the continued therapy he'll do at home, so she can prepare."

Back into her hands went Mrs. Claus' face, fingers pressing against her forehead. "How do I even go about finding a place to stay, here?"

Stephanie's heart went out to the woman. "We do have a social worker assigned to your husband's case. She can help you with that. But I would mention it to the President, when his office calls to check up on how you're both making out. Perhaps he can provide you with a place, just as he's provided you with health care and protection."

"Protection?"

Stephanie nodded. "There are Marine guards present, making sure no unwanted attention makes its way to either you or Santa. We're not sure if word will get out or not, but if it does, no one will be permitted closer than you'd like. The other staff won't even think much of it. They're used to seeing guards around from time to time."

"The shield," she whispered.

"What?"

"The shield around the North Pole that keeps outsiders from seeing us. It doesn't work here. It's one more thing I didn't stop to think about."

Stephanie tried to give her a comforting grin. "I know you have a lot to contend with right now. I'm sorry life is being harsh to the both of you today."

She made wide-eyed eye contact with the therapist. "What are we supposed to do about Christmas? If he can't make the deliveries... What do I do about that?"

Stephanie bit her lip. "I don't know, Ma'am. Maybe the elves can think of something."

"Ma'am?" a military officer asked from the doorway.

"Yes?" Mrs. Claus responded.

"I'm sorry to interrupt."

"It's alright," Stephanie said, standing. "I think we were done, for now."

"Thank you for explaining the process to me," Mrs. Claus told her.

"You're very welcome. I'll be back just as soon as cardio gives me the go-ahead to get started. In the meantime, make sure you take care of yourself. It's stressful on a body to be someplace strange, while worried for your spouse."

Mrs. Claus nodded, and Stephanie took her leave.

"The reindeer," the officer said, when Mrs. Claus' gaze settled on him. "They're still on the roof and we'd like to get them settled at Andrews Air Force Base."

"And you're from Andrews?"

"Yes, Ma'am. I've spoken at length with a... with..."

"Chip?"

"Yes, Ma'am. With Chip. He's given me copious notes about Vixen and Cupid's care. But neither will... lift off? Or be loaded onto a helicopter. I was hoping you could come up to the roof with me and get them moving."

She nodded. "Of course. I think it's easiest if I fly them over and then be given a ride back. But let's move quickly. Santa is in surgery."

"Of course. If you'd like to handle it that way, I'll make the arrangements for your return transportation."

"They're exhausted and just as worried about my husband as I am. They're bound to be less tolerable of strangers. If I escort them, they'll have more confidence they've been taken to a place with people that will care for them."

Within forty-five minutes she'd flown the reindeer over to the Air Force Base, gotten them to go into the small aircraft hangar the men had quickly turned into a makeshift barn, and had them reasonably convinced that they would be in good hands. She'd made arrangements with the caretaker for her to be transported back and forth no less than every other day to visit with them.

Now she stood, back in the Presidential Suite of the hospital, watching an orderly stare at her while trying to set a food tray down on the small dining table.

"I thought I'd arrived after food service hours," she said.

"Oh... Your husband's nurse had me go down and fetch sandwiches we keep on hand, after hours, for patients coming in late or new mothers who didn't finish their labor until late at night." He looked down when he lifted the dome off the plate.

"How hungry do you suppose I am?" she asked, eyeing the multitude of sandwiches on the platter.

"Well, I... I wasn't... I didn't know what you would like. And being in the Presidential Suite, we aim to please."

"I see."

"There are menus here for both of you, for tomorrow. If you'd like to circle your preference of the choices, I can submit them for you."

She nodded and he handed her the papers. She found a pen on a side table, made the selections, and when she turned around to hand the pages back to the orderly, she realized he'd been staring the whole time. She smiled, "Can't believe I truly exist?"

He shook his head. "I grew up Muslim. Santa never visited me. I couldn't ever figure out why it worked that way."

Mrs. Claus nodded in understanding. "That's always seemed so unfair to me, too. The history of that one is long. Bottom line, he was never invited in. He was never believed in by your religion. The explanation is far more cumbersome, but that's the gist."

He nodded. "I'm sorry you weren't believed in."

"I'm sorry you never received a present."

"Can I get you anything else?"
"No. Thank you so much."
"Goodnight, Mrs. Claus."
"Goodnight."

5 CALL ME JOY

"Mrs. Claus?" Dr. Hershey said, coming into the room.

Mrs. Claus looked up from some knitting she'd been doing to pass the time. "Is it finished?"

Dr. Hershey nodded. "It took us a little longer than normal, but the surgery was successful. He's going to be monitored for a little while longer in post-op, but then we'll bring him up here. You'll see a significant increase in the amount of machinery hooked up to him. But it just means we're keeping a very close watch on him, to insure his recovery."

She put her knitting down and stood. "Why did it take longer?"

Dr. Hershey let out a sigh. "We were very careful and tentative in every step. Not knowing how much the magic has and has not affected the flesh, and the flesh itself having existed for so many centuries, made us very cautious. I cannot express to you how very much our team did not want to have a part in Santa's death. We wanted to be the team that saved him, not the team that failed him."

Mrs. Claus nodded her head in understanding. "It must be difficult to always stand on the precipice of being the hero or being the failure. Thank you for being the hero today... or yesterday, now, I suppose. It's well past three in the morning. You must be exhausted."

Dr. Hershey shook his head, trying not to tear up. "Anything for Santa, Mrs. Claus."

"Joy."

His eyes zeroed in on her, "What?"

"My name is Joy. You saved my husband. Call me Joy."

"Joy," he said with a half-chuckle. "That's fitting."

"A bit of a weird coincidence, don't you think?"

"Yeah, actually."

"Did you ever stop and think that maybe the word joy is associated with

Christmas because my name is Joy?"

"You're just out to break my mind, now."

She smiled. "If actually seeing Santa didn't break your mind as you pushed the gurney through the streets of North Pole Village, I think your mind is safe."

"It's certainly been a day I'll never forget. I'll be in a nursing home, somewhere. Grey and half-bald, rambling on about all I've seen today and how I saved Santa, and everyone will think I have dementia and am just babbling."

Joy let out a chuckle. "It'll add variety to all the rambling about treating the President."

He sobered. "You know, this isn't the first time I've worried about the government offing me, if I ever do develop dementia."

Joy started to say something comforting, but then didn't know how to word it and feel confident in speaking truth, so she shut her mouth and just smiled.

"What, no words of wisdom and encouragement?" Jacob's phone buzzed in his pocket. He reached into his pocket and pulled it out, reading the text. "Santa's vitals have remained stable. They're going to move him up here, now."

"Why here and not intensive care?"

"Security and the need to keep a low profile. Intensive care is too public a place for our comfort. This suite is equipped to handle whatever accommodations are necessary."

"Ah. The Presidential Suite, of course."

He nodded as people began to bring in equipment ahead of the patient, everyone smiling and nodding to Joy as they came and went.

Within moments, the hospital bed was wheeled through the doorway and Joy got her first glimpse of Santa, post-op... Post crisis.

Her face fell. He looked so... small. And old. It was eerie.

Jacob took in her expression. "It's perfectly normal," he murmured as the team wheeled Santa into place and finished hooking him up to all the monitors. "You're used to seeing him healthy and full of life. When someone's personality isn't shining through, they can look very different. But Santa, your Santa, he's still in there. He'll slowly return to you, I promise."

She nodded, trying to regain control of her emotions. "How long until he wakes up?"

"He did wake briefly in post-op. But he'll probably sleep through the rest of the night. It's just the remnants of the anesthesia, and all the pain meds."

She watched as the team smiled at her and headed for the door. "Thank you," she called after them.

"Their training for high-profile patients is to not speak unless spoken to, unless they have to impart information."

"Yes, well, it feels strange."

"It's to keep them from ogling the patient and crowding them. Patients come to recover, and we try to respect that. But, if you're looking for conversation, I'm sure they will be more than happy to hang around for as long as you'll tolerate them."

She nodded with a chuckle before glancing back at Santa and her face immediately falling again.

"He's going to be okay. He's just been through a lot. He will perk back up. And in a few weeks, he'll be back to his old self."

Joy's bottom lip trembled slightly.

Jacob saw it and tried to stop the tears before they began. "What's your middle name?"

She bit her trembling lip and sniffed as she looked back up at him. "What?"

"What's your middle name? I've never thought about what your full name might be before, but now I've got to know."

"Noel."

The look on his face was comical.

She couldn't help but grin as she wiped away the one tear that had managed to fall. "Middle names weren't a thing yet, where we came from. Even if they were, neither one of us was highborn enough to have one." Her attention immediately shifted back to her husband.

He shook his head at her, thinking that she must surely keep his patient's life interesting enough for neither of them to mind their constant seclusion.

"Is this the beginning of the end for him, for us?" she asked, wide-eyed as she turned around to face the doctor again. "I don't think I ever considered our limited mortality. I just figured that with him only leaving one night a year, he would live forever. Or, at least until people stopped believing altogether, when the world was ready to let him go."

Jacob shook his head. "I don't understand the ins and outs of the magic, so I can't say. What I do know is that people can have this surgery and then go on to live full, long lives. He'll go through a few weeks of physical therapy, and they'll help teach him how to move and live and such with this operation. It doesn't have to be the beginning of the end. It can be the beginning of his next phase of life."

"I used to joke that, relevant to him, I was getting younger than him. Especially when he set out for three weeks of training with the tech companies."

"You've never left the North Pole since arriving?"

"We've taken a vacation here and there, but not really."

"The seclusion must get to you."

"Oh, I've always been a homebody. And the village is quite large. And the internet has certainly filled the need for varied entertainment. Plus, I'm surrounded by elves. I have many friends."

He smiled. "The different ways people live their lives has always fascinated me."

"It's an odd life, but it's mine and I do love it. It is strange to be around so many other humans, though."

He chuckled softly with her. "I should check the monitors and make sure he's settling in well, after the trek through the building."

"And after that, you should find a bed."

"I will. And so should you."

"After I call Claude and give him an update. He'll update the others for me, then I can settle down for the night."

"How are you doing today, Mr. Claus?" the morning nurse asked.

It took Santa a few seconds to process that some strange woman was standing in a room he'd never seen before, and that she was speaking English to him. "Where am I?" he asked, taking a good look around for the first time.

Joy sat up in her bed, blinking, as the night before came back to her in a flash.

"You're in the hospital, sir," the nurse answered.

Santa eyed the woman up and down. "I take it I'm not at the North Pole."

The nurse smiled, "No, sir."

"You're in Washington, DC," Joy answered. "Don't you remember anything from yesterday?"

"Bits and pieces. What happened?" he asked.

"You had a heart attack, mid-flight, and the reindeer flew you the rest of the way to the North Pole and landed," Jacob declared from the doorway, coming into the room. "Mrs. Claus reached out to the world leaders, and the US President offered his personal hospital accommodations. The Coast Guard flew up with me, to retrieve you. My name is Dr. Jacob Hershey, your cardiothoracic surgeon. I performed a double bypass on your heart last night. You're on a heavy cocktail of meds, and you're expected to make a full recovery within the next several weeks."

Santa was looking more aware of his surroundings now, "By Christmas?"

"Not very likely at all, no."

"I have to be better by Christmas Eve."

"You have to survive this Christmas, so that it's not your last."

Santa thought about that for a moment, not knowing what the answer to the problem was going to be. He let out a sigh and turned to the nurse, "You think the world would buy into a true Christmas in July?"

The nurse was looking like she didn't know if Santa was kidding or not. "It's possible."

"Good. You do a round of news cycles and break it to all the children in the world for me, would you?"

She did smile at that, "There's not enough money in the world to pay me to do that."

"One. Billion. Dollars," Santa said.

The nurse's body froze, "Really?"

He rolled his eyes, "No, not really, I just knew you had a price." He shook his head. "The kids will not understand. Even if they do, they'll never be okay with it."

"That's a problem for another day," Jacob said. "We need to discuss your heart health. From everything I've seen of your heart in the last twenty-four hours, I'm led to believe you've been dealing with undiagnosed hypertension."

"High blood pressure?"

"Yes. It causes damage to the heart, and coupled with high cholesterol, fat, and plaque buildup, you basically became a ticking time-bomb."

"You're about to bury me in pamphlets, aren't you?"

"And lectures, yes. But I'll spare you from hearing it all at once. I'll spread it out. Let's just start with wrapping your mind around this one thing... No more cookies."

"But I only eat cookies one night a year," Santa grumbled.

Jacob shared a look with Joy before turning back to Santa. They both stared at him, hard.

"What?" Santa asked.

"And how many millions of cookies does that amount to?"

"Do you have any idea the amount of energy I burn on Christmas Eve?"

"Eat the carrots left out for the reindeer."

Santa shook his head. "Cupid will boot me off the roof again, if I go out there with carrot breath."

"Then pack your own snacks."

"And have kids crying on Christmas morning because I rejected their cookies?"

"Okay, at some point, there will be a press conference about your heart attack. They'll wait for as long as they can, but before rumors hit every news station in the world, they'll make me do a press conference. I'll be the bad guy and tell the world that you can't be eating cookies on Christmas Eve anymore. I'll give them heart healthy snack options, to give them ideas for things to leave out for you."

Santa thought about that for a moment. "That might work."

The nurse shook her head but said nothing.

"Yes," Mrs. Claus said, pretending to agree. "It's not like you'll have millions of children blaming themselves for their cookies causing Santa's heart attack, and their being the reason he can't make his trip this year."

Jacob let out a sigh, "You know what, I'll be telling it to the camera. I won't have to see any of their faces. I can do it."

"You'll get hate mail," the nurse warned.

"How many will track down the address?"

"The postal service will get letters addressed to 'Santa's doctor' and they will forward all those letters here," Joy told him.

"Oh, they will not."

"Oh, yes, they will. They get very lenient where Santa is concerned."

"I'm your Physical Therapist, Stephanie Bellini," a young woman introduced herself to Santa.

Santa cracked open an eyelid and looked her straight in the eye, "I know."

"I'm sorry?"

"I know who you are. I also know how many times your name appeared on my naughty list."

"And you know that I became a physical therapist?"

"Yes."

"How?"

"Because I'm Santa."

Stephanie smiled. "Okay. Do you also know I'm here to begin your torture?"

Santa's eyebrow raised, "Going for another naughty list year?"

She hid her grin and shrugged, "It's my job."

"Your job is to rehabilitate."

"Yes, by torture. Would you like to consult with my prior clients? Call the President, mention my name, and ask him about his knee." Her smile was both proud and smug, more than ready to indulge a grouch with some banter.

Santa narrowed his eyes and moved his head, to focus on the bathroom door, "Joy!"

No answer.

"Joy!" he called again.

The door opened and Joy rounded the door, "Yes?"

"Either I'm on too many drugs, or I need you to kick this woman out. She says she's here to torture me!"

Joy smiled. "Good afternoon, Stephanie."

A hint of laughter echoed through Stephanie's voice, "Good afternoon, Joy."

"She's naughty, kick her out," Santa said.

"She was naughty one year, and you left her a gift anyway, because you understood what was going on. Leave her alone," Joy answered with an eyeroll.

"Yeah, and look where it's gotten me," Santa grumbled.

"The year my mom got cancer and almost died three times?" Stephanie asked.

Joy nodded.

"Yeah, not my most shining of moments," Stephanie agreed, before turning back to Santa. "Now, sit up."

"What?" Santa all but sputtered.

Stephanie winked at Joy, then looked back at Santa, cocking a hand on her hip. "I know you're used to leading a large staff. But, in this room, you aren't in charge. If you want to return home, to return to your life as it was before, you're going to have to listen to not only your doctors, but also your therapists. Many patients refer to therapy as torture. It's going to be hard work, a lot of hard work. But you have to bear in mind that what happened to you was no small matter."

"And submitting myself to your torture will have me better by Christmas?"

She grinned at him. "With hard work, excellent cooperation, and great listening skills, we'll have you fully recovered and back to your old self by next Christmas."

Santa was nonplussed.

"You'll be good by February," Stephanie told him.

Jacob walked into the room, "Did you really think that asking someone else was going to get you a different answer?"

Santa rolled his eyes, "You know, people usually bend over backwards to please me, when they see me."

"We're not capable of magic, around here," Jacob told him.

"Son, I'm in the mortal world and I'm still breathing. I think you're plenty capable of magic," Santa said.

"Him, you call son?" Stephanie asked.

Santa's head turned back to her, "You told me you were here to torture me."

Stephanie pointed a finger at Jacob, "He fileted you open and rearranged your parts!"

"To save my life."

Stephanie crossed her arms over herself and shifted her weight to one foot. "Okay, sit up, stand up, go retrieve your reindeer, and head on home."

Santa's look of consternation would have made any toddler cry.

"Exactly," Stephanie said. "And that's where my magic comes in."

Santa raised a surly eyebrow and shut his mouth.

Joy started giggling. "Never would I have advised anyone to take that approach with him," she said, pointing to her husband. "But darned if it didn't work. So, good job."

Santa landed a stink-eye on Joy, "Maybe you're the one out to make the naughty list this year."

Joy smirked at him. "Make your way through Stephanie's list, here and now, and I'll be as naughty as you want me to be."

Stephanie turned wide eyes to Jacob, "I'm not mature enough to have heard that from the two of them."

Jacob fought off a smile. "Santa is not allowed to get naughty until I clear his heart for such activities."

Santa's head snapped to Jacob, "Are you trying to take all the joy out of my life?"

"No. I'm trying to make sure Joy has you in her life, for the rest of her life."

Santa's eyes darted to Joy, "He caught my play on words."

Joy nodded, playing along, "They're both proving to be smart enough to take you on."

"I don't think I know how to take orders from anybody."

Joy shrugged her shoulders, "You seem to take them from me just fine."

"You make suggestions."

"And so will they."

Santa laid his head back on his pillow, "Okay, that's it. That's all the protesting I have the energy for."

Jacob and Stephanie shared a smile. Jacob turned back to Santa. "I heard you're running a bit of a fever, so I'm going to have some blood drawn and sent down to the lab. We'll keep an eye on it. In the meantime, I'm going to start you on an antibiotic. I'm guessing you've never had one before, so keep me apprised of any side-effects you may have."

"How would I know if it's a side effect? My whole body doesn't feel like it's mine."

Jacob smiled. "How're the pain meds? Are you loopy? Are you still feeling any pain?"

"I think they're fine. I'm not feeling much of any pain, I'm just very tired."

"That's to be expected, given everything you've been through."

"Then I guess I'm right on track."

Stephanie stepped forward, "And that's my que to begin the torture. Sit up."

Santa looked back at Jacob, "She's bossy and mean."

Jacob smiled. "That's what we pay her for. You'll probably feel a bit of pain and soreness by the time she's done with you. Get used to that." He turned and headed for the door, "I'll check back in, a bit later."

Stephanie's grin spread from ear to ear as her gaze sharpened on Santa. "And now you're all mine."

Joy lost herself in laughter.

Santa shook his head, "Am I really supposed to just sit straight up?"

Stephanie shrugged, "If you can."

"Do you have any idea how old I am?"

She nodded, her expression solemn, "Very."

Santa gently put a hand to his chest and broke into laughter. "You and I are going to get along just fine."

Joy shook her head, pleased to see her husband smile again. "I'm going to leave you two to your therapy session. I'm going to grab some fresh air and check on Vixen and Cupid."

Santa called out to her, as she headed for the door, "You brought those two?"

Joy snickered as her hand landed on the doorknob, "You have your favorites, and I have mine."

6 A LITTLE SOMETHING

"Good morning, Santa," Jacob said, coming into the room. "Anything new to report?"

Santa let out a half-chuckle. "Well, I seem to have remastered the art of sitting up on my own."

Jacob smiled at him and looked to Joy, "Good morning," and turning to the last person standing in the room he said, "and good morning to you, Stephanie."

Stephanie smiled. "Good morning, Jacob."

"How's he doing?" Jacob asked her, head-nodding to Santa.

"He's on schedule, so far."

"*Hmm.* Good, but his chart says he can't seem to shake the fever. The meds aren't working for it."

"Anything show up on the bloodwork?"

"No, which is encouraging. I'm going to switch his antibiotic."

"Intravenously?"

"Yes. But I don't think it's going to prolong how long he needs to be tethered to the pole."

"Do you think infection is the cause?" Joy asked.

"It could be," Jacob answered. "He's been around a lot of germs that he's not usually exposed to, up in the North Pole. In the meantime, given that he's not in the habit of having antibiotics, it won't cause him any harm. It could also be from any number of other factors, including a reaction to all the drugs."

"I don't feel feverish," Santa grumbled, not liking the way they were all talking about him.

"You're on so many pain meds, they're masking the symptoms of the fever," Jacob said.

"Is it possible," Stephanie asked, "that his normal body temperature is a bit higher than what we consider to be normal? There are studies that show normal body temperature to be lowering over the last hundred years, or so. I mean, he was birthed in the 1200s."

Jacob looked at her as he considered her question. "I suppose it's possible, given that it is only a low-grade fever. I'll have to call Claude and see if he has Santa's normal temperature documented."

"Who's Claude?"

"He's head of the Sniffles Ward at the North Pole."

Stephanie tucked her lips between her teeth, but her eyes belied her withheld laughter.

Mirth hid in his eyes, as well, "Yeah, ya heard me. I said, 'Sniffles Ward'."

Stephanie couldn't help it, a snort escaped. "Joy told me what is was last night, but hearing you call it that just tickles me."

"Uh-huh." He turned to Santa, "I'm going to call Claude for a consult before I order the change in meds. I'll be back shortly to finish checking in." He turned back to Stephanie, "I'm going to grab a coffee on my way back before I have to go into surgery. Do you want one?"

"Yes. Large. Thanks."

"No cream, three sugars?"

"Yes, and none of that fake sweetener stuff."

"Yes, ma'am. That is not a mistake I'll be making again."

She smiled. He winked and left the room.

Santa and Joy shared knowing grins when Stephanie turned back to them, still smiling.

Stephanie saw the exchange, dropped the smile, and looked from one to the other, "No."

"No?" Joy asked.

"No."

"I'm pretty sure I sensed at least a little something between the two of you."

"No," Stephanie said, her hands gesturing with her denial.

"He knows how you take your coffee."

"We work together."

Joy turned to Santa. "Have you noticed?"

"I have," Santa answered with a nod.

"Noticed what?" Stephanie asked.

Joy smiled at her. "How he seems to come into the room every time you're here."

"I handle all his cardiac recovery patients. Our paths naturally cross throughout the day."

Joy gave a little shrug, "If you say so. But I still contend that there's something between the two of you."

"No," Stephanie said, gesturing again, the slightest of smiles on her mouth.

"No?"

"No. I'm involved with someone."

Santa snorted. "No, you're not."

"Yes. I am."

"You hardly see the man. And you use him as a convenient excuse to keep your parents off your back about finding somebody."

"He travels extensively for his job, and I'm kept plenty busy by mine. It's an arrangement that works well for us."

"Is it because you have no interest in Jacob?" Joy asked.

Stephanie sighed and pinned Joy with her eyes. "Please don't push this."

"Please push this," Santa said to Joy. "She's been pushing my buttons for the last forty-five minutes. Go ahead and push hers."

"Jacob is married to his career," Stephanie said with an air of finality.

"But maybe, if he met the right woman…" Joy hinted.

Stephanie was nonplussed as she looked to the ceiling and shook her head. "He has met the right woman, a couple of times."

Joy didn't know what to say to that.

Satisfied that Joy was going to lay off the topic, she turned to Santa. "You've sat up long enough for now. Let's get you back into the bed, where you can adjust the back to whatever incline is comfortable for you."

"Okay," Jacob said, coming back inside the suite, "the general consensus is that this could very well be your natural temperature. So, as a preventative measure, I'm going to continue your current antibiotic and we're going to watch your temperature and see whether it changes or not."

"Sounds good," Santa said.

Jacob turned to Stephanie and handed her a cup, "This is yours." He looked around at all of them, "You guys all have a good day. I gotta run. I'll be back to check in, later." With that, he turned around and left the room.

"He has a surgery scheduled," Stephanie explained as she helped to resettle Santa. "At any rate, I need to get going, too. I have to get to my next patient." She gathered her supplies and set them on her cart. Wheeling for the door, she looked back with a smile, "You two have a good one!"

Joy smiled until Stephanie left the room, then she lost her smile and turned to her husband.

Santa was adjusting his blanket over his lap when he looked up to see her eyes on him, waiting. "What?"

She moved back to the chair she'd taken to sitting in, by his bedside, and sat down. "Spill."

"I'm sorry, but no."

"No?"

"He's been through a lot. Things he may not want everyone to know."

"What? You always tell me about people when I ask!"

"Sure, when you don't have a personal connection to the person."

"But actually knowing the person makes me care more."

"Exactly."

"What?"

"The moment you know is the moment you're going to set about trying to fix things."

"Well, someone has to help him."

"That doesn't mean he wants help from you."

"But I'm excellent at fixing things."

"It's up to him, whether or not he wants to share that part of his life with you."

"But you know it's going to seriously bug me, not knowing why he's closed the door on love."

"I know it will. But it's his decision."

"What about after all this is done and we're back home?"

"Maybe, after I'm sure we're long past me needing to see him anymore."

"You know, it's not often that I'm jealous of your gifts that I've not been given."

"Just know that those gifts come with responsibilities, like not blabbing everything I know about a person to people in their lives."

"Does Stephanie have a love life?"

He rolled his eyes at her.

"That means, no. And wouldn't it be nice if she did?"

Santa shook his head at her.

"She does enjoy the company of men, right? Or did I misread her? Or maybe I misread him?"

He let out a sigh. "They both enjoy the company of the opposite sex."

"Is he already married?"

"No, he never married."

"Excellent."

Santa shook his head at her again.

She pinned him with her eyes, "I'm sorry, did you want to remain my sole focus of attention?"

He quickly shook his head, "No, no. That's quite all right. Just... go gently on them. I need them to stick around, not run away from my nutty wife."

7 WHAT ARE WE GOING TO DO?

"Stephanie brought you breakfast this morning," Joy reported, when Jacob came into the suite.

Jacob chuckled. "Yeah, I got her text."

Stephanie looked at Joy, "Stop it. He was in surgery most of the night, so I brought him a breakfast sandwich and a fruit salad. It is not a big deal."

Jacob grinned. "Stephanie is a valued friend. She spoils me a little when I need it the most."

Stephanie's shrug reflected in her voice, "We help each other out. It's not a big deal."

He looked from one woman to the other. "Okay, what's up?" Jacob asked Stephanie. "You only say something isn't a big deal, when something actually is a big deal."

"Not to me," Stephanie said with a gesture at Joy, "to her."

He looked at Joy. "And why is it a big deal to you?"

Stephanie answered, "She's matchmaking."

Jacob wrinkled his nose at Joy. "Oh, no, don't do that."

Santa let out a hearty chuckle. "I tried to tell her."

Joy held her hands up to fend them off. "I am not matchmaking. Neither of you are interested in having yourselves a little romance, so who am I to doubt that you both know what you're doing with your lives? At this point, I'm just trying to get to know you both better. Is there any harm in that?"

"As long as that's all that it is, then there is none," Jacob said.

Stephanie raised an eyebrow at her.

Joy shook her head, "It's your own business if you two want to live the rest of your lives alone. Go ahead and forge your lives without a partner. I'll just be grateful that the two of you have found a like-minded friend to talk to, when needed. In the meantime, I'm stuck in this room with nobody but

38

my husband and yet, I'm flying a bit high from being around other humans. That's why I'm a little nosey. Forgive me. I'll try to not overstep, I promise."

Stephanie swung her gaze over to Santa.

Santa shrugged. "I'm Switzerland. I won't be telling her any stories that are yours to tell. And I certainly won't be caught trying to matchmake anybody."

"Alright," Stephanie said, "then we should be able to proceed as planned."

"Very good," Joy said, looking back and forth between Stephanie and Jacob. "Now, while you do your rounds on him, and you do his therapy session, I have some errands to run."

"What errands?" Santa asked.

"Never you mind, what errands," Joy told him.

"If you'll be checking on things back home, wait until these two are done with their torture tactics. We can connect virtually. I want to talk to—"

"No," Joy told him. "You are recovering from a heart attack and an open-heart surgery. No working for you."

"But the board—" he stammered.

"No, wifey is right," Jacob told him. "Absolutely no stress allowed."

Santa gestured at Stephanie, "All that one does is stress me out, ordering me around. Besides, it's little more than four weeks until Christmas. I need to check in with them. We have to come up with some sort of plan."

"You are on sick leave," Jacob told him. "There will be no calls to the North Pole for you. Let your wife handle it."

"I'm Santa Claus. I don't have a substitute. She doesn't know how to run things, up there."

Joy cocked a hand on her hip and eyed her husband down. "Are you implying that I cannot handle checking in with them? I seem to remember handing things easily enough to get you here, to save your life."

Santa let out a long sigh. "It's not that you can't. It's that you don't know how."

"Oh," she said, nodding to herself. "Well, maybe we'll just see how much I can fake my way through." With that, she turned her back on them and moved into the bedroom and changing area the suite held for the spouse to use. She grabbed a couple items, then sent a text to the officer at the Air Force Base, who oversaw her transportation to and from the reindeer.

Santa turned to his torture team. "So, what other parts of my life would you two like me to do away with?"

"How is Santa doing?" Figgy asked, once the Present Makers Guild Board Members were seated around the table, with Joy sitting in Santa's seat.

"He's stable and recovering. He was having a physical therapy session when I left," she said.

"Now that a couple of days have passed," Plover said, "I'm wondering if we can now have some answers to a few questions?"

Joy nodded. "It's why I requested a conference. Santa is going to recover, of that they seem most certain. It's their medical opinion that he'll eventually be able to return to full duty. Albeit, with some dietary changes, of course."

"Excellent," Bip said. "How soon can we expect his return?"

Joy tucked her lower lip between her teeth for the barest of moments. "I'm afraid that he might be there for a few weeks, until he completes this intensive stage of therapy."

"But we only have a few weeks," Bip said.

"No matter," Figgy said. "We can handle completing the remaining present orders."

"Just so long as he's back up here by Christmas Eve, ready to go," Plover said.

"See, that could be the real problem," Joy said. "Since we don't age normally within the realm of the North Pole, doctors are telling us that they are unsure that Santa can heal properly within the realm. It was an idea that I initially balked at, but the more I thought about it, the more I realized that we've never mixed the ancient magic with modern medicine before. I'd rather not experiment with Santa's life when their medical treatment is working. And all that's in addition to not having cardiac professionals up here to oversee his care. So, we now have to stay down there until we know for a certainty that he is well on his way to recovery."

"So long as he's back by Christmas Eve," Plover reiterated.

"See, here's the thing… Even if he's back up here, he's not going to be cleared to fly on Christmas Eve. Although they said people recover at different rates, the doctors all agree that doing his deliveries this year is forbidden."

The three elves sat back in their seats, flabbergasted.

"What are we going to do?" Bip asked. "How are we supposed to get the gifts to all the children?"

"Isn't there any way a few of the elves can get together, and get the job done?" Joy asked.

Plover was already shaking his head. "You know that's not how the magic works. We're elves, we have our purpose. We can't survive for very long outside of the protection of North Pole Village. And we still have a very real fear that someone would capture one of us, just to unlock our secrets. Besides, we don't have a cross-reference that matches the child with the present. That's all part of Santa's magic. We'd have to set a team aside, trying to match each gift with a name and an address. And as you well know, not all children have a home, and not every home has an address."

Joy was already nodding her head in agreement. "I know. I'm sorry. I just don't know what the answer is. Though, you really should put together that team and get it started. It may come down to needing that to be done."

"Did you wish us to become no better than a shipping business?" Bip quipped.

"She's trying to be practical," Plover told him. "I'll get started on assembling a team," he reassured Mrs. Claus.

"Maybe," Figgy began to suggest, "if we worked it like a relay race. We send out groups of three to head out for a couple of hours, then fly back here and trade off. Then that group goes out for a couple of hours…"

Plover had begun shaking his head from the start of the suggestion. "You'll exhaust the reindeer past their point of tolerance with all that extra flying. Plus, that would require a lot of retraining for them. To come home and turn right back around like that… They're just not conditioned for that kind of use. After a certain number of trips, they'd all lay down and refuse to go any further."

"What if we quickly make three more smaller sleighs? What with each one only needing two deer, we could…" Joy's voice trailed off as Plover shook his head.

"You're grasping at straws," Plover told her. "You know it takes six months to properly imbue the wood with the necessary magic."

"But maybe we could use the smaller sleigh," Bip said. "We could just send out the gifts for a particular leg of the journey, with just the two reindeer. Then every time the sleigh comes back, we trade out gift bags, elves, and reindeer."

Now Figgy was shaking his head. "On the surface, that plan would work. But Dasher and Dancer are the lead reindeer for a reason. It's one thing to take a couple of reindeer out to a specific destination. It's quite another to expect each pair to be able to guide the sleigh to so many places. Never mind that Dasher and Dancer keep the others in line, while waiting for Santa to complete each delivery. You can't expect that same kind of behavior from the other six reindeer. It's just not going to work."

"Perhaps if I spoke to Chip and Toot," suggested Joy, "maybe they can come up with a solution."

"You're welcome to consult with them, of course," Figgy said. "But it's not as though a number of us, up here, haven't been trying to come up with ideas, just in case. When it comes to the sleigh and reindeer, I'm sure there's not a thing we've thought of, that they haven't."

"Ma'am, I don't know what to tell you," Toot said, sitting at the table across from both Joy and Chip. "We've thought about delivering the toys early, one smaller batch at a time, and having parents hide the gifts until the big day. But not all children have parents. Many have very simple homes that lack a proper space to hide the gifts. Some lack homes to live in. And all it takes is a small percentage of nosey kids finding their presents early, rumors will take flight, and they will all stop believing. If we deliver them late, then we're no better than any other delivery service out there in the human world. What sets us apart, what makes us magical, is the fact that no matter what is happening on the planet, no matter what is happening to a person, Santa can always be depended upon to be there for them on Christmas Eve. To be the one consistent, caring, loving, entity that a believing child can count on, no matter what happens."

"Ma'am," Chip said, drawing her attention, "I think you have to break it to the people. I think you're going to have to let people know that Santa just can't do it this year. No one is going to respond well to it. But telling them upfront will go a long way in helping them to understand that this is just a onetime blip on the spectrum of history. Santa is human, and his age caught up with him. You're going to have to ask them to understand. No one will like it at first, but they'll come around, as long as you're honest with them."

"You know," Toot said, "that sounds perfectly reasonable. But the problem is that if we prove to the world that we actually exist, and more and more people believe in us, the more that will be demanded of us. Can we handle making presents for a population of over seven billion? Can Santa even make that many deliveries? And if he can't, then he'll fail to live up to his own hype, and everyone will stop believing. And once they stop believing, the magic will start to dissipate. It'll be the beginning of the end for us."

Joy looked from one elf to the other.

Toot and Chip had no more suggestions to offer.

8 THE PROBLEM AT HAND

"Mrs. Claus, come in, come in!" the US President greeted as soon as he'd opened his secretary's office door and spotted her.

He ushered her into the Oval Office and over to one of the couches, before taking a seat in a chair. Pointing to a woman sitting on the couch opposite her, he said, "This is my Secretary of State. It's her job to help me keep dealings with other countries smooth and easy going. I invited her because I heard that you're in need of further assistance. And helping you can have global repercussions, so the Secretary might have questions."

Joy nodded. "That's fine."

"So, tell me," the President began, leaning forward in his chair, "what more can the United States offer?"

Joy was brought up short by his phrasing. "If asking for more aid is asking too much, I can go to the UN. I just wouldn't want to do that behind your back, while under your nose."

The President shook his head. "There's no need to go through the UN. It's just been a busy day, and I apologize if I made it sound like your being here is an inconvenience. In fact, seeing you made my day easier, because I got to bump meetings with two senators off my appointment list for the day. So, please, how can America help?"

"Well. First, once Santa is released from the hospital, we'll have to find accommodations somewhere, because returning to the North Pole might hinder his post-op recovery and prevent him from healing properly. Those accommodations will have to be within reach of trained therapists, for him to continue his recovery."

The President nodded. "That won't be a problem. Several hotels keep a suite or two available for me to use for special guests. I'll give you the use of whichever one is the closest to the hospital. I'll have my secretary make the arrangements. I'll also give you continued use of a military guard, just in case word gets out."

"Yes, about that... I need to find a way to break it to the world that Santa cannot make his trip, this year. Christmas is falling just too early into his recovery for him to make the deliveries."

Joy watched the expression that fell upon the President's features. Then the President shared a look with his Secretary of State, before rubbing his hands together briefly and leaning forward once again. "Surely there must be a secondary plan for such an occurrence."

Joy could only shake her head. "If only there were. The head elves and I have discussed it at length. The way the magic works... The limitations... We just haven't been able to come up with a practical option. Santa made mention of having an actual Christmas in July as a joke, but maybe the thought has some merit? I don't know. What I do know is that he isn't going to be cleared for anything like a round-the-world trip until, possibly, February. What I need from you is a proper forum to present the news to the world. You may want to get your Press Secretary involved."

The President nodded, sharing a few more looks with his Secretary of State, mulling over what Joy had just said.

Joy sat, not knowing if the silence was a good thing or not. Her attention was suddenly drawn to a clock on a shallow shelf, ticking the seconds of time and mortal life away.

"What if you hold off on telling the press? What if you allow me to present the problem to a gathering of Christian nations, much like the party line? Let us see if we can't come up with a plan or an alternative."

Joy smiled. "I was hoping you might have some suggestions. I'm more than happy to have you put some feelers out, to see if anything else can be done. My team of elves and I would be happy to discuss the feasibility of any thoughtful ideas you may present."

"Excellent. Now, I also heard that you left and returned to Andrew's Air Force Base, today. Will the elves have the presents prepared, or should we come up with a workable alternative for that, as well?"

"Oh, not necessary. They're running right on schedule."

"Any problems with the reindeer?"

"No. Vixen and Cupid were happy to return to the base with me, even after it was offered for them to swap out with another from the team. Their caretakers at the base are absolutely spoiling them. I do believe they feel like they're on vacation."

The President chuckled. "Well, at least something is working out as well as hoped."

"How did your meetings go?" Santa asked when she arrived back to the suite, trying with everything he had in him not to sound jealous and bitter over her handling things for the moment.

"About as well as I expected them to go," she answered, stepping into the bedroom area to put her things down.

"Just so I know, are you going to make me play twenty questions in order to find out what's going on, or are you going to tell me on your own?"

"Just so I know, are you going to let me get settled first? Because it's been a bit of a day for me, and I've just come through the door."

He wrinkled his mouth in slight contrition as he watched her walk over to the bathroom and close the door behind her.

He held his silence, despite the sigh that exited his nose. Sitting around, while everyone else took care of everything, was not a role he was used to serving. He was a doer. He was used to being busy. Right about now, he was feeling quite left out of his own life.

Joy reentered the room, went over to the kitchenette area, and proceeded to make herself a cup of coffee. As the coffee filled the cup, she took her phone out of her pocket and returned a text message, before retrieving the cup and moving to take a seat next to his bed. "So," she said, "good day?"

He regarded her a moment, using it to filter the snark out of his response when he answered, "As good as it's going to get, couped up in here."

She nodded. "Did you have any big accomplishments, today?"

"Yeah. I walked over to the bathroom and used the toilet on my own."

"Well, good. Job well done."

"Stephanie gave me a gold star."

Joy snorted in her coffee, while trying to take a sip. "How'd that go over?"

"I stuck it in her hair, when she walked away."

Joy's mouth dropped open, "You did not."

He nodded. "I most certainly did. If she wants to treat me like a child, then I'm going to act like one. Now, what happened at the meetings? How many meetings were there?"

"There were a handful. I talked to the house staff about some of the changes that need to be made for you."

"I don't need any changes at the house."

"Yes, you do, which is exactly why I left you out of the meetings, altogether. Our diets need to change. And some small tweaking here and there, can go a long way in making our lives more comfortable."

"Like what?"

"Like, don't worry about it."

"Fine," he said with another sigh. "What else?"

"The Guild says the toys will be ready by the deadline, no problem."

"Well, that's a piece of good news."

"But they rejected every idea for delivery that I, or anyone else, brought up for discussion. And no one at the barn had any practical options, either."

Santa's sigh was long. "It's not like I can just cancel or even postpone Christmas. It's not all about me. And the thought of it going on without me drives me crazy."

"I went over to the White House."

"To speak with the President, or with his handlers?"

"I spoke with him and the Secretary of State."

"And?"

"I asked for help in arranging a press coverage, to break the news."

Santa's gaze was cast downward as he nodded. "When do they want to do it?"

"They actually want to kick ideas around with some allies, see if they can come up with a plan for Christmas."

"Well, that's encouraging. I don't know if humans can come up with a solution to this, but I love knowing that it will have been thought about from every angle before we just announce that it's not happening this year. I really do not like disappointing children."

"Sweetheart, I think if there's anything we need to learn from this whole experience, it's that we're still human, too."

His sigh was long and lamenting. "I think I'd managed to forget all about that."

"I know. Me, too."

"What do you think would have become of us, if we hadn't become Santa and Mrs. Claus?"

"I'm not sure. But it wouldn't matter now. We'd be dead."

"Our old lives, they seem more like a dream than a memory."

He nodded. "Do you ever regret agreeing to it?"

"In the beginning, I did. It was hard to know that our family was aging while we didn't. To only check in with them once or twice a year. It was harder still to hear of their passing, one by one. To meet their descendants, and watch them age, as well. And now? Our given lives are so far removed by time that no one knows our true story. And our own familial descendants aren't even aware of a connection. I wouldn't even recognize someone that we're distantly related to."

"I would."

Her eyes drifted from her memories to him. "...What?"

His eyes met hers. "I know who our descendants are."

"In all these years, you never told me?"

"You never asked. I always thought that maybe it got too painful for you to remember. To think about what we missed out on, by not staying to live out our natural lives. When you stopped talking about it, I stopped bringing it up. I didn't want to cause you to feel more pain."

She was utterly flabbergasted.

Silence reigned in the room as the nurse opened the door and entered. "Time for meds and vitals," she declared with a smile. Her eyes swept over the two of them, their silence washing over her.

She quickly dropped her smile and let professionalism take over. She grabbed her blood pressure cuff and went to Santa's side. "How's the pain level, this evening?"

"Better than yesterday."

"Any loopiness when the meds kick in?"

He shook his head. "I get very relaxed. It's cozy and warm."

The nurse smiled. "Don't be surprised if the doc takes that as a sign that he can start lowering the dosage."

"That's fine by me."

"I read in your file that you're able to use the bathroom again. Please don't hesitate to ring your bell if you need help. Sometimes patients get themselves to the bathroom, then lack the energy to get themselves back to bed. It's normal, it happens. Just please pull the cord in there and ring me, instead of your wife or I having to find that you've fallen in the middle of the night. A fall can set your recovery back if you hit the floor the wrong way."

He smiled. "Stephanie warned me. I promise to be a good boy."

The nurse proceeded to give him his pills, check his IV line, and run his vitals.

Joy sat there, stewing in the revelation her husband's confession had caused. Her head suddenly came up, "Do you hold all the babies?"

One of the nurse's eyebrows rose, but she said nothing.

Santa turned his head to her. "And risk waking them up and their parents having a bad night because of it? No."

"So, you do nothing to acknowledge it?"

He let out another sigh, "I give them all the same gift for their first Christmas."

"All? How many are there?"

He looked at her but didn't answer. Instead, he looked to the nurse, "How are my numbers looking?"

The nurse was transferring the readings into his file on her tablet. "Your temperature has not budged. But I'm told they are no longer worried about it unless it goes up. Pulse is a little elevated. And your blood pressure is up, at the moment, but still within the normal range. Pulse ox is good."

"How long has his blood pressure and pulse been elevated," Joy asked.

"This is the first time since surgery," the nurse replied. "But I'd imagine they'll both be back down, the next time he's checked."

"Why is that?"

"Because I'd imagine whatever conversation was happening in here, before I came in, is the cause of the elevated levels."

Joy looked stricken.

The nurse saw her expression and stopped tapping buttons on the screen. "Don't blame yourself. His levels would have risen no matter where or when the conversation happened. As long as they are returned to normal by the next time we check them, there's nothing to worry about." The nurse finished her ministrations and looked at the two of them. "An event like this, it's stressful on both people in a marriage. And spending so much time together, locked away from the world, conversations come up. And sometimes difficult feelings come up, for both people. The important thing to remember is that both of you need to remain calm. Because if one starts letting their hurt feelings rule their words and actions, then the other one starts doing it too, and that is not a healing environment. Now by all means, if you can talk your way through whatever is going on, calmly, then go for it. But if you can't, maybe stick a pin in it. Either way, I'm going to go finish the rest of my rounds. When I'm done, I'm going to come back in and rerun his vitals. It'll make all our evenings run more smoothly if they're back to normal when I return." With that, she turned and left the room, making a quick exit before either of them could sputter about or deny what she'd said.

Joy sat back in her chair, not sure whether to continue her scrutiny or not.

"Joy, honey—"

"What's the gift?"

"A knick-knack of Santa and Mrs. Claus holding a baby."

"Of us holding the baby?"

"It's two generic-looking people dressed up in full red and white fur costumes, holding a generic-looking baby. Tweedle has molds she uses to make them for me."

"How many are there?"

"Millions."

"What?"

"Honey, there's been dozens of generations between when we left our old lives and now. Our DNA in them is so diluted that I doubt the technology would even be able to trace it back."

"But you know who they are."

"It's part of the magic. My human brain certainly wouldn't be able to keep track of so many."

She started to say something but stopped herself. She shook her head. "I've never worried much about our humanity. But now it feels like I can feel every tick of an imaginary clock in my head."

"You don't have to be here. You can go home while I recuperate. You don't have to spend time aging here."

"You're not understanding my point."

"Then tell me your point."

"You've aged probably about two and a half years more than I have."

"Eight hundred Christmases."

She nodded. "Plus, trips to scout out new toys and learning how to make them. At some point, you will reach the end of your life. The more time away from the North Pole and me that you spend, the more you age ahead of me, the more likely it is that you will die, and I will be left behind. And for how long? How many years will I be left here, without you? You are the only link I have to that life we lived so long ago. And, more than that, what happens to me, once you aren't around to be Santa to the world?"

"You know the answer to that. You can either continue to stay with the elves, or you can finish out your natural years in a grand retirement community, anywhere you want to be. You know that's what the money is sitting in that account for."

"Yes, but we always said that would be for the both of us, if we grew tired of the seclusion and wanted to stop, or if the world stopped believing in us. I never let myself consider that you wouldn't be there with me."

He held his hand out to her, "Come here."

She scooted her chair closer and took hold of his hand.

He gave her hand a squeeze. "We've been married for eight hundred and thirty-two years. How much longer do you think we have a right to ask for?"

She smiled.

"No one ever promised us that we'd get out of one of us dying, and the other being widowed. We were only told that we'd be able to put it off for a while. Honey, for as different as we are from the rest of humankind, we're still just people. So, yes, one of us will die before the other. Yes, it will probably be me. Death is the most equalizing thing on the planet. We all die. But what a hell of a life to have lived, huh?" he said with another hand-squeeze. "I don't think we could have asked for a better life."

She nodded her agreement. "I know you're speaking truth. It's just a truth that has taken me this long to confront and try to process. At any rate, I'm not going anywhere. I'm not going to have you age weeks ahead of me. It'll be that much longer I'll have to live without you. I'm staying put for the duration."

The nurse popped her head in. "Are we all in calmer frames of mind, or do I need to give you two another twenty minutes?"

"You can come in," Santa told her. "My numbers should be back to normal, now."

9 SHE JUST CAN'T HELP HERSELF

"Good morning," Stephanie said, a little too bright and cheerful for a Monday morning.

"What has you in such a fine mood?" Joy asked, smiling at the girl's enthusiasm.

"Oh, nothing in particular. I just find that if I plaster a smile on my face and speak a little louder, I can fake an energetic mood. And, sometimes, it rubs off on the patients, and gets them moving a little faster."

Santa groaned from his bed. "That nonsense is not going to work on me. Now, why don't you call off sick and take yourself on a nice, little day trip? Maybe take a couple of days off?"

Stephanie laughed. "They'd just replace me with another therapist, and you'd still have to get up and do your exercises."

"Darn."

"How did your weekend go?"

"It was short."

"Are you this grumpy all the time?"

"Only when people are pestering me."

Joy sighed loud enough to draw both their attention. "Would you stop it, you old coot? You haven't been grouchy since they started letting you use the toilet again. Stop posturing for her."

"She's the one that introduced herself to me with an attitude. I'm just keeping up with her game."

Stephanie smiled. "I was just trying to establish dominance within the dynamic, that's all. Neither one of us needs to be short with the other."

Santa grunted. "You have three coffees with you."

"Yes, I brought one for your wife." She moved to hand Joy a steaming cup, "I didn't know how you take your coffee, so I brought up both cream and sugar."

Joy smiled her appreciation at the gesture, reaching over to retrieve a creamer and two sugars from the cup carrier.

"Is that other one for me?" Santa asked.

"No," Stephanie answered.

"So, you can bring up coffee for yourself, Dr. Candy Bar, and my wife, but you can't bring me any? I thought you were done being mean to me."

"No caffeine for you, until Dr. Candy Bar says so."

"Dr. Candy Bar?" Jacob asked, walking into the room.

"His new name for you," Stephanie said, pointing to Santa.

Santa rolled his eyes. "I was just giving her a hard time."

"Why?" Jacob asked.

"Because I'm bored and tired and she's here to bother me."

Jacob grinned as he looked over Santa's chart on his tablet. "I see you had some elevated vitals on Friday evening, but then everything resettled, later on." He looked up at Santa as Stephanie reached out to him and he accepted the coffee cup. "Did you experience any symptoms associated with the episode?"

"Yeah, marriage."

Stephanie snickered.

Joy cleared her throat. "We talked about a number of things, Friday night. The nurse took the vitals right after he'd made a confession to me."

"I was worried about how she was going to react," Santa admitted. "But we talked it through like we always do." He paused just long enough to wink at Joy. "All is well."

Jacob nodded. "Good. I'm glad to know it was caused by a conversation and not by a health complication. Better still that you two worked it out. You're both going to need each other, to get through this."

"Oh, I don't know," Joy said. "You two seem to be getting through your lives, each on your own."

Jacob used his stylus to point, "He needs someone by his side, to keep him focused on forward progress. And you have a life partner, who's going through a crisis, and that shakes up your entire world. It's different when you're single. I'd need support to get through the crisis, but I wouldn't be causing a crisis in someone else's world."

"But who would you have to lean on?"

"Joy," Santa said.

"What?" she answered.

"If I have to be nice to Stephanie, then you have to stop prying into their lives."

Joy wrinkled her nose, refusing to acknowledge that he was right.

Santa hid his smile at her silence and looked back to the doc. "Any other questions I can answer? Because the longer you and I talk, the longer I can put off Stephanie's torture session."

"Actually, yes, there is. Some patients, more than you'd think, have a difficult time wrapping their minds around all that they've been through. They have an even harder time coming to terms with the lifestyle changes they need to make. And those patients can find it very helpful if they have a professional to talk to. Someone who can help them gain perspective on everything that's happened and is happening to them."

"You're suggesting that I speak to a psychologist."

"It can be very helpful."

"I'll admit to being a bit humbug. But that's not because of the heart attack. It's about having to accept that I can't do the most important part of my job this year. I imagine that you can sympathize with the idea of a profession becoming an important part of your identity."

Jacob looked to the floor and nodded before looking back up at Santa. "Yes, I can."

"And so, I'm a bit grouchy. But, truthfully, bantering with Stephanie has been a wonderful outlet for me. I can give voice to the negative emotions, venting them, which helps me make room in my head for reason and logic to work its way in. I'm good, I promise."

"He's full of reindeer droppings," Joy said.

Both men turned to look at her.

"He's been speaking with Penelope. She's been keeping his head on straight," she said.

"How do you know about that? I only talk to her when you're out of the suite," Santa asked.

"Because I've been talking to her too. It started out as me just trying to keep the elves in the loop of what has been going on. But more often than not, she ends up counseling me. She let me know that you were talking to her as well."

"It seems that nothing in my life is sacred," Santa mumbled.

Jacob let out a chuckle. "Welcome back to human reality. Now have yourself a good session with Stephanie."

Stephanie clapped her hands together and began rubbing them back and forth. A low, diabolical, snicker emitting from her throat. "Let the torturing begin."

Joy's eyes widened, but then Santa let out a round of full, rich laughter. Joy found a smile of her own and shook her head at both of them.

"Oh, happy day!" Stephanie said, all but bouncing into the room. "Oh, happy, joyous day!"

"What. The. Hell," Santa said, genuinely both curious and grumpy about her bubbly attitude this morning.

"It's discharge day!" Stephanie beamed. "Everybody loves discharge day!"

"Yeah, but I don't get to leave until this afternoon."

"Oh, but I get to fill out your therapy papers and kick your case off my in-patient rotation, just as soon as we finish up this morning."

"Oh, well, that is happy news. You're too damn chipper in the mornings."

"And you're too persnickety in the mornings to deal with."

"You two are both ridiculous," Jacob said, walking in with their coffees. "Besides, I don't see what either of you are all that ecstatic about."

"Neither do I," Joy said, having watched the whole exchange from the kitchenette area. She turned to Santa. "You know they're going to assign you therapists to work with at the hotel."

"Yes," Santa said, "I know. But it won't be her, and it won't be so early in the morning." He turned to Stephanie, "You act like you're on some sort of caffeine, sugar, and cocaine kind of high every morning."

"And you act like you're hungover every morning," Stephanie retorted.

Jacob turned to Santa, "Who's to say that your next therapist won't be as energetic?"

"Well, it's not like all therapists can be morning people."

"You'd be surprised."

Santa's eyebrow raised, "Do you know who will be my at home therapist."

Jacob nodded, taking a sip of his coffee, "I do."

"Well, who is it?"

"A lovely woman," he said, and then a sly grin crossed his face.

"I don't like the way you just said that."

Stephanie cleared her throat. "High-profile patients get followed by the same therapist during their out-patient care, when they stay local."

"Oh, come on."

Joy began to chuckle to herself. "Will we be seeing you every day, as well?" she asked Jacob.

"At minimum, every other day."

"That's not normal, is it?" Joy asked, concern clouding her features. "Is there a reason you'll be checking in that often?"

"In part, it's because he's high-profile. But honestly, I manipulated the flesh and bones of an eight-hundred-year-old magical being. While I'm confident I've done right by him, I'm a little paranoid about how everything will hold together and heal. This is a case where I'm learning every bit as much as I'm treating."

Santa eyed Stephanie. "Tell me you don't plan on stopping by the hotel even earlier, like before you come in here for work."

Stephanie shook her head. "That's the good part. Expect me either just before, or right after lunch. I won't ever have to catch you just after waking up, again."

"Now that's the best piece of news, yet."

"I knew it would be, for you and me both."

"All right," Jacob said. "Let's get to today's round of twenty questions, so you can move on to today's torture session.

Jacob, sitting at his desk, looked up from his chicken salad sandwich, to see who'd just paused to stand in his doorway.

"Joy," he said, smiling brightly, "is there something I can help you with?"

She nodded. "But I can come back. You're eating lunch."

"Oh, never mind that. It's only ten o'clock anyway. Come in, have a seat."

She moved inside the room and took the closest seat, opposite him.

Two guards moved to flank his doorway.

"I was just wondering…" she'd begun, eyes moving to the wall behind him, noting his diplomas, before her gaze moved to take in the contents of the bookshelf. "Is that…?" She stood and drew over the shelf, her hand lifting to pick up a small knick-knack.

A smile fell upon Jacob's face, his sandwich now forgotten. "Do you recognize it?"

"Should I?"

"I've been told it came from Santa."

Joy frowned momentarily about why he would have to be told, but then it dawned on her that a baby wouldn't remember what was given to him on his first Christmas. His parents would have had to tell him. "I honestly wouldn't have. Santa only recently told me of its significance." Her finger glided over the smooth curves of the resin sculpture.

"Significance? Does it mean something to be gifted one?"

Joy bit her bottom lip, wondering if it was okay to explain what it meant. Wondering if he could handle the idea of it… Wondering what, exactly, his relationship to her was. And wondering how far the rule about not treating family extended. Perhaps it was best he not know until Santa was recovered, rather than having to chance Santa's case needing to be transferred to someone else, whom her husband may or may not like. "Well, yes. Not everyone is gifted one of these."

"What does it mean?"

She smiled. "That's Santa's secret." She moved to sit back down in the chair, trying to redirect his attention. "I thought it might be a good idea, if I had a checkup while I was here. But I don't really have a doctor. I was hoping you could recommend someone."

"That's actually a really good idea. It'll give us some baseline readings to

54

compare your vitals to, if we ever have need to treat you while you're ill. If Santa would have done that, we would have already known about his higher-than-normal temperature."

"Well, good. I can stop worry about being a bother, if I have a good reason for doing it other than paranoia."

He smiled at her. "I'm friends with a family medicine doctor that comes in right after lunchtime, to round on any patients he happens to have in the hospital. I'll give him a call and get him to do a physical before Santa is discharged. I'll send him a text right now."

"Well, that was simple enough," she said with a smile. "Thank you."

Jacob looked as if he wanted to say something but was holding it back.

"What? If doing it today is a bother, then I can just do it before we have to return to the North Pole. The hotel is within walking distance."

"No, no. I happen to know that he only has a couple patients in the building today."

"Then, what is it?"

"I trust my friend to do right by you. His reputation is excellent..."

"But?"

"Well, if you... If you feel as though he might be running extra, unnecessary tests, I want you to text me. I'm sure that given your lack of available healthcare at home, he'll want to check your health thoroughly. But I also don't want him to treat you like... Well, like a—"

"Mythological Guinea pig?"

"Exactly."

"Do you think that's a possibility?"

"With him, no. But I'm willing to admit that I might be misjudging him. If anything makes you feel uncomfortable, just text me, okay?"

"Okay."

"And please don't worry about being an inconvenience. People have heard the whispers going around the hospital. They've all been chomping at the bit to be called in for a consultation, in hopes of being able to meet either one of you. Trust me, every time you take a stroll through the halls, people get giddy with excitement just to get a glimpse of you."

"Speaking of which, since we're leaving today, I wonder if you can point me in the direction of the children's ward. I thought I would visit the kids staying here. I've waited because I didn't want any of the kids trying to sneak out of their rooms to try and track Santa down."

He nodded. "You're looking for the pediatric wing. I'll call down and have a Child Life Specialist come and grab you from Santa's room. She'll be able to walk you around and help you disengage from the clingy kids, so you have the chance to see them all."

"Well, thank you. You're being very accommodating, and I appreciate it."

"You're very welcome. I'll text you when to be back at the suite for your physical."

She nodded. "I'll be waiting. You should finish eating." She stood to leave and headed for the door.

"I'm going to miss having you around. You and Santa have made the last week remarkably interesting."

She smiled. "It's been good getting to know you, too." She gave him a wink and headed back to the suite.

"Why?" Joy demanded, just as soon as she entered the suite.

Guards standing in the hallway pretended not to notice the outburst, as they took a collective step back from the doorway.

"Why, what?" Santa asked, genuinely perplexed.

"Why did you not tell me?" she all bur yelled as she moved further into the suite.

"Not tell you, what?" he asked, purposely keeping his voice calm.

She narrowed her eyes. "You know what."

"Sweetheart, I am on too many drugs to play this game with you."

"What game?"

"The game where you give me a vague explanation as to what you're mad about, and then I have to guess what it is that I've not told you about, while you sit there and listen to my every guess, and you find out about three or more things I've omitted."

"It would be easier for you, if you simply stopped omitting things."

"Do you have any idea how much information I have floating around in my brain? I have no idea what all you want to know about, and what you don't."

"And you somehow think that I wouldn't want to know that Jacob is a descendant?"

Santa's brow wrinkled. "What?"

"Jacob. He's got one of those sculptures of Santa and Mrs. Claus holding a baby, that you talked about the other day."

"Are you sure it isn't just a knock off? You know how companies get a hold of one of the elves' creations and make their own version."

"He said it came from our workshop."

Santa tilted his head back and closed his eyes. A few seconds later, he shook his head. "I'm not seeing the connection." He opened his eyes and lifted his head. "But the drugs are all hitting me right now. It jumbles some things until they begin to wear off. Ask me again in a couple of hours."

Her sigh was long as she stared daggers at him.

He rolled his eyes at her. "Forgive me. I've had a not-so-great week. My heart went kaput, people cut me open and rearranged the contents, and they've been pumping me full of chemicals ever since. I'm doing my best."

She shook her head. "You're just full of excuses, aren't you?"

He smiled.

"Knock, knock!" came a voice from the doorway. "Dr. Hershey called down and said you wanted to visit the pediatric department. I've come up to lead you around," a fortyish woman said, with the biggest grin Joy had seen in years, on her face.

Joy couldn't help but smile in reaction. "Yes, ma'am, I do."

Santa's face fell, "You're going to visit children without me?"

Joy turned back to him. "You can't go down there in your condition. The kids are going to know something's wrong with you. And when they realize it, the first thing you'll be asked is if you're going to be better by Christmas. What would you, on drugs, tell them?"

"Well, aren't the parents going to find it odd that you're here? They're going to realize that there must be something to all the whispered rumors going on."

"People know I'm here. I've been spotted in the halls. You haven't. I'll ignore any questions about why I've been here for days. I'll just focus on the kids and asking them about how they're doing. Trust me, I've got this, I'm not the one on drugs."

"They've seen you, but that doesn't mean they recognize you."

"They all suspect. Rumors are rampant."

"Okay. I'll just stay here all by myself, while you go off, adventuring with adoring children."

"And you'll finally get a taste of what I go through, when you go off adventuring without me."

He pursed his lips, trying to come up with a response, but not able to because she had a point.

Joy turned to the Child Life Specialist. "Give me five minutes," she said, right before disappearing into the separate bedroom area, where she'd been keeping their luggage.

The Child Life Specialist had nodded, but then turned her attention to Santa. And in doing so, the full realization of who she was staring at hit her. She became a fangirl dumbstruck by his presence.

Santa settled his gaze on her, his mind's eye searching for information about her, through the drug haze. "Most people who can't find it in themselves to talk to me feel guilty about spending so many years on the naughty list."

That statement shocked her out of her silence. "What? No!... I never got coal! I just... I just stopped getting gifts."

He nodded. "That tends to happen when you stop believing in me."

Her eyebrows rose, "So, you just drop a person? You stop believing in them?"

"I've never questioned your existence. It's that you've questioned mine. And when my existence gets questioned, a person starts questioning who really dropped a gift off for them. A person starts accusing other people of sneaking in, or breaking in, and leaving a gift behind. Fights about such things have destroyed friendships. Accusations of spending money a couple didn't have has been the starting point of events leading to divorce. So, to prevent the shedding of tears and wrecking of lives, I catch it early and take you off my list."

Joy came out of the next room, dressed from head to toe in red clothing and white fur trim.

The Child Life Specialist's attention was drawn to her. "You mean you actually dress like that?"

"Not normally," Joy said. "But it does assure the children that I am who I say I am."

"And for the ones who don't believe?"

Joy smiled. "They don't have to believe in me, to get a kick out of seeing me. Watch, you'll see."

"Joy," Santa said.

Joy turned to him, a questioning look upon her face.

Santa crooked a finger, indicating that he wanted her to draw near.

She moved, coming to his side, and lowering her ear to his whisper when he tugged on her hand.

Santa whispered to her, giving her some insight on some of the kids he'd been sensing near him all week. Not enough to give away their secrets, but enough information to impress the kids and comfort a few parents.

She smiled at him when he was done and kissed him on the cheek before pulling away. She turned to the Child Life Specialist, "Okay, lead the way."

Through halls and down elevators, they went, with the Child Life Specialist trying to hold her cool along the way. She'd heard the rumors about the Claus' being here, but she hadn't believed those rumors until she entered the Presidential Suite. There'd been an air of magic hanging around the pair, never mind that military guards had stood outside, and two now trailed behind Joy, wherever she went.

Joy used the moment to take in the explosion of the holiday season that decorated the halls of the Pediatric Wing. A full smile graced her features as she watched a nurse's aide hang child-made ornaments on the tree at the end of the hall. Attempts at hand-cut snowflakes, and tissue paper wreaths, hung from the drop-ceiling. What must have once been cases of construction paper now comprised pieces manipulated this way and that, aided by endless glue sticks, into all kinds of decorations before being taped to any and every inch of empty wall space available. She was in awe.

Her attention came to rest on a few of the individual room doors, noting that some were decked out for Chanukah and Kwanza. Some held more traditional Christian Christmas themes. Some focused more on winter, and some were left blank. Joy smiled at the individual displays, loving that there was room for all expressions of the holidays in this wing.

"The parents were all told that you wanted to visit the kids," the social worker told Joy. "An open door means that you are welcome. A closed door means that they'd rather you not go in."

Joy nodded. And when they arrived at the first open door, she put on a big smile and began to work some magic of her own.

She told all the kids that she was doing some reconnaissance work for Santa. She needed to know if each child in question was going to be better in time to be found at home, or if he would need to arrange for presents to be delivered to the hospital for them. She asked them for their Christmas lists so the elves would be sure to get their gifts right.

The children were enchanted. A toddler who hadn't been able to stop whimpering from pain calmed for the first time, in Joy's arms. She then turned to the mother and told her to stop kicking herself for her moment's worth of inattention. "He was determined to climb the stairs. You gated the steps. You did what you were supposed to do."

"I never dreamed he would climb the outside edges of the steps, past the line of posts for the banister."

"Of course, you didn't."

"If I just hadn't screamed when I saw him up there. Then he wouldn't have been startled and let go. If I just could have run faster to catch him…"

"He would have gotten to the top step, realized there was no way through the banister to get onto the second floor, then panicked and let go. He'd have fallen from five steps higher and broken his spine. Your scream might have landed him in here, with four broken bones, but thanks to you, he won't be a paraplegic."

"…Really?"

Joy nodded. "Really."

The next room she entered held two unconscious children in their beds, and both mothers looked up at her with exhausted and bloodshot eyes.

Joy focused on the child to the right. "Jonathon, isn't it?" she asked the mother closest to him.

"Yes," the mother answered.

"And what is it that Jonathon wants for Christmas?"

The mother's expression turned weepy, "A life."

Joy smiled at the mother and moved to grasp the boy's hand. After a moment she nodded to herself. "Life isn't a gift Santa can grant. But I sense nothing indicating that your child is going anywhere." She looked up at the mother. "So, what do you think he'd like, that Santa can give him?"

"A Christmas at home?"

Joy shook her head, "Not this year. He's not quite done with his nap, yet."

"But he's going to wake up?"

"The brain takes time to heal, but he'll get there, eventually."

"He's into anything with wheels that makes noise."

Joy grinned. "Aren't they all, at his precious age?"

The mother grinned and nodded.

And then Joy turned to the other mother in the room, sitting by her son's bed, looking at Joy with the most expectant gaze she'd ever seen.

Joy gentled her features as much as she could, moved one of the empty chairs in the room over to the comatose boy and his mother, sat, and took the boy's hand in hers. While Joy's senses might not be as powerful as her husband's, she still knew the pull of death when it was close by. It was how she knew she'd arrived at the side of one of the children Santa had warned her about. "He has such a bubbly, jolly, personality, doesn't he?"

The mother's face brightened. "Oh, yes. So much so, it's hard not to smile around him."

"I bet he's helped you to make many special memories over these last six years."

"So many."

"How fortunate you've been, to have had him with you."

Something faltered in the mother's expression. "Yes, of course."

She put the boy's hand down, stood, and placed a hand on the mother's shoulder. "We'll leave a little something under the tree for him." Joy removed her hand and began to head for the door.

"He's not going to wake up, is he?" the mother asked from behind her, sounding utterly defeated. "I'm not going to be a mother anymore," her voice catching in her throat.

Mrs. Claus turned back to look at her. "You will always be a mom. His mom. The best mommy a little boy could have ever asked for. He will always be in your heart."

After she was done making the welcomed rounds, she came to stand outside a closed door, debating.

"Remember," the Child Life Specialist said, "a closed door means that they'd rather not talk to you."

"I know," Joy said, "but maybe I really need to talk to someone in there."

"If they don't believe in you—"

"They believe in me," she muttered. She debated another moment, before knocking on the door once and opening it, to head inside.

The mother sitting off to the side of the room immediately stood, "He really doesn't want to see you."

"I know," Joy said, her attention solely focused on the boy.

The boy's gaze was belligerent.

"Santa wanted me to tell you something," she told him.

"Yeah, coal, whatever," the boy scoffed. "Tell him that I don't care. You tell him that I'd do it all over again."

The mother stepped closer to Joy. "We're in the process of getting him evaluated."

"She thinks I'm nuts," the boy qualified.

"Not nuts," his mother said, her gaze shifting back to Joy, "More like, disturbed."

The Child Life Specialist stepped closer, to speak in a low volume. "He abuses his twin sister. He's in here because a teacher had to grab him and lift him off his sister, and then threw him into the wall, to get him to stop his latest round of torture. He has broken ribs from the impact and had to have surgery to stabilize them."

"He only does it at school," the mother said, looking like she was about to burst into tears. "We weren't being told about every incident. We thought he was only picking on her to impress his friends. We had no idea the extent of it, until my husband and I sat in on a meeting with the teacher and the principal." Tears did start to spill as she went on, "My husband and I feel like failures because we just didn't see it. We just didn't think things were so bad."

Joy clasped the hands of both the social worker and the mother. "I know." Then she stepped away and she moved to clasp the boy's hand, holding on tight when he tried to withdraw. She looked him dead in the eyes, "I know."

His expression looked doubtful. "Know what?"

"I know why you do it. Santa knows why you do it. And he wanted me to tell you that he understands, and that you are not on the naughty list."

"I'm not?"

"No coal for you."

Expressions flitted over his face, peeling away all the protective layers he'd encased himself with over the last few months, and before Joy's eyes, the boy's eyes filled with tears, revealing the nine-year-old underneath.

The mother stepped forward, "Why, Jeremy? Why are you torturing her at school?"

"I told you why!" he yelled through his tears.

"Yeah, to impress your friends at school."

"They're not my friends!"

Joy sat on the edge of the boy's bed, put one arm around him, and gently pulled him into a half-embrace, to quiet him before turning to the mother and social worker. "He's tried to tell the adults around him what's going on. But he lacks the skills to express it properly, to the right people. So, while people are trying to listen, no one hears him."

The mother stepped closer, "Then can you help me understand him?"

Joy nodded, "There is a team of three bullies at the school. They targeted your daughter. Jeremy overheard their plans for his sister. When he told a couple of the teachers, they said they couldn't do anything about it until or unless the bullies actually did something to her."

The mother swung her gaze over to the Child Life Specialist.

The Child Life Specialist nodded. "I can believe that much to be true. You can't punish kids for something they haven't done yet. At that point, the teacher doesn't know if what the kid is saying is true or if he's trying to stir up trouble for kids he doesn't like. When the teachers did nothing, Jeremy should have been allowed to report what was going on to the police, so they'd have it on record. An officer could have gone house to house, putting some fear into the bullies, in an effort to avert the targeting."

Joy cleared her throat to draw the attention back to herself. "Jeremy wanted to protect his sister. So, he did the only thing he could think of doing. He treated her badly, making sure to do something less mean than what the bullies had planned, but bad enough that even the bullies didn't want to add insult to injury. Every time Jeremy acted first, the bullies wouldn't bother following through with their plans."

"You held her down and poured glue in her hair. You used a marker to write on her face. You tore pages out of her favorite books. You punched her in the stomach," the mother said to her son.

Joy gave Jeremy an encouraging squeeze around the shoulders, so she wouldn't hurt him. "Tell them what the bullies were planning."

Jeremy looked down at the blankets. "They were going to cut her hair off. They were planning to write bad words on her face with permanent marker. They wanted to rip her books to shreds, I only pulled pages out so she could still put them back and read the books. And I punched her in the stomach so they wouldn't punch her in the face and break her nose."

"They asked you to join their gang," his mother said.

"Because I always seemed to be one step ahead of them. That doesn't mean I wanted to join them. But now, I either have to join them, or be willing to take on all three of them."

Joy took a breath. "It seems that in his misguided attempt to save his sister, he's put himself in a bit of a situation."

His mom's hand went through her hair. "That damned school. What are the teachers doing there?"

The social worker shook her head. "The teachers are put into impossible positions, each and every day. How can the teachers do anything about the three bullies, when your son is the one doing the torturing? And even now, the minute we corner those boys and tell them to leave your son alone, their parents are all going to jump and yell about how it wasn't their boys doing all the things your son has done. Those boys are going to see their own parents defending them, and believe they have the right to go on and do whatever it is they want to do. Situations like these are only the tip of the iceberg as to reasons why teachers are fleeing the profession in droves."

The mother let out a sigh, "What am I supposed to do?"

"Well, I'll be talking to the principal and his teachers, so they can be let in on what was actually happening, so they can be vigilant in trying to catch those three boys in some kind of act. I'm also going to suggest a few staff trainings on recognizing and countering bullies, and then confronting the bullies' parents. And I'm going to try to get the school guidance counselor involved. I'm going to suggest family counseling that focuses on both your children. Your daughter needs to understand that everything Jeremy did was out of a place of love, but they both need to understand that in no way is it ever okay to treat anyone like that, nor be treated like that. A family counselor can help repair the damage he's done to his relationship with his twin, and with you and your husband. And he, or she, will help you to understand that the blame for this is on those three boys and their parents, *not* the teachers. Teachers are paid to teach academics. It is the parents' job to send their children to school, ready to learn. And I'm also going to advise you on some free, public, charter school options that you and your husband may want to look into."

"Well," Joy said, "my job here is done. Though, I should specify that Santa does not believe you were right to treat your sister that way. It's that he understands you took on a problem no nine-year-old should be expected to know how to handle and did the best you could. You acted from your heart. He won't, however, be on your side, should you bring harm to someone again. Understand?"

Jeremy nodded. "Can I make a request?"

"What's that?"

"Can Santa leave doggy doodie in their stockings instead of coal?"

Joy smiled. "I'll pass along the request." She stood and moved over to the Child Life Specialist before whispering, "I can see myself back to the suite."

It was on her walk through the halls that she received the text from Jacob to meet his doctor friend for her physical, so she detoured in that direction and didn't make it back to the suite for another two hours.

"Where have you been?" Santa asked. "The nurse just said she'd be back in a few moments with my discharge papers."

"I was having a physical. They ran some tests and put me in tubes, scanning me for different things."

"Did they find something to be concerned about, that they ran the extra tests?"

"No. I think it's more that I'm so old and don't have access to regular health care, that they were looking everywhere for everything and anything. I'll get the test results later."

"Did anyone take a scalpel to you?"

"No. A couple of needles. And the scans were quite thorough, so as to avoid a multitude of more invasive tests."

"Sounds more like they went test happy so they could document their findings in some journal article," he grumbled.

She sighed, "Well, at least they haven't gone full-blown E.T. on either one of us."

Santa chuckled, "I have to tell you, that was a fear of mine when I woke up in here."

Joy shook her head. "They wouldn't dare. We're too high-profile for them to get away with it."

"It was a good movie, though... Were you able to speak with Jeremy's mother?"

"I was. That family has quite a bit of healing ahead of them."

"Yes. And now they're headed down a healing path because we found a way to interfere."

"How often do you do that?"

"I try not to interfere. But when it's a situation of poor communication and poor listening... I intervene often enough to keep things interesting. The thing though, is to only interfere when you know it's going to help the situation a person is in. Sometimes a person's fear of confronting the truth is well-founded."

"Is that why you won't tell me about Jacob?"

"My telling you his story isn't going to change what happened. The harm has been done, and he isn't in any kind of danger. He's not in crisis. Leave him be."

"Have you sobered up enough to remember his connection to us?"

"Yes. He possesses none of our DNA. I never gave him one of those sculptures."

"Then how does he have it?"

"It must have been regifted."

"Why would someone do that?"

"The people who get one have no idea that it holds any kind of significance. Just because a gift means something to me, doesn't mean they're going to cherish it. For all I know, it was donated to a thrift shop, and he liked it and picked it up."

"Santa," the nurse said as she came through the doorway, "as much as I'm going to hate to see you go, it's time to sign some papers and get you on your way."

10 CAN THEY REALLY DO THIS?

Secret Servicemen came in with computer equipment. Without even asking, they placed it on the dining room table, within the hotel suite the US President had gifted them with, for their stay. Joy and Santa stole glances at one another as they sat back, watching the spectacle of wires being connected and computers being turned on.

Once done, the Secret Service cleared the suite, and the US President entered. "Joy, Santa, I want you both to know that I tried to keep this whole mission simple. But word spread, and it quickly spun out of control." The President went over to the computer, pressed a few buttons, and up popped many blocks on the screens, one block per world leader. "Mr. and Mrs. Claus, won't you join us?" he asked, gesturing to the two chairs with cameras sitting in front of them.

Joy and Santa looked to each other, then moved to the chairs.

"Santa," the President said, "it's good to see some color back on your face."

"Thank you. I'm beginning to feel a bit more human, as they say," Santa said, completely intrigued as he watched the screens and the delays in everyone's reactions, realizing that the ones who didn't speak English were listening to translations. Santa did his best not to shake his head. Part of the magic was an ability to speak all languages, but he couldn't do it simultaneously, so he guessed this was the next best thing.

"As you can tell by the faces on the screens, leaders from around the world have come together to solve the problem we have in common."

"How to break it to the children of the world that I won't be making my trip?"

The President grinned. "How to make those deliveries, in your stead."

"And how do you and the other leaders propose to accomplish that?"

"The US Air Force will be sending an advance Tactical Air Control

66

Party to the North Pole, to coordinate efforts. And then, on Christmas Eve, every country who is willing and able will send Air Force teams in helicopters through the Confetti Tunnel, to the North Pole, to pick up loads, to then transport them through the Confetti Tunnel, and deliver the presents."

Santa's eyebrows rode high on his forehead as he considered the plan. "That's going to take a great many teams. How many do you have?"

"So far, we're at over a hundred who've committed to the task. We've put out the call for more. Frankly, we're about to extend the offer to teams from other military branches. If we do that, we'll only be limited by the number of helicopters we can find to use for the task."

"The two sleighs are the keys to opening and closing the Confetti Tunnel. Now, we can train a couple Airmen in using the sleighs, but whomever you send up for training had better know his way around reindeer. And, even then, that's going to take an enormous amount of coordination for the sleigh drivers to know where to be when. But you haven't accounted for slowing time, moving hyper-fast, and instinctively knowing which presents to deliver to which house. Not to mention the magic of getting into and out of a house, undetected. I don't know that you can plan for such an achievement in only four weeks."

"Yeah… We're going to have to let the public know what's going on. We'll be telling them that we'll be putting together a worldwide, military effort to distribute the gifts. We want people to answer their doors when we come knocking. And we'll let them know that we'll be making the deliveries until they're done, even if it takes us a couple of days. I think we might even start delivering a day early, in the hopes of getting everyone delivered to on time. Elves will have to label each gift with a name and address. We'll double check names and addresses when we make each delivery. It's the best we can come up with."

"Three things," Santa said, leaning forward in his seat. "One, the elves are in charge. Your advance team can act as liaisons between the rest of the teams and the elves, only. And that's only if the elves think your idea can work within the limitations of the magic."

The President pursed his lips as a few of the other leaders smiled. "And two?" he asked.

"If my elves catch one person trying to analyze the Confetti Tunnel, any equipment trying to measure anything, anyone asking too many questions about any aspect of the magic, the elves will shut the whole thing down. I will give interviews to any and all news outlets that the children won't finish receiving their gifts because the world's militaries couldn't play nice with each other."

Silence reigned in the shadow of not only Santa's words, but also at the expression on his face.

Santa made sure to not only meet the US President's eyes, but to then look into the camera facing him. "I will not live in a world where the magic meant to be used in bringing joy to the children of the world, is suddenly used in some sort of misguided political power play."

"Me and the elves," Joy said.

"What?" Santa asked.

She shook her head. "I know you. You may have said the elves will be in charge, but we both know you'll be on the phone with the elves every day, trying to determine how best to make this all happen. And you cannot handle that kind of stress, yet. I'll be the one to talk with the elves, they and I will be in charge of how this all happens."

"It's not your responsibility, it's mine."

"I think I did alright in managing things when you showed up unconscious."

Santa's sigh was long, "Fine. Joy and the elves will be in charge." He glanced at the President and looked into the camera. "If these two points cannot be agreed to, then we have no deal. I'd sooner have the children of the world deal without presents for one Christmas, than to have the secrets of the magic discovered. A human here and there might be able to be trusted, but no government on this planet can be entrusted with such knowledge. That country would either try to use the knowledge for some sort of gain, or another country would target it, in an effort to gain the knowledge for themselves. Our secrets are ours and ours alone."

"How do you propose to determine whether a helicopter is equipped with some sort of scientific data collection device?" one of the leaders on the screens asked.

"The elves will scan each individual aircraft."

"And how will they know whether something was added or not? Are you telling me that there won't be any pieces of standard equipment that the elves might misjudge? And some of these specialized vehicles have a number of measurement devices on them, to help gauge whether the team onboard is flying into an unsafe zone."

"Then I suggest you all disable that equipment when you enter the tunnel. I'm leaving it up to the discretion of the elves. This is not a condition which is up for debate. You have to realize what I'm risking in allowing multiple countries to enter my territory. The elves have been nothing but peaceful and giving, and you want me to allow an obscene number of foreign military vehicles into the village. Forgive me, but humankind has a terrible track record of being untrustworthy around the peaceful and generous populations of the world."

One of the European rulers queued up his microphone. "I'd be interested to know how unauthorized aircraft, like commercial airplanes, will be kept from accessing the Confetti Tunnel."

"Well," Santa said, "there are two choices. One, all governments ground all other aircraft, globally, from the start to the end of the special op."

The US President wasn't the only one shaking his head over that idea. "There's no way to enforce that, particularly with non-cooperative countries, especially at the precise time of year when travel is at its greatest height."

"Agreed," Santa said, "though it would have been easier for the elves… The second option is that we equip each approved aircraft with a tracking device. The elves will then track each aircraft, communicating to the sleigh pilots when to open and close the portal at appropriate times, for appropriate destinations. It'll slow things down, but it's the safest option I can think of."

"And what is the third condition?" the President asked.

"The elves, and/or my wife, can call the whole thing off, at any point, for any reason. And that they are under no obligation to even tell you the reason," Santa said.

The President nodded before looking into his camera, "Ladies and Gentlemen, let us vote, 'Yay' or 'Nay' in the chat box."

One by one, responses scrolled up in the chat box, all 'Yay'. Santa nodded, already planning on telling his elves to make sure the tracking devices also had the power to block other devices onboard from doing any data collecting, thereby killing two birds with one stone.

Then Santa glanced over to Joy, to gauge how she was taking all these developments, and quickly amended his thoughts to telling her to tell the elves about tracking devices and data collections blockers.

The meeting concluded with a lot of political formality. After the President closed out the window, he turned to Santa. "I'm sorry that I didn't have a chance to touch-base with you on the plan before the meeting. I know that whole thing caught you off guard. It was a task that I wanted the US alone to handle, but then others started voicing concerns and it snowballed. People got impatient for an answer, and too many others kept trying to add caveats or conditions of their own. Closing this deal quickly became the best option for keeping things simple."

"The elves are not going to like it."

"I know. I'm sorry. But we did have a prior meeting where we kicked around other ideas… Why can't the elves just do it for you?"

"Because they can't leave the North Pole."

"Why not?"

Santa just looked at him, expressionless.

"Yeah… okay. There are things I wouldn't tell you. I get it."

"What I don't understand," Joy said, drawing both the men's attention, "is why the militaries don't just start transporting the presents for their respective countries to large warehouses now, then have your existing package delivery systems distribute them all in time for Christmas? Wouldn't it just be simpler to take advantage of systems that are already in place?"

The President was already shaking his head. "Again, this is the worst time of year for a plan like that. Those systems are already operating at their breaking point, due to all the presents everyone already buys each other. The existing systems simply can't handle the added burden. As it is, companies like UPS are already renting U-Hauls to help make all the deliveries, because they simply do not have enough trucks to get the job done."

Joy let out a sigh. "Alright."

"Believe me, I would never suggest involving so many militaries, if we didn't have to. But they are the ones who are kept at the ready for such an unexpected occurrence. I just don't see how else we can come close to accomplishing Santa's feat. Besides, if we can pull this off, it will be the largest peacetime military operation in the history of humanity. God forbid we all learn that it's possible to work together for a common goal."

Joy nodded, her expression resigned, "If there's nothing else, Santa really should get some meds into him and lay down for a while."

"Sure, sure," the President said before turning to Santa. "I told my daughter that I'd pass along the message that she would like a pony for Christmas. And then I told my wife that I'd pass along the request that you not send a pony to the White House for Christmas."

Santa smiled with a silent chuckle. "You wouldn't believe how many parents attempt to cancel out their children's requests. How about a puppy that will grow to the size of a small pony?"

"How about we don't give a living being to a six-year-old?"

"You'd be surprised how many six-year-olds in this world are very knowledgeable in the area of animal husbandry."

"I hear you, and if I lived on a farm, had to raise my own animals for food, or lived in a country where it would be common to send her into the workforce, I might feel differently. But the White House just isn't equipped to house a pony."

"I think you could probably have that remedied."

Joy rolled her eyes with a sigh, "Would you please stop baiting our host? He's been nothing but gracious to us."

Santa grinned and winked at her.

The President looked from one of them to the other, then chuckled. "Alright. I'll keep you and your wife appraised as things develop. In the meantime, I have a job to get back to and you have some pills to take."

"And a nap," Joy reminded.

"How could I forget the nap?" the President asked with one of his signature charismatic smiles. "Have a good one, both of you." With that, he left the room.

Secret Service agents entered and began removing the technology.

After they exited, Joy and Santa both looked at one another.

"What the hell have we gotten ourselves into?" she asked.

He shook his head. "If this backfires in our faces…"

"I know."

"This is either going to bring out the best in world relations or trigger the worst."

"Alright, let me and elves worry about this. For now, meds and sleep. Let's go."

"I don't like it," Elvin, the elf in charge of flight security told Joy over the phone.

"Neither do we," Joy admitted, taking a seat on the couch in the hotel suite's living room. "But we don't know what else to do."

"Why can't they just use a handful of teams, coming in one at a time starting now, in rotation, and load those up and have them distribute to the respective countries? Then their teams can all distribute them on Christmas Eve."

"They'd still need the Confetti Tunnel to transport the gifts around their countries."

"But they wouldn't all need to come here."

"I got the distinct impression that no one wants to allow just one country to enjoy access, having to just trust that the country wouldn't gain some useful knowledge."

"Plus, they want to satisfy their own curiosity."

"True."

"Okay, so what about one team per willing country?"

"And where are they supposed to store everything? I can only imagine the targets some terrorist organizations out there would try to hit, to gain goods to then market. It's one of the many reasons for our shield."

"I don't know where they'd put it and protect it. That's not my problem."

"I'll pitch it to the US President. Maybe they have emergency bunkers that they can gather and organize the gifts in. But you need to start making moves to accommodate for their existing plan."

"It's too much chaos to have them all come and go in one night. And helicopters? They're not going to be able to fit enough. There's only one magic imbued bag for gift transport. They're going to need cargo planes, and you know it. And you also know we have nowhere to land them."

Joy put her face in her hands for a moment, already getting tired of being everyone's go-between. "I'll tell you what. I'll try and set up a meeting between you and the President, so you can discuss some of the issues with him. You're talking about things that I simply didn't think of, and Santa was too drugged to come up with. I was simply in a state of trying to take it all in. But Santa did make one of the conditions be that you and I both have the power to veto the plan. But I don't know that I'd get my hopes up about them agreeing to any other kind of plan. Although, any plan is worth considering, given the alternative."

"Here's something else you two didn't think of. Opening and closing the confetti tunnel with the sleighs is a proximity thing. But... if we employ both sleighs, in theory, we can use them to open a tunnel so that one sleigh is at one end of it, and one sleigh at the other. That only accounts for a beginning and an end point. They would all have to see their way clear to having all the helicopters working as a team and completing one area at a time. It will not be something where each country can just take care of their own."

"I don't know if that many militaries can participate together in such a large scale and agree on how to handle a joint distribution."

"I'll tell you what plan might actually be workable for us, and in our best interest..."

"I'm listening."

"If they could come up with one place for you to deliver everything to, you could take the gifts there, ahead of time. Then their militaries could do whatever they needed to do, to sort, distribute, and deliver them. It would just be you using the Confetti Tunnel. No other humans would need to come here, to the North Pole, where we don't care for many visitors."

"Yeah, okay. I'm going to attempt to set up that meeting for you, so you can pitch that idea."

Elvin harrumphed into the phone, "I would welcome that conversation."

"You have to go into it thinking he'll try to talk over you and undermine your concerns because he's probably going to view you as someone inferior."

"Give me an impressive title of some sort. Tell him I'm your Secretary of both Transportation and State."

Joy laughed. "That might not be a bad idea."

"How's the sleigh looking? Are those military guys messing with it?"

"Vixen bit the one who dared to touch it. The reindeer have positioned themselves as guards of the sleigh. Even as they relax, the sleigh is in the back of the hanger, and they are in front of it. They allow the airmen to look all they want but touch they shall not."

Elvin chuckled. "Good. Serves them right for trying to touch things that aren't theirs."

A noise at the suite door caught Joy's attention. "The doctor is here. I need to go."

"Alright. Let me know the President's response to the meeting request."

"I'm sure he'll agree to it, simply to take advantage of the opportunity to speak with an elf. Take care, Elvin."

"Goodbye, Mrs. Claus."

Joy cut the call and quickly shuffled across the room to open the door. "Good afternoon, Jacob. Come on in."

"Thank you. How's the patient?"

Joy raised the volume of her voice, "Determined to bathe and dress himself. He started about an hour and a half ago."

A voice boomed through the bathroom door, "That's because I soaked in the tub! I'll be out in a minute."

Joy rolled her eyes. "He's never relaxed in a tub before. I'm surprised he knew how."

Jacob chuckled. "How are you doing?"

"I'm good. Just trying to keep on top of everything happening back home and balancing the politics of the world against it."

His eyebrows raised, "I don't envy you that job."

She shook her head. "Would you like some coffee? The pot is only twenty minutes old."

"Sure," he said, moving to take a seat at the dining table. "I could use an afternoon jolt."

She smiled, fixed the cups, knowing by now how he took his coffee, and carried them over to the table.

He took his cup and put it to his lips, taking the time to smell the brew.

"Good day?" she asked. "You seem lighter than usual."

"I fixed a teenager's heart, and nobody died on me today. So, yeah, it's a good day."

"That's great news."

He nodded. "Any day I don't have to deliver bad news to family members is a good day, truth be told."

She winced. "That must be a heavy burden to bear."

"They look at you with all the hope they possess in their souls, and I have to rip it all away from them."

"I got a taste of that the other day. I don't envy you that job."

"What happened the other day?"

"When I visited the children, Santa gave me a head's up on a few of them, beforehand. I made the mistake of telling one mother to relax, that her child would enjoy many more Christmases to come."

"That sounds like you imparted good news, that her child would survive."

"Yes, but the mother of the child's roommate overheard me. And when I went to visit with her child, the mother's eyes followed me and my every move."

"And her child won't be enjoying more Christmases, I'm guessing."

"Her child has an inoperable brain tumor that won't stop growing. She knows he's not going to make it. I think she was hoping I could work some sort of magic. But those aren't powers we possess. All I could do was hug her and promise to pray for her and her son."

"Will he make it to this Christmas?"

"He'll be alive, but he'll remain comatose."

He nodded thoughtfully.

"Can I ask you a question?"

"Sure," he said, drinking from his cup.

"That little sculpture you have of Santa holding the baby. Santa says it wasn't gifted to you. Can I ask where you got it from?"

Jacob let out a breath and turned his head to look out the window, unseeing anything there. "Does it matter?" he whispered.

Joy waited the barest of moments before lowering her own voice, "You don't have to answer, of course. But those seemingly innocent knick-knacks do carry a significance with them. And I'd love to know more about the original giftee."

"Can't Santa tell you that?"

"He could only tell me that he never gifted one to you."

His sigh was long and deep, as a shadow fell over his face, and he looked back to her. "It belonged to my fiancé."

Joy briefly bit her bottom lip, not wanting to dredge up any past pain, and yet wanting to understand. "Oh. Past tense. Did she forget to grab it on her way out?"

"No. We didn't break up. She died."

"Oh. I'm so sorry."

"It was a hard-fought battle with breast cancer."

"I'm so sorry I brought it up."

"But you did, and harshed my buzz from a good day."

Joy looked utterly devastated to have caused another person pain, "I know. I'm sorry."

He let out a sigh, wavering between wanting to be irritated and wanting her to stop fretting over his past. "Do you know what would make me feel better?"

"What?"

"Tell me what the significance is."

It was her turn to let out an uncomfortable sigh.

The bathroom door flung open, as an exhausted looking Santa hobbled his way through the room, to the table. "The little sculptures mean that you're a descendant."

"A descendant... from who?"

"From us."

Jacob's head turned to look at one of them, then the other, over and over again. "...What?"

"We had children," Joy said. "Seven of them. They were grown and working on families of their own by the time we left."

"Plus, we had siblings with nieces and nephews, as well," Santa said.

"And he just told me about all this," Joy said. "I never knew part of the magic allowed him to recognize a relation. And for every descendant, he gives them one of those figurines like the one in your office. When I told Santa about it, he said that you were not a relation. But it did make me curious as to who the figurine belonged to originally."

Jacob was speechless. "Part of the lore is that you two were childless and sort of adopted the children of the world."

"Honestly," Santa said, "how much of the lore did you expect to be actual truth? Nobody wants to think about us leaving children and family of our own behind. The truth was simply that our children were children no more."

"So how did the two of you get... chosen?"

Santa winked at him, "You don't get to know all our secrets. It'll ruin the magical façade."

"So, you two... wait... so you left, and they all continued to age."

"Yes."

"That's horrible for you two."

"The joys of the life we've gotten to live, all these centuries, are rich and full. It was a big price to pay, but the payout has been immeasurable."

"How many of those figurines have you—"

"Millions."

"Wow."

"People would have a lot of kids, back then," Joy said. "And then people started moving around and meeting new people."

"And now we have descendants on all seven continents," Santa said.

"Seven?" Joy asked.

"One is a scientific researcher doing a stint on Antarctica. So, for a while at least, we can claim seven continents," Santa said.

Joy beamed, then a thought occurred. "Do all of our descendants believe in us?"

Santa shook his head. "No, but that doesn't stop me from dropping one off for each of their babies. They end up blaming a friend or family member. They might balk about people lacking respect for their religion or beliefs, and the parent might even throw the figurine away. But that doesn't deter me, I acknowledged our relation to the infant and that's all I care about."

Jacob shook his head, so entranced by the topic at hand that he'd fairly forgotten the reason he was even there. "She was my second fiancé."

Joy had been about three seconds from going into a rant over how much her husband was still not telling her about things she honestly thought she had a right to know, but Jacob's comment cut straight through to grab her attention. "She was your what?"

"Erin was my second fiancé," Jacob repeated.

Joy felt as though she'd completely lost control of the conversation. "Erin?" she repeated, committing the name of this lost relation to memory. "...What the hell happened to the first fiancé?" she stammered.

Jacob was so defeated by having the past brought up, he didn't even bat an eyelash over Mrs. Claus cursing at him. "She died."

"What from?!"

"Mountain biking."

"She crashed?"

"Her tire hit a rock the wrong way, jerked the handlebars as the tire twisted beneath her, sending her tire rolling towards the edge. It all happened so fast that she didn't have time to correct. The path was right next to the edge, and right over she went. By the time everything hit the ground below, she'd broken her spine with the boulder she'd landed on, and part of the bike had impaled her. She died, unconscious, in my arms."

"And this is why you consider yourself married to your job," Joy said, for a lack of knowing what she could say to him.

Jacob nodded. "I think I'm cursed."

"Not cursed," Santa said. "Just incredibly unlucky."

Jacob shrugged at the difference. "It doesn't matter what you call it. I can't go through it again."

"I don't blame you," Santa said.

"So, you're just going to live your life alone?" Joy asked.

Jacob took a breath. "I was lucky to find love the first time. Gabby was adventurous, athletic, loving, and bubbly. I couldn't have asked for anyone better. And that adventurousness came back and bit us both in the butt, and she died. And I mourned her. And then I met Erin. She was bookish, soft-spoken, cuddly, and so damn smart. She was perfect in so many different ways than Gabby had been. And I loved her, and I thought she was safe, and I fell in love with her so hard. But then she died on me, too, after an agonizing medical battle that my doctorate degree was unable to help her win. I had to take a three-month leave of absence to get past it. To get over the idea of the double-whammy. I'm not going for a third round of grief. No, thank you."

"But..." Joy said, trying to find words that would soothe him. "The third time's the charm?"

Jacob shook his head. "I'm not doing it, and you can't make me."

"Stephanie seems pretty healthy."

"Gabby was healthy. Erin seemed healthy. It didn't matter. Someone's bike tire gets diverted over a cliff, or your fiancé asks you to feel a lump she just discovered in her breast that was not there before. Things change in a moment, and I end up standing over a casket."

"But if she's going to die anyway, wouldn't you rather her passing with you having the knowledge what it was like to be loved by her? To hold memories of that person, that no one else could even guess about?"

"To a point, yes. To another point, I've done that twice. If you can't guarantee me at least a silver anniversary, with children, but without having to bury any of them, then it's not worth it to me. I don't have that kind of strength left in me. Gabby and Erin took it all. I cannot do it again. And I won't risk putting myself in the position to be left behind yet again."

"But if you're destined for someone else, and you refuse to accept that, then the other person has to go to their grave, never knowing love."

"That's the kind of thinking that landed me in the arms of your hundred times great granddaughter."

"Okay," Santa said, "we're old, but not that old. She was our thirty-four times great granddaughter."

Jacob rolled his eyes and glanced at the clock on the wall. "I gotta go," he said, downing the rest of his coffee. "I have a surgery this evening I have to get ready for."

"An evening surgery?" Joy asked.

Jacob nodded. "He's being flown in from overseas."

"High-profile?"

He shook his head. "Nah, but someone who means something to a high-profile person."

"I am sorry if I upset you," Joy said as he stood.

"Forget it. I knew you were going to pry at some point." He turned to Santa, "I'll be back tomorrow to check up on you, since I didn't get to do it today." With that, he spun on his heel and high-tailed it out of there.

Santa let out a sigh as the door closed behind his doctor. "And I didn't even get to tell him about the pinching chest pain I've been having today."

Joy spun to face him, "What? You didn't say anything about a pain! I'll go get him back! The guy flying in can wait another ten minutes." She picked up her keycard and took off for the door.

Santa's chuckles were rich and full.

She spun back around, "What?"

"There's no pain. I just wanted you to feel bad about taking up my doctoring time, dredging up that man's worst memories."

She fixed him with the stink-eye she'd spent centuries perfecting. "I already felt bad about it."

"That didn't stop you from pressing him, after I told you that he'd been through a lot."

"Can you honestly tell me that he's meant to be alone for the rest of his life? That Stephanie is, as well?"

He shrugged. "I can't see anything that hasn't already been set into motion. But even if they aren't meant to be alone, that doesn't mean they're meant to be together. Let them enjoy their friendship."

"But—"

"What if he is meant to be alone and you ruin that by putting Stephanie in his sights? What if she isn't meant to be alone, but just meant to be with someone else she hasn't met yet, and misses out on the perfect guy for her, because you were determined to interfere?"

She herself drew back. "I would remind you that my instincts for this have proven successful, in the past."

"With elves."

"With three of our sons."

"Oh, yeah, there was that…"

11 THE TRUTH, THE FULL TRUTH

"Do people at the hospital believe Jacob is cursed?" Joy asked Stephanie, the next day, when the therapist came to work with Santa.

Stephanie closed her eyes to cover the fact that she rolled them. "No. But we don't blame him for feeling like he is."

"If he were to start dating again, would people talk about it and start checking in on the girlfriend?"

"Don't be silly," Stephanie said, getting ready to shift her focus to her patient. "We wouldn't start checking on her until after he proposed."

Santa started chuckling. "It's nice to know I'm not the only one you're a smartass with."

"Oh," Stephanie said, "I'm a one-stop shop on sarcasm and attitude once you get me going."

Joy shook her head. "I was just trying to figure out if he was putting the idea of the curse onto himself, or if people were telling him such lies."

"I think he uses it as a defense mechanism, to keep himself from being tempted to date again. Honestly, if I'd been through everything that he has, I'd quit opening my heart too."

"It's just such a shame. He seems like such a good guy."

"He is a good guy."

"Oh?" Joy asked, her head coming up and her gaze sharpening. "How do you know what kind of guy he is, if he's just a coworker?"

"I never said he was just a coworker. I said he was a friend. Our friendship is how I know that he's a good guy."

"So, how do you two know each other?"

Stephanie flashed her eyes to look at her, but then just as quickly moved her gaze down to the resistance bands she'd brought with her and needed to get out of her bag.

Santa's eyebrows crashed together in concern. "It's none of our business, my wife knows this. But she's just going to keep pecking away at this, until she knows the whole story. I'm sorry."

Stephanie showed Santa the next few exercises she wanted him to do with the resistance bands and then turned her full attention to Joy. "He used to date my sister."

"Just date?"

"Yeah."

"Did he eventually propose?"

Stephanie gave Joy a cautious look. "Yes."

Joy's whole demeanor changed. "And are you Gabby's sister… or are you Erin's sister?"

Stephanie slowly blew out a calming breath. "Erin was my older sister. She was everything to me."

Joy looked from Stephanie to Santa. "So, that's what's been bugging me about her. Why I can't leave it alone. I was sensing it, without knowing it."

Santa closed his eyes between reps with the band and nodded his head.

"Why didn't you just tell me?" Joy asked him.

"Because. I wanted you to sense it out on your own. I wanted you to know what that pull you feel is. Because it's unique and unmistakable once you tune in to it."

It was Stephanie's turn to look from one of them to the other. "What. The. Hell. Are you two talking about?"

Joy looked at her, not quite knowing how to tell her. She looked back at Santa, "I understand why it is that you give them the figurine as an infant and then never say anything."

"What figurine? What are you two talking about?" Stephanie asked.

Joy looked at her and regarded her a moment. "Jacob has a knick-knack type of figurine in his office, that he got from Erin."

"Santa and Mrs. Claus holding a baby. I have one that matches it. My mother has one from when she was a baby, that she has wrapped up and put away somewhere. What's the big deal with them?"

"Santa has them made for all of our descendants."

Stephanie cocked her head as though she wasn't sure she'd just heard her correctly. "For all of your what?"

"Descendants."

"You're saying we're… related?"

Joy nodded, "Through your mother, apparently."

"So… wait. You had kids?"

"Seven grown kids, when our lives changed forever."

"And you're saying I have your DNA running through me?"

"Only a tiny bit," Santa said. "Honestly, a DNA test would probably say we weren't related at all, it's been so long, with so many generations between us."

"But, like, what am I to you?" Stephanie asked.

"You are our thirty-four times great granddaughter," Santa said. "In fact, if you want to get specific, you can trace daughter back to mother, over and over, through our family tree, straight back to our youngest daughter, Rose. You and Joy represent a direct feminine line, from one straight to the other."

Stephanie shook her head, trying to take it in. "Santa and Mrs. Claus are my Granny and Gramps?"

"I'm a bit shocked by it, too," Joy said. "I didn't know, either. He's been the only one that can sense and know those things."

Stephanie turned to him, "You knew?"

Santa nodded. "I don't tell any relatives I meet. I don't want it to be a thing."

"But why?"

"Because after our children had so many children, who had so many children, and so on, over hundreds of years, through so many generations, it's too many people who might want relationships to keep track of. We wouldn't have time to devote to every one of them. So, I acknowledge it with a figurine. That way, if anyone figures out the connection, when I'm confronted, I can point to the figurine and tell them I've always known about it."

"Has anyone figured it out?" Joy asked.

He nodded, "Mostly just in the first couple hundred years. But there was one in the 1700s that believed in all the whispered family rumors, and caught me one night, leaving presents in their home, and confronted me. I simply pointed to the shelf of matching figurines and told him that not only were the family stories true, but that the figurines were my acknowledgement to such."

Stephanie flopped into a chair at the table. "Oh, my God. All my cousins on my mother's side... We all thought our grandmother gave them to us. She denied it, but it was the only thing we could think of that made any sense."

"It's not really something I'd go around advertising since there's no real way to prove it. The number of thirty-four times great grandparents a person has can topple well over sixty-eight billion... well, providing there aren't many repeats of ancestors among the descendants leading to you along the way. Though, that's very unlikely. Before widespread travel, inbreeding was quite the thing."

"What?!"

He nodded. "That's why DNA won't prove it. Too many cooks in the pot. Still though, at least millions, from eight centuries ago."

"That sounds less impressive now. And if you guys had seven kids, who all had large families... who *isn't* related to you?"

Santa grinned. "I don't know, but your smart-assery certainly comes from me."

"Did Joy give you a hard time, when you went back to try checking on Santa again?" Stephanie asked Jacob, over sausage biscuits and orange juice in his office, the next morning.

"No. She was on the phone with the President, trying to put parameters on how many multiple countries are allowed to attempt to deliver presents on Christmas Eve."

Stephanie drew her head back, "Yikes."

"Yeah. Santa was telling me that people don't like to respect a tiny, stealth, sovereign nation, when they think they have something you need. Other countries now see a way in, and are balking about maybe not being granted access, after all."

"Geez. Well, at least you got to have a peaceful visit."

"She cornered you too, didn't she? She nailed me the day before."

"Yeah, and you spilled your guts to her. Her questioning started out all about whether your belief in being cursed was self-inflicted, or if you were being bullied in the workplace."

He snort-laughed. "Co-workers don't try to bully me. I get enough of that with patients."

"I know... But why did you tell her everything?"

Jacob shook his head. "I think she put something in my coffee."

Stephanie smiled over the rim of her cup. "Was it nutmeg?"

He shook his head. "I don't know. Maybe she's got some sort of magic of her own. All I know is that it came spilling out of me. She kept apologizing. And the more she apologized for bringing it up, the more I felt compelled to tell her."

"I know! I felt that urge too! It's like she asks you a probing question and then emotes so much sympathy that you just start telling her your woes."

"I swear she knows she's doing it. She came in here last week and saw that damned figurine of your sister's on my shelf. That's what she started the conversation off with. Asking about the freaking thing."

Stephanie diverted her attention to the sandwich, putting a bite into her mouth and chewing.

"You said it started out about me. What did it evolve into?" he asked.

Her eyes rolled as her gaze moved from her sandwich to him. "The freaking figurine. What else?"

"So... They told you..."

"That they're my long-lost granny and gramps? Oh yeah. You coulda done something to prepare me for that one, don't you think?"

He put his hands up in supplication. "Hey, I didn't know if they wanted anyone else to know."

"I do thank you for not bringing me into the story. I mean, it provided me plenty of fodder to fan the flame of her shock, as she found out you were engaged to my sister and we both had to watch her die."

"Well, I figured that part was your story to tell."

"What are we going to do about her?"

"We could start kicking her out of the room. We can tell her she diverts our attention away from Santa, thereby impairing our ability to provide proper medical care."

She set her sandwich down. "Do you honestly have the heart to make her feel like she's holding his recovery back?"

"Why not? We've kicked spouses out before."

"Because she's going to turn that gaze onto us. That half-horrified, half-heartbroken gaze she has, when she thinks either she, or someone else has done something wrong."

"Okay. Then what solution do you propose?"

She shifted back in her chair and put her feet up on his desk. "Fake it 'til you make it."

His eyebrows rose. "You want us to fake-date each other?"

She shrugged. "Why not? We know enough about each other, at this point. And it's only for a few weeks."

"But don't you think Santa will know? He seems to know things about people."

"Why would he even bother looking too closely?"

"Um, I'm pretty sure lying to Mrs. Claus will land us on the naughty list, instantaneously. He's going to have to check it out."

She was nonplussed. "We don't even get presents anymore."

"Because we doubted them. But we're obviously believers again."

"Do you honestly think he's going to blame us for lying? He knows how she is."

"Huh. You may have a point."

"And we're on to the fact that she possesses some sort of voodoo that has us telling her personal stuff. So, we resist the urge. We just gotta think before we speak, is all."

He narrowed his eyes at her. "What about your man friend?"

"What about him?"

"Is he going to have a problem with it?"

She rolled her eyes. "With our fake dating? No. You know very well that things are purposely not serious between us. My freedom to do whatever I want is fully intact."

"Just checking... So, what do we do? Do we hang out together in the evenings? Do we go out, so we have something to report back to her with?"

"I don't know. I mean, maybe we do something on the weekends, for an hour or two. Just so that we have something to talk about that matches up with what the other is reporting. But aside from that? We're two very busy professionals."

"You know, maybe we can actually benefit from this too."

It was her turn to narrow her eyes at him. "I don't do multiple friends with benefits, one is enough."

He grinned as he shook his head. "Not what I'm talking about."

"Then what?"

"Well, I broke my couch. And you have a better eye for home décor than I do. Maybe our first 'date' can be furniture shopping."

"Oh!" she exclaimed, letting the chair rock her upright. "That's good. Let's use that. We say you asked for help from a friend because friends do that."

"And it can spiral into dinner."

"And maybe we linger over a drink."

"And there was no kiss, but there was definitely a spark."

"Oh, that's good. That seems like a natural evolution."

"And we don't admit to the spark right away. We make her drag it out of us, a little."

"And we don't know if the spark was reciprocated, but we think that we hope that it was."

"Sounds like a plan. I'm fine to not do dinner, but I do seriously need a new couch."

"How did you break it?"

"I was watching the Olympics, enough said."

She giggled. "Which sport?"

"The skiers were hot-dogging."

She laughed a bit harder. "And were you trying to pull off a flip of some sort?"

"I started out just doing it from the couch cushions. But I needed more height, before I broke my neck. So, I stood up on the back of the couch, jumped to test my balance, fell, and took out the couch right along with myself.

"The Olympics were months ago."

He shrugged. "I don't like shopping, so I've procrastinated."

She held up her juice glass. "Operation: Expel Granny from Our Personal Lives, is on."

He held his glass up and clinked it with hers. "Deal."

12 SURE, YOU CAN

"How are you today, Jacob?" Joy asked when he showed up to check on Santa, that Monday afternoon.

"I'm doing well. But, alas, I'm not the patient."

She smiled and carried on, fixing some coffee for him, despite his obvious reminder. "The weather was just beautiful for a late fall weekend. We enjoyed meals out on the balcony."

"Oh? I hope the fresh air helped Santa feel more like his old self."

"I believe it did. How about you? Did you get outside much, this weekend?" she asked, carrying cups over to the table.

He let out a sigh, trying not to look at the table. If she didn't mention the coffee, and he managed not to 'see' it, then it wouldn't be rude for him to avoid it. "Not as much as I would have liked. I'm afraid I had some errands to see to."

"Oh? Anything interesting?"

The barest of smiles crossed over his features because he knew she'd just given him the perfect chance to lay the groundwork for their deception. "I needed to buy a new couch."

She frowned. "I hope you at least went out to a real store. You can't judge comfort online."

He smiled at yet another perfect opportunity to feed her the story. "It wasn't comfort I was most concerned about. It was coordinating it with the rest of the room. I mean, they have software where you can upload a picture of your room, so you can judge how it will look, but I have no clue about stuff like that."

"Did you have the sales rep help you?"

"No. I don't know how good any of them are with that. So, I asked Stephanie to go with me."

The biggest of smiles spread across Joy's face. "Oh, really?"

Jacob rolled his eyes. "Yes, really."

"Well, that sounds just lovely."

"You know," he said tentatively, "it was rather lovely."

Her smile turned sly.

He nodded. "It's lovely having a *friend* I can turn to for furniture purchases."

She didn't let his comment sour her hopefulness for them. "Santa will be out in just a moment. He was napping, until I woke him a moment before you came in."

"You know, it's interesting how often he's conveniently in another room when one of us comes."

"I know you're trying to blame me, but the man is habitually late for anything personal. Professionally, he's always on time. But aside from that, all bets are off."

The door opened and Santa came out. "She's talking about me again, isn't she?"

Jacob smiled, "Always."

Santa, moving a little faster than the week before, made his way over to a chair at the table and picked up a cup. "Coffee?" he offered, gesturing to the third cup on the table.

Jacob found that it took everything in him to shake his head. "I really shouldn't. Your tardiness is soaking up all my time. So, how are you doing?"

Santa let out a sigh as his eyes darted over to Joy and back to him. "I got lightheaded a couple of times."

Jacob nodded, any thoughts about Joy and her coffee gone, "Did you pass out?"

"No."

"How long did the dizziness last?"

"Just a few seconds."

"And what are you doing when it happens?"

"Once when I shifted sitting positions. Twice when I first stood up."

"Okay," Jacob said, nodding. "You're probably experiencing some blood pressure fluctuations." He pulled out a portable blood pressure machine and cuff. "I'm going to leave this here. And I want you to take your blood pressure every two to three hours, throughout the day, and write the times and readings down. And if you're sleeping, don't worry about it. Just take it when you get up."

Santa grumbled.

"I'll make sure it gets done," Joy promised, any questions about Jacob's personal life forgotten.

Jacob caught Santa's gaze again. "Anything else?"

"No."

"What about skin pulling against the stitches?"

"Yeah. Sometimes."

"Let me see the incision."

Santa lifted his shirt.

Jacob inspected the stitches closely. "Yeah, I can see the two causing the problems. They look a little more raw than the others, but at least you're doing a good job at not popping them. Just try not to move in the ways that make them pull, because they'll take longer to heal. The good news is there's no sign of infection, just tenderness."

"Okay."

"Anything else?"

Santa shook his head.

"Alright. If the lightheadedness gets worse, call me."

Santa nodded.

"And if you pass out, call 911."

"What's 911?" Joy asked.

Jacob turned in her direction. "911 is an emergency number... I don't know if your phones will know what to do if that's all you dial. "I tell you what, you pick up the hotel phone. Dial 9, then pause for it to get you an outside line, then dial 911. They'll ask what your emergency is. You give them the hotel address, it's on the stationary, and tell them your room number, it's on the phone, and tell them he's post double bypass, and has passed out."

Joy started writing notes.

"You'll also tell them my name, and the name of the hospital."

Joy nodded.

"Alright, you two," Jacob said, straightening away from his patient. "I need to get going."

Joy walked him to the door. "How worried should I be?"

"Enough to keep an eye on it. Not enough to lose sleep over it."

He gave her an encouraging smile, crossed the threshold, and she shut the door behind him.

Walking down the hall and pressing the down button for the elevator, he took his phone out of his pocket. The elevator doors opened, he moved inside, hit the button for the lobby, and dialed Stephanie.

She answered on the first ring. "Did you lay the trap?" she asked.

"I only told her about the couch shopping."

"But you were supposed to tell her about the dinner, to thank me for the shopping favor."

"I couldn't do it."

"Why?"

"It's the kid in me. It's definitely a naughty listable offense."

She laughed in his ear as the doors opened and he exited the elevator and headed for the entrance. He let her continue to giggle until he got out onto the street. "I can't lie directly to a Claus."

"Sure, you can. You and Erin used to lie to my parents, right?"

"Well," his eyebrows scrunched, and lips puckered, "anyone can lie to parents, especially when they're your girlfriend's parents. It was the only way to have any fun."

"Exactly."

"What, exactly? You lie to family to keep the peace. What family doesn't know can't hurt them."

"Exactly. They're my grandparents, and you've lied to my family before. So, there's your loophole."

"But you're not my girlfriend."

"So? Your prior offenses to the truth with my family give you the loophole you need to continue to lie to my family members."

"I don't think—"

"Then stop thinking."

He laughed hard in her ear.

"Look, it's okay, this time. I'll tell them about the fake dinner and drinks, it's fine. But she's going to ask you about them, the next time she sees you."

"Yeah, I'll work on my moral compass. In the meantime, he's been experiencing some dizziness. He's supposed to be logging blood pressure readings every few hours. So, when you're there, just put your eyes on the log and make sure they're doing it and that the numbers aren't dangerous. And if they're not logging, or if they are dangerous, give me a call, okay?"

"Absolutely. Anything else?"

"Nope. That's all I got."

"Alrighty. Talk to you later."

"Yep." He disconnected the call and kept on walking.

"Good afternoon!" Stephanie boasted, her smile glowing as she crossed into the hotel suite as soon as Joy opened the door.

"Well, your Monday certainly seems to be going well," Joy said with a grin.

"It is," Stephanie said, crossing the room to Santa. "How are you doing? A little birdie told me your head's spinning around."

Santa grinned. "Blame the wife. Even centuries later, she still turns my head."

"Oh!" Stephanie said, feigning shock and turning to Joy. "Look who's flirting! But don't you listen to him, Joy. No hanky-panky until Jacob clears him. Which won't happen if his blood pressure isn't stable."

"A little flirting goes a long way in calming her down, especially after finding out about the dizzy spells," Santa said.

"Oh," Stephanie said. "Very well then, carry on."

She set about giving Santa his list of exercises while Joy watched.

"Must have been a good weekend," Joy said.

"Oh, yes, the weather was gorgeous," Stephanie said.

"You know, that's what I said to Jacob, earlier. Santa and I ate our meals out on the balcony. The extra lighting on display for the holidays really helps to give our view a cozy feel to it. Did you happen to get out this weekend?"

"I got a good amount of yardwork done, yesterday."

"I hear that's a good workout."

"You don't have a yard?"

"Well, it's the Arctic, so… nothing really grows."

"Well, I don't really grow anything, either… But how do you obtain food up there?"

"When you don't age within the Pole, you don't really need to eat very much. Meals tend to only follow energy-draining tasks."

"It is a treat, though," Santa said. "Sometimes we'll make a run to somewhere interesting and order up some catering to take back."

"Wow," Stephanie said, taking that in. "I think I'd miss food."

"You know, living the way we did, before we became who we are to everyone, food was limited where we were. We didn't have all the different items available, with dozens of ways to season and prepare it," Joy said. "So, in many ways, it was a relief to not have to worry about where we were going to find food next, only to sit down to the same boring meal that was taken in solely for survival."

Stephanie considered that for a moment. "Wow, then your time here, surrounded by all the food choices must be quite overwhelming."

"It's been a chore," Santa said. "Having to make all those meal choices. It honestly makes me want to just order the same thing, over and over again."

Joy nodded. "And yet, I'm anxious to try it all."

"Except that our digestive systems are not used to such abuse," Santa said with a chuckle.

Stephanie chuckled right along with him, "Oh, no."

"Yeah," Santa said with a chuckle. "I'm particularly grateful to be holed up in a country with reliable indoor plumbing."

Stephanie let out a snicker.

Joy let the conversation lull while Stephanie gave Santa more instructions. But once she was done, Joy said, "So Jacob mentioned you two spent some time together on Saturday."

Not missing a beat, Stephanie nodded. "We tried that little Italian place, down about two blocks from here. It was good. You should try it while you have the chance."

"Italian? Do you mean the two of you shared a meal? Jacob didn't mention that."

"Well," Stephanie said, stealing a glance at her, acting as though she were trying to minimalize the 'slip' in revealing too much, "it was just as a thank you, for helping him pick out a couch."

"Well, that was very nice of him."

"It was, actually. Choosing the couch really only took twenty minutes."

"You know what I find interesting?"

"What's that?"

"How you know the interior of his house so well that you could pick a couch out for him, to coordinate with the décor."

Stephanie flashed a look at her and let out a sigh. "The couch is the first thing he's changed since before my sister died. They were living together for six months prior to her death. I was over to his house plenty of times. Plus, he'd taken pictures to refresh my memory."

"Oh," Joy said, looking down at her hands. "Sorry. I thought maybe you'd spent some time at his house this weekend."

"No. And honestly, by the time we'd gotten done shopping, eating, and then having drinks, it was more than enough time for me to have spent with him."

"Drinks?"

"Well, yeah. It was an Italian restaurant."

"So that means drinks?"

"I thought people lingered over coffee, after dinner, in this country," Santa said. "Or am I mixing up my world cultures?"

"Depends on what's offered. I have a weakness for good Amaretto. He knows that, so he offered."

Joy's face lit up. "Well, it certainly sounds like the two of you stretched a simple chore into a very enjoyable evening."

"I have a Roger," Stephanie informed them.

Joy raised an eyebrow in question to Santa. "She has a Roger?"

"She does not have a Roger," Santa answered.

"Well," Stephanie grumbled, "I have something going on with a Roger."

Joy's phone rang. She looked at the number and let out an exasperated sigh. "Excuse me," she said. "I have to go do battle with a bunch of spoiled brats." She stood and headed for the bedroom.

"Elves, or politicians?" Stephanie asked.

"Poli-freaking-ticians," Joy muttered as she entered the bedroom and closed the door behind herself.

Stephanie didn't even try to hide her smile. "They made Mrs. Claus say 'freaking'."

Santa watched his wife walk away but grinned at Stephanie's comment.

"Mrs. Claus has a bit of a potty mouth when she's riled and thinks no one is listening."

"Really?"

He nodded, waiting until he was sure the door had fully closed behind his wife, before turning back to Stephanie. "What did you have for dinner at the Italian restaurant?" he asked.

"Chicken parmesan."

"And what did he have?"

"Carbonara."

"Did you have dessert?"

"No, we were too full. That's why he opted to offer drinks."

"What drink did he have?"

"He had an Italian coffee."

"You weren't worried he was trying to liquor you up?"

"*Pfft.* It was Jacob. I'm safe with him."

"Uh-huh."

She was failing at hiding her smile as she packed up her stuff.

"For the record, I know exactly what you two are up to."

She paused to look him straight in the eye. "We figured you would. Are you gonna let it fly?"

He pretended to mull it over for a moment. "…This whole thing has been hard on her. She's doing a decent job at not letting it show, but I can tell. She's stressed. And, admittedly, her having a pleasant diversion, even if it is fake, might do her more good than harm. By the time the disappointment hits, hopefully I'll be well on the mend and can start alleviating some of her worry."

"Really?"

"Yes. But don't be surprised when I try to act like I didn't take the time to realize what was going on."

She grinned. "Understood."

Moments later, passing by the guards in the hall, and getting on the elevator, Stephanie pulled out her phone, hit the button to call a contact, and waited for the person on the other end to answer. When he picked up, she said, "Guess who just got Gramps' blessing."

13 SLOW GOING

"I called into your office with a question on Friday, and found out you had a three-day weekend," Joy said.

Santa grunted as a small, fleeting smile crossed Stephanie's features.

"I flew down to Florida, to celebrate my mother's sixtieth birthday," Stephanie said.

"That's a bit early, to retire to Florida," Joy murmured. "Is your father significantly older than her?"

Stephanie chuckled. "No. I grew up in Florida until I was twelve. My Dad became a Florida Senator. That's how we ended up here in DC. We bounced back and forth between Florida and DC for years, but my sister and I both went to college up here. Dad stayed in the Senate long enough for Erin and me to graduate, then stopped running for re-election. He gave Erin and I the house to live in, and he and Mom went back to Florida, permanently."

"Why didn't you want to settle down there? I mean, it's Florida."

Santa raised an eyebrow at his wife.

"I'm not saying I would want to live there," Joy muttered. "I'm just saying, a lot of people act like that'd be the thing to do."

Stephanie shrugged even as she smirked at the two of them. "I made it my goal to work in a prestigious hospital. I guess you could say it feeds my ego to work with VIPs like Santa. I like knowing first-hand that these people with big names are just regular people, living extraordinary lives. And when I see them on the television, I know that I had a hand in helping them along the way. Knowing that helps me not to be intimidated when I see other influential people around town, that I don't know through my profession. And, truth be told, I get off on not being impressed by a person just because they have some sort of lofty job title."

Santa grunted again.

Stephanie turned to look at him. "You're different. I'm impressed by how damned old you are."

He chuckled in response to that one.

"So, I guess you didn't get a chance to see Jacob over the weekend." Joy said.

Stephanie rolled her eyes and abruptly cleared her throat, turning to Santa with her whole body, shifting her attention to focus solely on him, and gave him a bright smile. "Let's get you started on these exercises. It's time to start upping your game."

Joy watched the pair work throughout the hour. Stephanie was unwilling to be probed for more information about her weekend, but Joy wasn't fazed. She was paying enough attention to know that Stephanie hadn't been so laser focused until she'd brought up Jacob's name. Obviously, something had happened between the two of them. Maybe he'd given her a ride to the airport, or something. And the fact that they seemed to be trying to hide it was adorable.

"So, which do you want first?" Stephanie asked, spreading lunch out across Jacob's desk. "The Santa update, or the Joy update?"

Jacob rolled his eyes at her.

She smiled. "Santa, of course, yes. I momentarily forgot who I was talking to. You're Jacob. Unless you're humoring a patient or spouse of a patient, it's always business first."

He raised an eyebrow. "He had a heart attack."

She quickly nodded. "I know, I know. And it's a serious thing. I'm just teasing you a little."

"You're not the one who holds people's hearts in your hands."

"Please do not gear yourself up to tell me your job is more important than mine. You may save lives, but I get them back on course."

He immediately gentled his features. "You know I'd never do that. I only meant that you get the more relaxed side of cases."

She nodded in acknowledgement of that truth. "Precisely why I went into therapy. No one's waking me up in the middle of the night with a therapy emergency. I get a more relaxed life because of it."

"So, Santa," he said, reaching for one of the bottles of water.

She handed him a fork for his salad. "Yes, Santa. It's not high blood pressure causing his dizziness. It's low blood pressure."

He sat back in his chair. "Huh. Are you sure?"

She nodded. "Joy circled the readings she took when he was having the dizzy spells. His pressure is dipping."

He nodded and opened his tablet to update the chart, "I'll knock down the dosage of his medication and see how he does."

"He's also not progressing along in his therapy as quickly as I would like."

He looked up at her. "What do you think is the cause? Do you think he just isn't doing his exercises as often as you assign?"

"No. I think Joy would be all over him, if he wasn't."

"Do you think it's psychological?"

"Eh. He might be reacting to the idea that even if he beats records in recovery, he still won't be cleared to deliver in time."

"What's your gut telling you?"

"I'm kind of thinking he's enjoying being human again."

"You think he's using this as a vacation?"

She nodded. "Think about it. You think the heart attack was brought on by untreated hypertension. Now, all of a sudden, his blood pressure is dipping? I mean, don't get me wrong. Maybe he doesn't want to push himself with the dizzy spells and the threat of popping stitches, making his scars bigger and him having to live with them for however many more centuries he may have left. But," she paused to shake her head, "he went from upset that Joy would have to handle all the calls and business back home, to not even blinking when she gets a call and has to leave the room to talk business with world leaders."

"She gets those calls while you're there, too?"

Stephanie nodded. "It used to bug him, to watch her walk away with the phone. Now it doesn't even phase him. I think it bugged him that he'd miss the deliveries, and I think he's come to accept that, so why should he push himself? I think he's taking a step back and relaxing, for once. And if that's his mindset, I don't think he'll be in a hurry to get back."

"So, they won't be going home at the end of this week?"

She shook her head, "Maybe next week."

He nodded, making mental notes for when he went to visit the famous duo that afternoon. "Okay, now Joy."

Stephanie sat back in her chair. "I played it not cool. I told her I went to Florida for the weekend. And then avoided the topic when she tried to pry enough to see if I saw you at all over my three-day break."

"Got it."

She glanced at her watch, groaned, and started shoveling her salad into her mouth. "I've got ten minutes," she mumbled around her bite.

He grinned. She might give him grief about his job dedication, but that didn't mean that she wasn't incredibly dedicated, as well. You didn't get assigned to the cases she tackled without having some serious levels of job commitment, and the ability to keep her mouth shut about who she was treating... *Huh*.

That may be the reason she seemed so eager to play this game with Joy, and to have someone to play it with.

94

He couldn't help the gentle grin that settled around his mouth as he glanced at the clock and realized he wasn't doing much better in the time department.

"So, how did you enjoy your three-day weekend?" Joy asked when she opened the door.

Jacob blinked his eyes and shook his head for her benefit. "First of all, I haven't even gotten into the room yet, and you're already prying. And secondly, I didn't have a three-day weekend. I had post-operative patients to attend to, and an emergency surgery on Friday. That's the only reason you didn't see me."

"Oh," Joy said, with no small amount of disappointment in her voice.

"Can I come in, now?"

"Oh! Of course," she said, scrambling out of the way to let the doctor in.

Santa was at the table, shaking his head at the scene. "She was so sure you and Stephanie were together over the weekend."

"Well," Joy said, defensively, "far be it from me to think that he'd be the type to be invited to a family affair, by his dead fiancé's parents."

Jacob let out a long and tortured sigh. "I was invited to the sixtieth birthday party."

"I knew it!" Joy said, plopping down on a chair at the table. "You couldn't be bothered to take a day off and go?"

Jacob raised both eyebrows at her. "First of all, they only invited me because they appreciate how I stood by Erin's side throughout her fight for survival. And, they also believe I haven't moved on from it, either."

"So, you didn't feel obligated in any way to pay your respects in their daughter's stead," Joy said, nodding.

Jacob closed his eyes and took in a breath. "Not that it's any of your business, but I took a late flight down on Friday night. I slept the whole flight and the stewardess had to wake me for the landing. I got to the hotel at, like, two a.m., all so I could attend the party."

Joy looked thrilled.

He turned to look at Santa, sitting down in the chair next to him, exasperated. "She got on me like that just so I'd break and tell her I ended up in the same place as Stephanie, didn't she?"

Santa chuckled, nodding his head. "It's rather entertaining to watch, from this side of things."

A phone rang and Jacob's hand automatically went to his pocket before he realized it wasn't the right ringtone to be his.

"Son of a bitch," Joy muttered when she pulled out her phone and looked at the number. "Toddlers, all of them." She stood and left the room.

Jacob watched her walk away and then turned to watch Santa watch her.

"Politicians," Santa said. "They don't want to do things the way the elves want to do them, and vice versa. Meanwhile, they all suddenly feel entitled to our airspace, just because, for once, we're the ones needing someone to do something for us. You show one sign of momentary weakness, and they're all looking to pounce."

"And yet, you don't seem stressed by that."

"Are you kidding? She's gone into full-blown Mama Bear mode."

"Should I be worried about her stress level?"

Santa shook his head. "Her abilities have been suppressed for ages. For the first time, I'm seeing what she's really made of. Watching her take all this on, planting her feet on a line and refusing to let others bully her into agreeing with them, it's amazing for me to see it. It's something I always knew was inside of her. I mean, you can't handle the life we've led and not be capable of all this. But it's never bubbled over the surface like this before. And, son, I've got to tell you, it's a real turn on for me."

Jacob threw his head back and laughed.

"What?" Santa asked. "Is it that you so associate us with kids that you can't imagine that there's a sexier side to our marriage? Or is that we've been married for so long that everyone thinks we're above such things now? Or is it that you all believe we're too damned old to make some body parts work properly anymore?"

Jacob shook his head, trying to get the images out. "It's probably all three. But that's beside the point. Stephanie told me your blood pressure has been dropping and that you're lagging a little behind in progressing through your therapy. We kind of thought you were beginning to treat this all like you were on some sort of vacation. Here, you're just enjoying the hell out of watching her stand her ground."

"Oh, well, I do admit to staying out of her way. What with the warpath she's been waging, part of me is eager to stand aside and let her fly."

Jacob chuckled enough that his shoulders shook.

"How behind am I? I don't want to worry Joy, because God knows she'll focus all that attention on me, and that is something I do not find to be cute."

"You're still bumping the curb. But you won't be returning home this weekend. You've bought yourself another week down here."

"Huh. Another week without the chaos of life up there, this time of year? That does sound like a vacation."

"Santa…"

"I'll get back on track."

"Now, if you go back up there, before Christmas, are you going to stress yourself right back out, or are you going to hole yourself away from it?"

"Are you kidding me? She's not going to allow anyone to come to me with anything."

"Alright."

"To your point, though, admittedly, once I wrapped my mind around letting others take care of everything, it sure has been nice to have a reason to sit back and just let it all go. So, in many ways, it has begun to feel like a respite. But if I've gone overboard on the whole taking it easy bit, I'll get back on the horse."

"And here's where I cause you to become confused by reminding you not to overdo it, either. Just listen to your body, how hard to push, when to back off. Some people recover slower than others. It's just that you were clipping right along, and now you're slowing."

"Got it. I'll make fewer goo-goo eyes at my wife and work a bit harder at recovery."

"Alright, in the meantime, just as Stephanie saw in these logs, your blood pressure is dipping, so I'm going to tell you to cut those hypertension pills in half and then keep taking your blood pressure periodically. I want to see if that solves the problem."

"But do you think once I get back up there, after recovery, and get back into the swing of things, that my blood pressure will rise back up?"

"I think taking daily blood pressure readings upon your return will become part of your new routine. At least for a while."

He nodded. "Do you think it'll fluctuate once inside the North Pole?"

"I don't know," Jacob admitted. "But that's what daily readings will help us figure out. If it doesn't, then maybe we only medicate you when you're outside the bubble, so that it reads normal once you're inside. If your pressure somehow freezes, let's let it freeze at a good reading."

"Alright," Joy said, bursting through the door to the bedroom, "I was afraid I wouldn't get back out here before you left. Now, did you and Stephanie get to spend some time together?"

Jacob let out a sigh and winked at Santa. "Well, she was pretty much the only other person I knew down there, aside from the immediate family."

"And what about coming home, yesterday?"

"We sat next to each other on the plane."

"And how did that go?"

"The flight was uneventful. Not even a bit of turbulence, with a smooth landing. Everything you could want from a pilot, plane, weather, and crew."

Joy let out a frustrated sigh as Jacob tried hard not to smile.

14 ANNOUNCEMENT

"News out of Washington this morning. Doctors at Walter Reed Medical Center, in conjunction with the White House, will be holding a press conference later this Friday afternoon.

"The White House has remained tight-lipped about the topic to be addressed. Rumors run high that the announcement will address the health of the President, or a member of the President's immediate family, given that Walter Reed is where the President would go for medical care."

"For the record," Joy told Santa, as the newscaster finished with his theorizing, "if you ever decide to declare the North Pole enough of a sovereign entity that you become a true politician, I'm divorcing you."

Santa grinned. "There are no paper documents proving our existence. What lawyer would you find, never mind what court would you go to, to prove the marriage even exists?"

"I don't know, but I'd figure it out," she muttered.

"Legally," Jacob said, "I'm pretty sure that, at this point, you could just walk away from it all. Without proof of marriage, how could he contest it?"

Joy nodded at Jacob, "Very true."

Jacob turned to Santa, "Are you sure you don't want to speak to the press? Maybe take some questions."

Santa shook his head, "I don't want everyone knowing exactly what I look like. It'll ruin the magic and the mystery if they see that I'm just a human, after all. It's bad enough they'll be hearing about it. Plus, I like having the ability to blend in when I'm away from home and not doing deliveries."

"But you'll have a chance to speak for yourself."

"Son, the first thing they're going to do is ask me to prove that I'm Santa. Then the second thing they're going to do is try to fix the situation by asking me why I'm not taking whatever approach to preserving Christmas flings itself into their heads first. I'm not interested."

"He's also an introvert, but I'm not supposed to admit such things about him," Joy said.

"Well, okay," Jacob said. "But if I start getting hate calls from Cupid, I am not going to be a happy camper."

"Now there's an idea," Joy said. "I should talk to Cupid about your situation."

"My situation?" Jacob asked. "What is it that you think your reindeer can help me with?"

"I thought you were talking about the actual Cupid, not the reindeer we named after him."

"I was… You mean Cupid is real, too?"

Santa chuckled. "We're all real. Did you really think I was the only one?"

"Well, it's not like Cupid actually runs around on Valentine's Day."

"It's not like people only fall in love one day a year," Santa said. "It's just that they celebrate that love on a specific day. Which is why Cupid doesn't mind our plan. We're good, you're safe."

Jacob turned to Joy. "If Cupid is real, then yes, talk to him about my situation and ask him if fiancés dropping dead on me is my lot in life, or was he just screwing around with me."

Joy smiled. "He's not to blame for relationships cut short. It's not like he sets up every couple. If that were the case, he'd have been fired long ago. It's humans that choose a lot of the wrong people."

Jacob turned to Santa, "I know the hospital held drills for you needing care, but…"

"But what?" Santa asked.

"Is there a vet, somewhere, lined up to help care for the Easter Bunny?"

"I actually haven't asked," Santa said.

"But is he an actual bunny?"

Santa blinked twice before consternation took over his features, "I'm not your mythical, mystical figure guru. I'll speak for myself, and occasionally for my wife, but that's it."

"Of course," Jacob said, immediately letting the subject drop.

"At any rate," Santa said, "this is how I'd like to handle it, as long as you're good to handle the press conference."

Jacob nodded. "No one expects a doctor to pull off a perfect press conference, so low expectations play into my favor. I'll handle it."

"Here now, from Washington, at the Walter Reed Medical Center, is chief cardiothoracic surgeon, Dr. Jacob Hershey."

The camera cut from the network news anchor at his desk in-studio, and opened to a team of healthcare professionals, sitting at a table in the lobby of the hospital. The man sitting in the center seat sat upright and reminded himself not to lean into the microphone, but to just speak clearly.

"Good afternoon. My name is Dr. Jacob Hershey. For the past few weeks, I have headed a team who has been treating and working with a very special patient. And I'd like to start my report by reassuring everyone that this patient is set to make a full and complete recovery.

"Approximately four weeks ago, world leaders got the call that Santa had suffered a heart attack. The news was followed by a plea for immediate help, as the healthcare at the North Pole is lacking for such an event. Many countries offered help, but it was the US President that offered to send Coast Guard Special Forces to move Santa from the North Pole, to here for medical treatment, and an offer to provide lodging for his recovery, as well. The Claus' accepted our President's offer, and Santa was brought here within hours.

"I, and my team, performed an open-heart, double-bypass surgery, to repair Santa's heart. The surgery was successful, and he has spent the time since then recovering. And while Santa has been making strides in his journey to better health, it is my job to inform all of you that he will not be able to make his deliveries on Christmas Eve this year. It's simply not enough time for Santa to make a full recovery and go back to the intense work that is required of him, to perform the task.

"At Santa's request, I'm making the next announcement on his behalf: Santa wishes for families and friends to celebrate Christmas without him, this year. As for your gifts from him and the elves, Santa needs your patience and understanding. His presents to the world will arrive, but they will be late. Santa will be making his deliveries on Valentine's Eve, instead.

"While he understands it can be difficult to wait even longer for the goodies he brings, he knows all of you can understand that he needs to be in tip-top shape, so that he can complete his mission, and not leave any believers without a gift.

"Santa's presents have always been about spreading love and cheer, so what better day to substitute his famous ride with but Valentine's Day? Santa has assured me that Cupid doesn't mind this change, at all, and joins Santa in wishing everyone a merry and joyous holiday season. Thank you."

Jacob sat back in his chair, and just as he was expecting the director to call 'cut', questions started being asked by the reporters standing opposite him.

"Are you sure it's actually the real Santa?"

"Did you consider other treatment options?"

"Have you tried any holistic treatments?"

"What is his recovery regime?"

"Is he at risk for a second heart attack?"

"Is Santa still in the hospital? Where is he staying?"

"How did he get to you within hours? Why didn't you go to him?"

"Is this a conspiracy to cover Santa's death?"

"How is he human? Is he human?"

"If he's as old as to be believed, how did the magic allow him to get sick?"

"Will this force Santa into retirement?"

"Why can't the elves deliver the presents?"

"Why can't we send up our military to get the gifts?"

"Were you paid for your treatment? Does Santa have insurance, or is everything to be paid by the American taxpayers?"

Jacob sat up in his chair again. "I'll not be taking questions at this time. Any further details to be released will not be at my discretion. But, yes, I've seen enough in the past month to know that he is the real Santa, and he is most assuredly still alive. That's all I have for you. Thank you."

Jacob sat back in his chair and gave a pointed look to the director. Either the guy was going to call 'cut', or Jacob was going to stand and leave.

The director got the point, pushed the button, and called, "Cut. Clear."

Jacob nodded, ignoring the reporters who'd resumed calling out their questions. He stood, turned, and left, heading straight for his office. The rest of the team, who'd been present merely for show, all stood to leave as well. Stephanie pushed her chair back under the table, and followed behind Jacob, all the way to his office.

"Way to stand your ground," she said, closing the door behind her as she entered.

"Patient-Doctor confidentiality," he said, collapsing onto his office chair with a relieved sigh. "That sucked."

"It did," she said, sitting down across from him. "You gotta love how you prepped them by saying you'd be taking no questions. And they prepped you by saying they'd immediately cut. But then they think they can just keep rolling and maybe you'll cave."

"Meanwhile, they're doing good just to get a doctor to talk about a case at all." He let out a sigh, "Whatever. It's done now."

"Do you think it was smart for Joy to change the public announcement, before telling the world leaders that they won't be accepting military help, after all?"

"I don't know. And that's not my problem to figure out and solve. Only one thing was for sure, I wasn't going to stick around long enough to hear about it. I'm not even going to watch the news, to find out how they twist and turn it. I would like to remain oblivious."

She giggled. "Why? You're not responsible for their choosing to postpone the trip."

"I prefer not knowing how my actions have ripple effects," he said, and gave a little shiver.

The motion hadn't escaped Stephanie's attention. Working on the high-profile patients that had come and gone, she knew that whether someone with a lofty title was able to return to work or not had repercussions on the laws and actions that shaped not only the country they came from, but sometimes the world. She knew the last thing she wanted to feel was responsible for a past patients' ability to make poor decisions. But, in this particular case, she didn't think that was the reason for his reluctance. "You don't want to watch the commentary of people trying to obliterate the messenger."

"Exactly," he said with a nod.

"You could have told them that you were going to stick to the medical facts and denied passing along the additional message."

He shook his head solemnly. "When Santa asks you for a favor, you don't say no."

She smiled with a half-chuckle. "Yeah. I agree. A smart person doesn't chance crossing Santa if you can help it."

"I can't believe you used a medical press conference to send out that message," the US President said in his next phone conference with Joy.

"Well, I didn't much care for it, either. But it seemed to be the most efficient way to cease all the bickering that was going on," Joy said, more than a little annoyed with the situation.

"I wouldn't call it bickering."

"What would you call it?"

"Politicizing."

"Well, Mr. Claus and I both believe that people have politicized Christmas quite enough. And there was no way I was going to sit through another meeting where world leaders went about trying to explain to me how they were going to handle their intrusion into a sovereign territory that isn't theirs."

"We were coming to diplomatic solutions—"

"Well, we've come to our own diplomatic solution. He's delivering everything seven and a half weeks later. If you don't want to give him clearance over your airspace, fine. Go ahead and try to catch him in the act. Santa is never seen unless he wants to be seen."

There was a long sigh in her ear. "I'll give Santa clearance anytime he wants it. But good luck with some of the other countries."

"You'll understand if Santa doesn't install NORAD's tracker this time. If he has to return to stealth-mode, so be it."

"They'll still know he's been to whatever country opposes you, by way of the trail of toys he leaves behind."

"That's mere evidence. Without actual, physical, proof of his presence, the UN isn't going to tolerate anyone trying to stop Santa from doing what he does for children who believe."

The president's sigh was long. "There's already an outcry for intervention in this country."

"They're only upset because the gifts won't be here on time. If you want my opinion, America could use the lesson in practicing some patience. They're all lucky Santa is going to be able to return to his deliveries, at all."

"I could still try to continue negotiations—"

"No. Thank you. There will be no more fighting over who gets to come inside our airspace. They aren't interested in helping someone in need, so much as they're hoping to gain knowledge in order to replicate our magic. This is exactly why we keep ourselves closed off from the rest of the world. It's too much knowledge that can be turned into evildoing. So, thank you, but no. We'll be handling things by delaying the deliveries."

"Well... okay."

"Okay."

And he hung up.

Joy pressed her lips together, then nodded to herself as she hit the 'end' button.

Santa shook his head. "It's going to be interesting, moving forward, to see if all this mess and you putting your foot down is going to make dealing with them harder or easier on me from now on."

"You know, when those elves first came to us, with the whole cockamamie notion, I didn't want to do it. But you said it'd be an adventure."

"Yes, I did."

"Well, consider this all part of the adventure."

He chuckled. "I don't think I was counting on you leading any of it, outside of the North Pole."

"Well then, this is what happens when you underestimate me."

"Speaking of not underestimating you, what do you think your matchmaking duo will be doing this weekend?"

"I don't know. What have you heard?"

"I haven't heard anything. It's just that they spent last weekend together in the company of her family, and the weekend before furniture shopping. I was merely wondering if they'd have an excuse to get together again."

"It's going well, wouldn't you say?"

"Look at the smile on your face. Are you thinking you should be taking credit for their sudden need to be near one another?"

"No. I don't know them well enough to use any magic on them. But the power of suggestion can be forceful."

He grunted. "I'm thinking there was at least a little magic involved."

She glanced around the room. "Well... maybe just a smidge."

"Maybe?"

"Maybe just enough to make them more agreeable to spending a bit of time together. And just enough time for them to start getting used to having each other around. Just so that we can see if they start to miss each other when they're not around one another."

Santa shook his head. "I knew you'd done something."

"It's just a smidgeon of magic. A dash of it, maybe."

"Who needs Cupid when you're around?"

It was her turn to shake her head. "You know I don't have the power to make people fall in love."

"Oh, please."

"All I do is encourage people to see the best in another person, despite their flaws. And if love happens to develop, then all the better." She set about tidying up the room a bit.

Santa watched her for a moment. "You know what you should have done?"

She lifted up a bag of chocolates from the side table, "What is this?"

"Those are my treats."

"Do you honestly think you should be eating chocolate while recovering from a heart attack?"

"I'm allowed one piece of chocolate a day, and I've only been eating half of a piece. It's fine."

She looked closer at the pieces in the bag. "These are chocolate Santas."

"Yes. That's all the corner store had this time of year."

"And you've been biting the heads off all of them."

He grinned. "I know."

"Why?"

He shrugged. "Because I felt like it."

She was incredulous as she stared at him.

"I thought it was funny the first time I did it. Now it's just my thing."

She rolled her eyes. "Okay." She put the bag of chocolates down, dumped the few pieces of garbage she'd gathered into the trashcan, and looked back at him. "So, what's the thing I should have done?"

"Used your magic on the politicians."

She snorted, which made him smile. "If I could figure out how to use the magic without being face-to-face with someone, I'd have brokered world peace centuries ago."

"But you were face-to-face with them, via the internet."

"I tried. It doesn't work. I think it must be transmitted eyeball to eyeball, not eyeball to camera to display to eyeball."

Santa grinned as an idea struck. "We should create a special elven task force. They travel straight to a leader's home, kidnap them, then bring them straight back to the North Pole."

Joy's mind tried to picture elves tackling leaders and securing them with tinsel. "Why?" she asked with a smirk.

"So, you two can have yourselves a little staring contest. You can work your way down a list, one-by-one. No one would know where the elves would strike next. Could you imagine the news coverage? *Mrs. Claus Tackles Santa's Naughty Politician List.*"

She grinned. "Give me Putin, first."

15 THE LAST WEEK DOWN SOUTH

"Looks like you'll get home just in time to miss listening to everyone really launch into bitching about their inconvenience," Stephanie said to Santa, that next Monday morning.

"Yes. I love how the reaction immediately following the announcement was encouraging. People were concerned about me. I was getting messages to take my time recuperating. Well wishes about how much they cared. I was sent so many virtual hugs it was ridiculous. But now, the closer to Christmas we get, the more they realize that I really won't be coming around this time, and the more they start complaining. Now I get messages about how disappointed their kids are that there won't be anything under the tree this Christmas, and how dare I allow that to happen. And Joy has been sending messages back with alternative suggestions as to how the parents can respond to their kids. But most just really want to complain and make demands. When is it that the world became so selfish and cynical?"

"Joy should make mention that any further complaints will result in placement on the naughty list for the remainder of their lifetime."

"If it would work, she'd do it. Honestly, the whole thing makes me want to stop doing the deliveries altogether. Maybe just take a century off. Then, when I resume making the deliveries, everyone would just be thankful that I've opened my heart back up."

Stephanie shrugged, "Maybe you should."

He sighed. "But it's not the kids' fault that their parents can be such jerks."

"No, but they are being raised by the same jerks, so maybe you can use this opportunity to teach them to not act like that."

Santa shook his head in annoyance. "Honestly, they're all probably so testy about it because they know they lack the ability to give good, meaningful gifts."

"Oh," she said with a chuckle, "are you about to get cocky over your gift-giving abilities?"

"I'm just saying, there are times I, and the elves, can really hit it out of the ballpark."

She grinned at him.

"I mean, sometimes we purposefully downplay the gifts I leave behind, so a parent's gift can be the highlight of a child's Christmas. But that's just me letting the parents have the glory, in cases where the parents need a boost of confidence."

"Oh, you're a sly, old man. Taking credit for a failure like it's actually a win."

"It is a win," he grumbled. "You have no idea how many letters from children I get where the parent has read the letter first, before mailing it, and crossed off the items on the list that they plan to purchase themselves. If that isn't parents trying to steal my glory, then I don't know what is."

Stephanie chuckled at him.

"How are your Christmas preparations coming? You're just about out of shopping days."

"Do I really need to bother? Aren't you going to have to cancel Christmas?"

"First of all, if you think I have that power, you really are missing the point of the holiday. Secondly, didn't you listen to the press conference you attended? Everyone is supposed to carry on without me. And thirdly, if I can't distribute gifts, then I'm going to need the rest of you humans to pick up my slack."

She winked at him. "I finished the last of my Christmas shopping on the plane ride back from my mother's birthday party. I'm afraid it's going to be another Christmas provided by Amazon."

"What's wrong with that?"

"I miss going out and seeing all the displays as I rush around, trying to take care of everyone on my list. I miss the freebies some stores provided if you shopped with them. I miss listening in on other people's disagreements about their relatives and what they liked. I miss getting together with my mom and sister to shop and have lunch out."

"Ah, there it is."

"Having a career you're good at keeps you busy, especially when you're trying to climb up the ladder."

"Is that really why you're not dating?"

"I have Roger."

"He doesn't count. He's merely a distraction and you both know it."

"Stephanie," Joy said, coming into the suite after having checked on the two reindeer that morning, "good to see you again!"

"Good to see you, too. How was your weekend?"

"Oh, did Santa tell you? We dressed up like regular people and took a few evening strolls, taking in the sights, looking at all the Christmas lighting."

"Walking?" Stephanie said, eyebrow raised with a smile. "It's the best form of exercise you can do. I'm glad you finally got out further than the corner store," she said, glancing at the bag of chocolate Santa bodies.

Santa nodded, ignoring her reference to the bag. "It did feel good to get out."

"Well, I commend you on your stealth skills. It's all Jacob can do to get from point A to B, without being bombarded by people asking questions about you, demanding to know where you are. As it is, he has to put on a disguise before he leaves the hospital with two agents in plainclothes. Then, when he gets to where he's going, he quickly takes off the disguise, before anyone sees him. It's insane."

"What about you?"

"I've only had a couple people recognize me because I was off to the side. I just give them a quizzical look and tell them I wish I were in on the case. That doesn't make getting through all the added hospital security measures any easier, though."

"I hadn't realized what a ruckus this was going to cause for the hospital."

"Eh, don't worry about it. It's not the first time. We've all been through it before."

"I know what you mean, though. Traveling incognito is something I've become very good at, over the years."

"Good. I'm glad. I know you won't feel back to normal again until you get home but moving around is good for your heart and your mental state."

Joy moved to stand in front of her. "Speaking of going home, are you sure he's going to be ready by Friday? To go back to the North Pole, I mean?"

Stephanie smiled. "He really has made strides. As long as he keeps making forward progress, I'm comfortable with sending him home at the end of the week. I know you have an elf to guide the physical therapy up there, but her experience with humans is lacking. She and I have arranged for me to lead your sessions, via the internet. The elven therapist there can set equipment and such out, but then I can guide you through the exercises, so I can track your progress. That makes both Jacob and I more comfortable about him receiving proper continued cardiac care."

"Speaking of Jacob," Joy began.

Stephanie didn't even try to cover her grin at Joy's predictability. "Yes?"

"Did you and he happen to spend any time together, this weekend?"

"You know, I don't think you're quite grasping the concept of a man and a woman just being friends."

"Oh, I can grasp it. I can even celebrate such a relationship. I just don't think that's the destiny of your particular relationship with Jacob."

"Then maybe you should leave us alone and let us get there all in good time."

"Now why would I do that, when I could see the two of you happy now?"

Stephanie shook her head. "Ah, there lies my point. Neither one of us is unhappy."

"The longer he hides within the shadows of his lost relationships, the harder it's going to be to get him to come out."

"How do you figure?"

"Because he's not still in mourning. He's in hiding. Hiding from any further pain. And the longer he hides, the more comfortable he's going to get while doing it. And the more content he'll become, in avoiding chancing further pain."

"Stop it."

"What?"

"You're going to guilt me into trying to start something with him that I don't want."

"Why wouldn't you want him?"

Stephanie lifted her head and gave Joy a look of warning that belied the pain simmering just underneath the surface. "Because he's Erin's. He's hers. And, yes, I've accepted a lot of her hand-me-downs in my life, but I draw the line at hand-me-down husbands. She and I, we had a pact. We don't share men, period."

Joy closed her mouth and sat down in a chair.

Santa looked from one woman to the other, not sure how to react. When Stephanie finally shook herself out of her own thoughts, she turned to him. He said nothing. Instead, he quickly started doing the exercises he knew she was about to direct him to begin.

"I'm sorry, I truly am," Joy quietly said, after the silence had stretched into awkwardness. "I thought you'd be onboard for going after something more with him, given how close you two seem to be. And your sister? She would understand, given the circumstances."

Stephanie shrugged. "When Erin got sick, he and I were who she relied on. And after she died, we leaned on each other, to get through the grief. We've become each other's family, despite Erin dying. There's no way in hell I'm chancing anything romantic with him, having it fail, and losing the only person I have left in this town that I can truly count on. So, no, I have no interest in pursuing anything further with him. I need my friendship with him too much to risk it."

"But if it worked out—"

"But you can't guarantee that it'll work out. I'm not interested in taking the gamble. The wager buy-in is just too high."

Joy let out a sigh as she watched Stephanie attempt to get back to work by directing Santa and reviewing her notes on his case. She let Stephanie show him a couple new exercises and waited until the flush of anger left Stephanie's face before saying anything more. And then, "So, I take it you didn't spend any time with him for a third weekend in a row?"

Stephanie rolled her eyes and let out a low snort.

Joy turned to Santa and whispered, "I think that means she did."

If looks could kill, the sneer on Stephanie's face would have gotten her arrested for murder on the spot.

Jacob watched as Stephanie emptied the takeout bag he'd brought into her office. She all but flung the Chinese containers onto the desk as she laid the items out. He raised an eyebrow and tried for a laugh, "Mondays suck."

She snorted, "Yes, they do."

"Bad case?"

"Bad case of button pushing."

The second eyebrow joined the first. "Ah. And who dared to push your buttons and get you all riled?"

"Who else?"

"Joy," he said with finality as he popped the lid off his entrée and sat down. "I thought we weren't going to let her matchmaking get under our skin?"

She let out a groan as she slid down into her seat. "She asked why I was so set against the pairing."

"Oh," he said, nodding. "She hit the sister button."

She used her chopsticks to point at herself. "I'm loyal."

He nodded without hesitation. "As loyal as they come."

"And she just... she just... she made me feel like my loyalty was... unnecessary."

"Because Erin is gone?"

She nodded, and he could tell she was on the verge of fighting back tears.

He took the chopsticks out of her hand, put them down, then took hold of her hand in both of his. "Do not let her talk you out of being the person you are. Your loyalty is not a character flaw. It is an intrinsic part of what makes you, you."

She blew out a long, slow breath. "I almost told her where she could shove her opinions."

He fought off laughter. "And your professionalism stopped you," he said with a nod.

She shook her head. "It seems I'm incapable of telling Mrs. Claus to shove anything, anywhere."

"Yeah, I don't think I could even bring myself to say the word 'ass' in her presence, let alone mention hers directly."

She let out a sigh and smiled. "Damnable, meddlesome family."

"No one can simultaneously push your buttons and meddle in your life like family can. But there is a bright side," he said with a smile.

"Oh, yeah? What's that?"

"Interfering grandmothers do tend to want to make their transgressions up to you, when you've made it known they've overstepped."

"Huh. I'd forgotten about that. Wonder what I could get her to do?"

"So how was your weekend?" Jacob asked before Joy could open her mouth.

Joy blinked at him, before the smile overtook her face and she began laughing.

"Better than my morning," she managed to say.

"I heard at lunch about part of your morning," he said, walking past her and into the suite, to get to his patient.

"How much did she tell you?" Joy asked, trailing after him.

"Enough to know that I agree with her. I'm only in this town because of the prestige of the position I was offered within the hospital. I have no family here. I'm kept so busy that I don't have time to develop much of a social life. I need her friendship, because she understands the kind of pressure I live with in my life. I refuse to do anything to jeopardize it."

"Do you want to know what I just heard?"

"No, I don't. I have no interest in you twisting anything that either of us have said."

"Very well," she said with a sigh.

"I'll tell you what I've noticed," Santa said. "I've noticed that neither one of you have actually answered any questions about your weekend. Which tells me the two of you did spend some time together."

"We spent it working," Jacob answered.

"Together?" Santa asked.

"We were helping each other, yes," Jacob admitted.

Joy had the decency to turn her back to them, busying herself with making coffee, before letting her smile spread.

Jacob shook his head as he sat at the table, brought up his case notes, and began the check up with Santa.

It was after Jacob had left that Santa turned to Joy, "So did you and I hear the same thing, in everything those two said today?"

Joy nodded. "I heard a shared, unspoken, sentiment."

"Me, too."

"The only thing holding them back is the fear of losing each other."

"And not a lack of interest."

"Exactly."

"It's a valid concern."

"I wish you could tell if it would work out. I mean, maybe if it didn't work out between them, maybe they could save the friendship."

"I think they're too dependent on each other for that. I don't think they could both handle the rejection. And I tell you, I worry about a certain amount of depression settling in on him. He's already been through so much. I don't know if he can take another loss."

She sighed. And then her face lit up.

"What lightbulb just turned on inside your head?"

She looked at him. "I think I'm going to phone a friend."

Santa wrinkled his brow. "I think you've been watching too many gameshows."

"I'm not going to deny that's a possibility. I'm also not going to deny the fact that I absolutely want to play on a celebrity edition of one of them." She winked at him before turning and hurrying into the bedroom.

"Who are you calling?" he called after her, but she'd already shut the door. So, he dug into his bag of chocolate Santas found an intact one, peeled back half the foil, and bit the head off. He looked back down at his Santas and wondered if he shouldn't maybe think about taking Jacob up on his offer of matching him with a psychologist, just to check in with...

Nah. He knew where the head biting was coming from. It came from him not living up to the fake persona that the world had projected onto him. More like, his rebellion against the world for not seeing him as he actually was. Peel back the layers of the job title, and he was just a human, just like all of them. Like Stephanie had said before, he just happened to be living an extraordinary life.

"And this, is our home," Joy said, leading Stephanie through the entry.

The two women had come to the North Pole, so Stephanie could spy the most appropriate placements for the equipment she'd be instructing Santa to use.

Stephanie's eyes moved to take in the living room. Her gaze crossed over a preserved drawing on the wall, and she moved over to it. Two adults standing in the background, three people sitting side-by-side on a bench, four sitting on the ground. Stephanie's eyes refocused on the two in the back. "Is this you and Santa?"

Joy nodded. "My sister was very gifted. She drew Santa and I with our grown children, over the last two days we spent with them. It's taken a bit of magic, and a lot of care, to keep it intact all this time."

"The magic being that things don't age, here?"

She nodded. "Pretty much." She moved to point to the woman sitting on the ground. "That's my Rosie."

Stephanie touched a fingernail just beside the woman, careful not to smudge the glass. "What about their spouses and kids?"

"To fit us all, and have everyone be recognizable, she would have needed a much larger animal hide and we just didn't have one at the time. But, every year, she'd leave parchment drawings out for me, for Santa to pick up when he delivered. I have albums of all our children with their families, grandchild portraits. My nieces and nephews with their families, too. It wasn't until the year that the drawings stopped, that I realized she had passed on. I regret that she'll never know just how much her drawings carried me through those early years of seclusion."

"Would you be willing to show me the drawing of Rose with her family?"

A soft smile crossed Joy's features. "I'd be more than glad to show all of them to you, before we head back."

"Do you think I could take pictures of them? I won't use a flash."

"Absolutely, but first, let's get things set up for Santa, shall we?"

"Oh, of course. What room do you think he'll be doing his exercises in?"

"Right here. We only have a few rooms, this being the largest. Plus, we still have that bar mounted to the wall," Joy said, pointing. "We put that in when I injured my shoulder and had to do exercises for therapy."

Stephanie nodded, "I did see that before I got distracted. That bar will come in handy." She pulled a resistance band out of her pocket, looped it around the bar and started trying various exercises with different muscle groups.

"You carry those bands around in your pockets?"

"Every working day of my life," she said, making mental notes on which muscles could be worked. "This is quite a bit high for my liking, but it'll do. Can I ask why you left it here, after you were done with your recovery?"

Joy moved over to the bar, reached up, grabbed the bar, then bent at the knee, lowering herself until the bar took enough weight to allow her spine to straighten.

Stephanie heard no fewer than four pops come from the old woman, before Joy let out a relieved sigh and stood up.

"That's why," Joy said.

Stephanie continued to grin as she nodded. "That's what staff use them for in the therapy rooms, too."

"If you would like another bar attached to the wall somewhere below this one, just mark the height you want on the wall. I'll track down Woody to make a matching bar and he'll have it installed before Santa comes home."

"And Woody is a carpenter?"

"A happy coincidence. He's not much of a toymaker, though. He handles construction."

Stephanie pulled a mini marker out of her pocket and moved to put marks on the wall.

"How many things do you keep in those pockets?"

"Hey, Santa has his never-ending bag of gifts, and I have my pockets." She lined her black dots up to where the ends of the bar would attach to the wall. "I'm going to put marks for two bars."

"Alright."

"Then, I'm going to show you a couple exercises you can do with the bar and bands to strengthen your back, for after you pop it, like you did."

Joy nodded, "I'm all for that. And then I'll show you those albums."

"Sounds like a plan."

"Well, Stephanie is beside herself," Jacob declared Thursday afternoon, walking into the suite after Santa opened the door.

Santa chuckled. "Is that a good or bad thing?"

Jacob smiled. "She went from putting on a purely professional face, when she left the hospital this morning, to sending texts that were downright giddy, once she got to the North Pole."

Santa nodded. "Joy hoped that Stephanie would be so overwhelmed with everything she was seeing that Stephanie would forget to be irritated with her."

Jacob laughed. "I'd say, mission accomplished. Stephanie couldn't believe it when Joy extended the invitation. And then she just couldn't find it within herself to turn her down."

"Well, no. Not when she knows the level of unpreparedness going on, up there."

"Yeah, but Joy could have taken a checklist with her, and the elves would have gotten it done. You and I both know Joy wanted to smooth things over with her."

"She did. Joy can't handle it when someone ices her out, right in front of her face."

Jacob nodded. "She told me you were going to be her sole focus, while here, this week."

"Not to mention that Stephanie has been integral in my recovery. I think Joy wanted to do something special for her. And how much more special does it get than inviting her to the North Pole for the day?"

"She actually doubted whether all the equipment she wanted to take up there with her was going to fit in the sleigh."

Santa snorted. "She doesn't grasp exactly how much can fit on one of my sleighs, does she?"

Jacob grinned, put his tablet down, and since Joy wasn't around, poured himself a cup of coffee from the pot. "I tried to tell her that your small one should be able to pull the weight, but she was stuck on size." He shook his head, then took a long sip of the brew.

Santa had a sparkle in his eye as he looked at Jacob and said, "Muggles."

Jacob laughed mid-swallow, choked, and sputtered a spray of coffee all over the table.

Santa belted out rich and hearty laughter as he grabbed a few napkins and tossed them in Jacob's direction.

Shaking his head and wiping up his spill, he said, "Regardless, the women will have everything set to finish out your recovery upon your return, tomorrow. And Stephanie will feel better about the whole idea of conducting your therapy over the internet, knowing that you have all the proper tools at your disposal."

"So will Joy."

"She's more hellbent on monitoring your recovery than I am. She's less convinced of your ability to heal within the magic. If your progress slows, she's going to want you to come back."

Santa nodded. "I've wondered about that, myself. I'll make sure not to slack off any, so that we'll know for sure if it's the magic."

"Good deal. And, in the meantime, let's discuss how much TV you've been watching."

"You leave my TV time alone. All my exercises feel like they go by faster when I'm distracted with the television. Plus, once I return to my work, I won't have the chance to indulge nearly as much to be as satisfying."

"I'm sorry, what is this for?" Stephanie asked Claude, the head of the Sniffles Ward, who currently stood in front of her.

"If Santa straps this over his bicep, it will count how many reps of whatever exercise it is that he is doing. As long as he has the display on the inside, he'll be able to read it."

"What's the reliability on this thing?" she asked, taking a closer look.

"Ninety-five percent on legwork, one hundred on arm work."

"How? We have nothing that reliable."

"Elven technology," the elf leaning against the wall to the side answered.

"And what does this do? Is it a resistance band?"

"Yes. You can change the settings on the small display on the corner and it will change the tension of the material."

She silently blinked at the items Claude had brought with him, processing. "I thought your technology was behind human technology."

The elf to the side snorted.

Stephanie turned to him, "Who are you?"

"Toodles, the head of Elven Technological Advancement. And I'd appreciate it if you didn't spread the word about what kind of equipment we do and do not have up here. Joy said you had honorable level of discretion."

"But you didn't have the items necessary to treat a heart attack."

Claude answered, "Because while injuries happen due to clumsiness, heart attacks are caused by wear, tear, and aging. We're prepared for things we see happen up here. Heart attacks don't happen. We have emergency meds, in preparation for the unexpected, but that's about it. Beyond that, exactly how many humans do you imagine that we have cause to treat?"

She shook her head, trying to reconcile the information she was learning. "But I thought Santa was returning from a trip he spent learning about our technology and brought back samples, for the elves to learn how to make."

Toodles straightened away from the wall. "We reverse engineer human technology so we can match the current level and replicate it. Upon rare occasions, it contains something new to us. But nearly always we have to learn how to dumb our technology down, in order to give kids items that will communicate with other devices of your era."

"I don't understand why you wouldn't just give us things that use your level of technology, so that the knowledge can spread."

He shook his head, "We tried that, once."

"What happened?"

"Eventually? NASA."

Claude shot Toodles a look. "He's kidding," he told Stephanie.

Toodles shook his head, "No, I'm not."

"And putting in place a toy that led to NASA was bad?" she asked.

"It led to an international frenzy to get to the moon. Which led to the Cold War. Which damned near led to an actual war that could very well have wiped us all off the planet."

"Ah. So, now no one is in any hurry around here to advance the humans along."

"Exactly."

Stephanie tilted her head, "Your magic isn't really magic at all, is it?"

"Humans use the word magic to explain what they can't understand. So, yes, it's magic."

"Coming to you live, from Washington, we are moments away from Santa Claus,

116

himself, making a statement in reaction to all the comments and criticism that has been coming at him about his decision to postpone his annual flight, due to recovering from a heart attack.

"Reports from the President have been that while well wishes have been plentiful, criticism has been overwhelming, both towards Santa, and to world leaders, for failing to come up with another viable plan."

The head reporter paused in his dialogue, changed the angle of his head as he listened to the words coming through his earpiece, and looked back into the camera. *"Here now, for the first time in human history, Santa Claus."*

The camera cut on the station broadcast, and Santa appeared on televisions and monitors around the globe.

"Hello," Santa said. *"To give everyone an update on my recovery progress, I'm set to return to the North Pole today. I still have weeks of rest and therapy ahead of me, on my road to recovery, but I will be able to complete them from the comfort of my own home.*

"To the leaders of the world, I would like to extend my sincerest gratefulness for all the help and support you each offered, upon hearing about my medical crisis. I would also like to single out the support I've gotten from the United States.

"They sent up a medical transport to bring me to the help I needed. The hospital, surgeon, support staff, nurses, and therapists have formed a professional and welcoming team, all of whom have helped me through one of the worst periods of my life. Not only them, but also the staff at the accommodations the United States has offered have been the very best. The love and support offered not only to me, but to my wife as well, has been so appreciated. I will forever be grateful with how fast a plan was conceived and put into place, to ensure that I would survive and recover.

"Now, to address the complaints about my need to delay my ride, and the demands that I come up with another plan. I'd like to remind everyone that I have been serving in my position for just about eight hundred years. And in that time, I have never missed my deadline. I've never inconvenienced the world by wanting to take some vacation time, claiming to have the sniffles, a lame reindeer, a broken sleigh, a toy shortage, or even overall exhaustion from preparing all the gifts. In eight hundred years, I've had perfect attendance. I've done this because I know how much I'm depended on to come through on the expectations set upon me.

"But I've had a heart attack. A heart attack that I didn't get to choose the timing of. Now, I apologize that my health crisis is causing you to have to wait a few extra weeks for your deliveries. But that's the reality. And, quite frankly, I've given so much of myself to all of those who believe that I don't think I'm out of line to ask this of you, just this once. Just one favor, in exchange for all I've given to you.

"As for having another plan. The magic of the elves is not something that can simply be bestowed upon another entity, whenever it's convenient for all of you. The militaries of the world tried to come up with an agreeable plan, but they turned it into a political nightmare. Then, after the announcement, UPS, FedEx, and Amazon all tried to produce plans, and we might have been able to work something out with them, but then they turned it into business politics. Everyone was so afraid that someone else would learn

the elven secrets and not them. They were so afraid that they would then take those secrets and turn it into a way to phase the others out. It has put us in the position to have to deny those offers of help. One night's worth of help is not worth shifting neither political, nor corporate, balances that help make our world go 'round. Human fear and greed are to blame for a lack of a better option than postponement.

"If seeing your way through to forgiving me the transgression of requiring everyone to practice a little patience with me, then perhaps it's time for the world to retire the whole idea of Santa, because I'm not here to fight with you. The Mrs. and I can quietly retire and find somewhere to live out what remains of our natural, human lives, in peace and calm. And if that's the case, if it is time for that, then I thank you for allowing me into your homes for as long as all of you have, and I'll bid you goodbye, knowing that all good things must and will eventually come to an end.

"Thank you for your time and attention this morning. May you all live on in peace, patience, and prosperity."

With that, Santa stood and exited the lobby of the same medical facility that had hosted the initial press conference.

The camera cut back to the reporter in the studio, who set about recapping and unpacking everything that Santa had said.

"Well, that was quite the high-handed angle of attack," Joy said, when Santa returned to the hotel suite.

"Don't get me started, I don't want to take my anger out on you," he said. "I have given my entire life over to being Santa. I've lived for centuries, all in service, and the one time I need something from the world, in return, people have the audacity to complain."

"I know."

"And I understand that it's part of the human condition. I understand that they look forward to what I leave behind for them, and that for many, Christmas gifts can be the highlight of the year. I understand. But I've been down here for weeks now, and maybe everyone else needs to understand that beneath the magic, I'm human too. I'm just as susceptible to having my feelings hurt as they are. I'm hurt, I'm disappointed, I'm frustrated, and *my* patience is shot."

"I know."

"Not to mention, by their behavior pushing me to come forward, my face is going to be plastered all over the place. I will no longer hold anonymity. Which means I'll never be able to travel anywhere incognito again. So, all things considered, how nice was I supposed to play that?"

She took a breath and moved towards him with her arms lifted.

"No," he said, shaking his head, sullen. "I'm riled."

She smiled, continuing her advance. "Yes, you are."

He moved backwards, "Don't do it. I'm not in the mood."

"Oh, I'm going to do it," she said, closing in on him.

"No," he said, picking up a little speed in his retreat. "I'm set on brooding."

"Not with me around, you're not." Once close enough, she launched herself at him, arms wrapping around him in a hug meant to quell the most irate of beasts.

He stopped his retreat and focused on fighting the overwhelming feeling of calm enveloping him. "It's not fair to use your magic against me."

She grinned. "I'm using it for you."

"You're stealing my emotions," he grumbled.

"I'm merely guiding them," she corrected, clinging to him.

His tense muscles eased, and he let out a disgusted noise. "Alright, alright, get off me, woman." He turned in her arms to return the embrace. "You know what happens when you overdo it with me, and the doctors haven't cleared me, yet."

She grinned and quickly kissed him. "At least you'll stop grumbling."

"Ah, no. I'll just start grumbling for a whole new reason."

She laughed, kissed him a bit more thoroughly, and let go of him.

Santa shook his head. "This whole being human thing, twenty-four hours a day, is exhausting. I'm tired of feeling like I need a nap."

She grinned. "We'll be home soon enough, don't you worry."

16 BUSY WEEK

Excitement hung in the air as elves gathered along the walkways throughout the village. The six reindeer who'd remained at home joined the elders standing along the runway. Whispers travelled on the breeze, wondering and discussing how different things might be for them, going forward. The shimmering ring of the Confetti Tunnel opening above their heads ceased their murmurs.

Joy held the reins as Cupid and Vixen guided the sleigh in for a landing. Santa looked over the edge of the sleigh and took in the sight below.

His hand raised in a wave as a jolly smile lit his face. "Ho, ho, ho!"

A wave of cheers broke out from the elves as the reindeer landed and came to a stop in front of the elders.

"Welcome back, Santa," Penelope told him. "It's truly good to have you home."

"I feel like our lives are less interesting, now," Stephanie said, sitting across the coffee table from Jacob, in his living room, a half-empty pizza box between them.

He grinned as he picked up his can of soda. "It's Sunday. We haven't even had a workday without them, yet."

"Doesn't matter. I know I won't be seeing them tomorrow."

"You have an online appointment with him on Wednesday."

She shook her head in only half-feigned forlornness. "It won't be the same."

"You knew it was going to end at some point."

"I know," she said with a sigh. "I just didn't count on the idea of missing them."

"She drove you nuts."

"Yeah, but her heart was in the right place."

"Stephanie."

"It was nice having someone in town to bug me the way that only family can."

He was going to roll his eyes, but then he realized she was serious. "Alright. I get what you're saying, I do. But refocus. We have a big week coming up."

"Yes. Your surgery on the Sultan's son, and my interview."

"We've spent the past two weekends drilling and studying for them. How do you think we'll do?"

"I don't know. But if only one of us succeeds, then that person has to treat the other to a night of drinking and drowning the loser's sorrows."

"What do you want to do to celebrate if we both succeed?"

She thought about it a moment, and with a nod she said, "Drink."

He rolled his eyes.

"We never let ourselves have time to really let loose and relax. We both deserve a night of letting go of responsibilities."

He grinned. "Should we drink over a fancy dinner?"

"Absolutely not. Fancy food is disgusting. Cheeseburgers and fries if we both win."

He chuckled at her. "Done."

"Now what are you, a cardiac surgeon, doing with fried chicken tenders and curly fries?" Stephanie asked Jacob when she walked into his office for lunch on Monday.

He smiled at her. "I know it's your favorite meal on Earth. I figured whether you nailed your interview, or bombed it, you were going to deserve it."

She started giggling. "Our bodies aren't going to know what to do with us by the end of the week."

"That's what these are for," he said with a grin, as he pulled out a bottle of antiacid tablets.

"Oh, appetizers!" she said, sitting down and claiming her portion.

"So, how did it go?" he asked, taking a few of the tablets for himself, and pushing some ketchup packets in her direction. "You were gone all morning."

Her eyebrows rose as she sucked in a deep breath and slowly let it out. "I think I held my own. They really took their time going over my one-year and five-year plans for the department. They asked question after question, and I kept watching their expressions for feedback. As far as I can tell, I don't think any of my answers ticked them off. Once I realized that, I figured the longer they kept me, the more they liked me as a contender for the position."

He nodded. "I actually hoped that you were kept in the interview for longer than expected, and not that it was a patient keeping you from texting me that you were done."

"They said I should know within the next couple of days, whether I've gotten the promotion or not." They began to dig in, eating their lunch. "What about your case? The son arrives today, right?" she asked.

Jacob was already nodding. "He's in the air now. I'm going to have some bloodwork and scans ran on him today, and his surgery is first thing tomorrow morning."

"And you have to monitor closely for forty-eight hours?"

"Yep."

"I know you plan to stay here the whole time. So, let me know if you need me to grab you anything from your house."

He nodded. "I packed last night, so I think I'm good. But I'll keep the offer in mind."

"Has the President made any promises on your behalf?"

"Just that if he can be saved, I'll get it done."

"You still have that other surgeon joining you via the internet?"

"Yeah. She's the only surgeon doing this procedure with any kind of reliable success rate."

"I still don't understand why they can't just get her the security clearance and bring her in to do the surgery with you."

"Because she has familial reasons for hating the particular government the father rules over."

"Oh, geez."

"Yeah. She doesn't even know who the patient is. She just knows that he's high enough profile that he's being brought here, to me, and I'd like some experienced company during the procedure."

"Got it. I've got therapy blocks scheduled for him, starting Wednesday, but you let me know when you want me to start."

"Of course. For now, I'm just enjoying the calm before the storm."

"Oh, my God. Pizza. You're my new favorite person," Jacob said, coming into his office, to meet Stephanie for lunch on Tuesday. "I could smell it out in the hallway and hoped it was coming from here. Thank you."

Stephanie beamed a smile at him. "Bacon and onions, with extra sauce."

His face lit up like a little boy. "My favorite."

"Yep. How's the kid? All you texted me was that the surgery was over."

"He's alive. He woke up fine. And he's in the ICU for close monitoring. So far, so good."

"How much did you have to rely on the other surgeon?"

"I started to second-guess myself. And I know I only did it because I knew I had backup, but still. So, I got her a closeup of the situation and she let me know my instincts were right."

"You're not used to being the second most successful surgeon in the room, are you?"

"No. But when I am, I do dive into a lot of self-doubt."

"But only because you want to perform so well."

"It's because I know I've screwed up in the past."

"You haven't screwed up when it comes to new procedures. You've simply discovered ways in which experimental procedures do not work. It's that everyone's still trying to figure something out, seeing what's going to make it more reliable, going forward. What you like to call screw ups are research contributions."

"The thing is, you don't get to where I am by making mistakes."

"That doesn't mean you can be the best at everything, every time."

"But it does mean that everyone expects me to be."

"Okay, so, just for the record, you're determined to remain stressed out by this, even though the kid survived, and the heart is repaired. So, it doesn't matter what I say or do, you won't be calmed."

He looked towards the ceiling a moment, considering. "Yeah, pretty much. This kid could still code on me and die. His heart has been through a lot today and wasn't in great shape to begin with. He's not out of the woods."

"I get it. But you're still going to eat this pizza, though, right?"

"Oh, I'm gonna tear this pizza up. Move aside."

She giggled and plopped down in her chair.

"What happened to you at lunch?" Jacob asked, from her office doorway, at the end of her workday on Wednesday. "I saw that you came into my office and grabbed your lunch at some point, but you didn't respond to my texts."

She looked up from her computer and winced at him. "Sorry. It's been a crazy day. I got pulled into a second interview over lunch. Apparently, they're torn between me and one other candidate. And then I had to onboard your kid. And then I had to do Santa's virtual session. I've been buried in paperwork ever since."

"How'd the interview go?"

"I think I nailed it, but I don't know who they're comparing me to. They said they talked with the other candidate yesterday, so I can't even keep an eye out for who my competition might be. But one of them implied that whoever it is, isn't already working here. So, I'm guessing they're trying to decide whether to make a lateral move with someone experienced in the position, or if they want to promote from within."

"Got it. What'd you think of the kid?"

"I liked the kid. He's got a constant smile, despite what he's been through. He's polite, respectful, and was willing to follow any direction I gave him."

"And his mother?"

"She's just scared for her child, and way out of her comfort zone, being here. But, yeah, she's enough to drive you crazy."

"And their handlers?"

"They looked like they were going to grab me at any given moment. I actively thought my every movement through before I did something stupid like touch the kid to help him."

He nodded. "And how's Santa doing? I'm not set to meet with him until Friday."

"He's doing fine. Pressure and pulse were good, his spirits are as high as can be expected. He's happy to be back in familiar surroundings."

"And Joy?"

"In meetings with some of the elves."

"Awesome. You didn't have to deal with her questioning."

"Yeah, but..."

"But what?"

"Santa said that he was called by a hospital board member, asking questions about me."

"Looking for a patient reference, most likely, considering the job you're up for."

She let out a breath as she shook her head. "He said he really talked me up. Said that I dealt with Mrs. Claus' meddling in my personal life, and that I was a trooper in treating someone whose spouse couldn't respect the line of professionalism."

"And you did it without complaining to anyone about it, except to a friend. You should be good."

"Yeah, but was I too good? Am I too good?"

"What do you mean?" he asked, eyebrow raised, and head tilted in confusion.

"I mean, if I'm deemed as being so good with patients and families, will I be deemed too valuable in my current position to be moved up the ladder?"

He drew his head back, "You know, that's not something I've ever had to worry about."

"Yeah, well, until I hear their final decision, it's all I'm going to worry about."

"And if they do hold you back, at least you'll be spared having to worry about transitioning to a more administrative role. Dealing with coworkers that you now have authority over is quite a bit different than dealing with patient and family care."

"Yeah, but now that I know I'm a viable candidate for this level of position… If they hold me back, I have to consider trying to move up the ladder outside of this hospital."

Jacob hung his head for a moment. "I was afraid you were going to say that. I'd really hate to see you go somewhere else, but those are for selfish reasons. Hell, it'd be bad enough to see you move up. We work well with one another."

She hung her head slightly, "I know."

"We'll still have lunch meetings, even if we're not discussing patients we have in common, right?"

She smiled. "Lunches as friends instead of coworkers? What a shocking revelation. Sounds right up my alley."

By Thursday's lunch, they were back to salads when they met at his desk and sat to eat.

"Your kid is still alive. That's got to feel good," Stephanie said.

"Definitely. Now I have to worry about the mother, who can't wait to get him back to their home country. She keeps going on about security."

"Oh, I know. I had to listen to her go on and on about it, through his whole therapy session. All I wanted to do was yell at her that nobody here even knows who the hell they are."

He grinned. "No one who was onboarded with the case here had even heard of the country before."

She shook her head. "I can't even imagine living with that kind of paranoia. I have to wonder if it's somehow justified, or if she's just so far out of her element that she can't help herself."

"Well, I kind of think she's not used to having to make any decisions. All the pre-arrival stuff went through the Sultan. Any time I give her an option of something, she says she thought everything had been decided already. And she has no idea how to comfort her own child. I'm surprised they didn't send the nanny, instead."

"Okay, now I feel bad. We don't know the truth of it. Maybe the technology barrier, the language barrier, and the culture barriers are all getting the better of her. With all the tubes hooked up to the kid, maybe she's scared to death to touch him, thinking that she'll hurt him somehow. And why isn't the father here? His kid could have died."

"Both the Sultan and his wife have lost two other children to this same heart condition. I get the distinct impression that he doesn't want to take an interest in a child until they've proven that they won't succumb."

"You've got to be kidding me. Is that why he doesn't have their version of a prince title?"

"That's my best guess. It could also be why the mother doesn't know what to do with herself. She might have counted the kid out, and now here he is, with an increasingly excellent chance at a full life."

She raised her hands to the ceiling, "Oh, my God. That's why she's paranoid about security."

"How do you mean?"

"She's realizing she gets to keep this one. And with her coming to terms with that, she's scared something else is going to happen to him. She wants to love him and is afraid to, because the two she lost broke her heart and she knows she can't take that again."

"Wow. In a twisted way, that makes sense… Have you heard anything more about the job?"

She shook her head. "Just that they're supposed to take a final vote this afternoon and let me know tomorrow."

"So, they're going to know their answer for a whole day before they share it with you?"

Her eyes rolled of their own volition. "They want to vote, then sleep on the decision, and then check in with each other to make sure they're all still onboard with the choice."

He deadpanned a look at her that clearly indicated his thoughts on that kind of decision-making system.

She nodded, "I know." She stabbed her fork into the salad and lifted a bite to her mouth, before starting to nod again. "I know."

"So, I tried to add a patient to your roster for next week, but the system wouldn't let me," Jacob said, meeting Stephanie at the door to his office with chicken salad sandwiches in his hand. "Is there a known reason for that?"

Stephanie nodded, pushing the door open and setting the lemonades down on the desk.

"Tell me good news," he said, his whole face lighting up.

The smile that overcame her face was huge. "I got the job!"

"Well, look at you," he said, coming inside and putting the food on the desk, before turning to her for a hug. "Department Head, extraordinaire."

She hugged him back, just as hard. "Yes. That's exactly what they'll engrave on my nametag."

"They should," he said, not letting go of her.

She let out a happy sigh. "I can't believe it. Everyone else said I was too young, and they'd never move me up, yet."

"They made me department head without being old enough."

"*Pfft,*" she said, pulling away.

"What?"

"You're a man, that's what."

"And unmarried, which makes me unsettled, so what?"

"Okay, let's face some facts. The only reason they dared to move me up is because I'm single, without kids. I gave them no reason to Mommy-track me."

"They still Mommy-track women?"

She stared at him, hard.

"Okay, okay. Sorry I asked."

"Do you know that they nearly picked the other candidate over me because he makes it a point to sign everything with his doctorate title?"

"Why don't you?"

"Do you have any idea how many therapists have their doctorate title and don't use it?"

"But why?"

"Because patients don't view us as saving their lives. They come to us for exercises. We have to be more personable. We have to make small talk during their sessions. And doctorate titles do not accomplish that."

"Will using it be a requirement for you now?"

"Well sure, because I'll be dealing with the administrative pieces, so using my title is the only way anyone will pay attention to me. But my point was that these people forgot I had my doctorate, altogether."

"They what?"

"If anyone ever truly dug into the psychology of medical field professionals in relation to other medical field professionals, they'd unearth a plethora of behaviors to theorize over."

"Is that how you got them to vote in your favor?"

"No. It's the fact that I know how to handle high-profile cases. It's how they come away from treatment with me, singing my praises, regardless of my feelings about them. That's something the people at the top need the person in my new position to be able to do, and I've already proven myself capable."

"So, no new cases for you?"

"I'm still the high-profile specialist."

"Ah, I get it. You get the best of both worlds. No low-profile patients for you, while you oversee the department."

"Exactly. Give me the fun weirdos and leave the rest for the others."

"Which is why I can't add a new patient onto your load."

"Yeah. I'm going to train Lainey to focus on the regular cardio patients."

"Oh, I've worked with her before. She's competent."

"Yeah. She and I share the same sense of humor, so you two should get along just fine."

"Good. So, you and me, burgers and beer tonight."

She lifted an eyebrow at him.

"Are you too good for beer, now?"

"Head of the Department and the Savior of a Future Sultan sitting here, beer is beneath us both this week."

"Margaritas?"

"You're getting closer."

"Strawberry margaritas?"

"So close it's amazing you still haven't hit the mark."

"Frozen strawberry margaritas?"

"Ding, ding, ding!"

17 WHAT THE HELL WAS THAT?

"We're not going out?" Stephanie asked, having showed up at his doorstep, straight from work, and seeing the takeout boxes on the coffee table behind him.

"The last time we went out drinking, I had to thwart three different guys from trying to pick you up. I don't have that kind of energy tonight. It's been a good week, but a long one, and I would also like the luxury of getting drunk off my ass tonight. So, I got us cheeseburgers and fries, and brought them here."

"And the frozen strawberry margaritas?"

He crooked a finger at her and led her into his kitchen. "I bought a frozen margarita machine. I mixed everything right in the tank and it should start slushifying any minute now."

"*Hmm,*" she said, seeming to think it over. "It would be nice to enjoy myself without having to keep an eye out for lechers or figuring out who has to be sober enough to order the car to get us home."

"Speaking of which," he said holding a hand up and pointing in the direction of the far corner of the house, "I set up the guest room for you."

She grinned. "You mean you put the flannel Eeyore sheets on the bed for me?"

He nodded. "Of course, I did. How could I not?"

"Well, alright." She dropped her backpack from her shoulder. "I'd brought some clothes to change into before heading out, but I guess they just became clothes for tomorrow. I'll go throw my bag in the room, and then let's get to those cheeseburgers before they're completely cold."

Jacob had put on a favored movie by the time she came back downstairs. They then sat on the living room floor, eating at the coffee table with their backs resting against the couch. They talked and chatted until the food was gone, and then the margaritas began to flow.

Three full glasses each were downed before Jacob was lounging back against a chair. "You know what I could go for, and haven't had in maybe two years?"

"Oh," Stephanie said, her eyes lighting up as she hugged a couch pillow, "funnel cake."

He nodded. "You think that place still makes them?"

"They'd better," she declared, pulling her phone out of her pocket.

"What are you doing?"

"Seeing if I can get someone to deliver them to us."

He tilted his head back, resting it on the chair cushion. "Freaking genius."

"I keep trying to tell you that I was always the smarter sister."

"Erin could have gone for her doctorate," he said, staring at the ceiling.

"Yeah," she said, tapping buttons on her phone with a sigh. "But she didn't."

"She didn't need it for her career."

"Whatever."

He grinned, now contemplating redoing his ceiling with tiles. "I always admired how a well intoned 'whatever' could end any disagreement you two had."

She looked up from her phone. "You want a topping?"

"Apple pie filling."

"Oh, my God. I'm getting vanilla ice cream. We can mix them together."

"Apple Funnel Pie a la mode," he said with a chuckle.

"Freaking genius idea," she declared, placing the order. She looked over to him and focused in on him. "What are you doing?"

"Thinking about ceiling tiles."

She looked up, "Oh, well…" She sat up, spun on her rear, laid the couch pillow on the floor behind her, and laid down to look up. "What kind of tile."

"Decorative."

"Why?"

"Why not?"

"Because the room is already decorated?"

He sighed, grabbing a pillow, and moving to lay next to her. Then he brought up ceiling tiles on his phone. "Look at them."

She took the phone. "What color are we talking?"

"Silver."

She tried to picture it. "Shiny or matte?"

"I don't know."

"Matte will look grey in here. And who wants a grey ceiling pressing down on them?"

"Okay, shiny, then."

She wrinkled her nose. "And when the sunlight comes through your sliding glass doors, bounces off the hardwood in the dining room, and hits this ceiling? It's going to blind you."

"Hmm. White's just so boring to look at, though."

"Spend a lot of time staring at your ceiling, do you?"

He shrugged. "Sometimes, when I'm picturing a surgical procedure all the way through, I stare up at the ceiling as my mind's eye helps me prepare."

"But then, you're not really paying attention to the ceiling then, are you?"

He shrugged. "Maybe we could go out next weekend and look at some. Obviously, I need help in thinking my choices through."

She giggled. "Silly, we don't have to keep coming up with reasons to spend time together, so that we have something to report to Joy. They're not here, anymore."

He turned his head to look at her. "We still have to talk to them, to treat them, right? I know Joy laid low this week, but I imagine she'll figure you've had enough time to cool off."

"Nah, I was already pretty chill about everything after she took me to visit the North Pole. I imagine she had her hands full with business, up there. And with Christmas this week, trip or no trip, she'll be busy. Politicians and people will be complaining nonstop up until the last minute. And then after Christmas Eve, the elves will have to start in with making toys for next year, with no room to put them, because this year's toys will still be there. I wonder if they could just stuff all of this year's presents into the sack until Valentine's…"

"Maybe I just like spending time with you."

He'd said it so quietly, she'd wondered if he'd just said what she thought she'd heard. Her head turned to look at him. "What?"

"You have to know that you're the best friend I have."

"Oh! …Oh. Yeah. Well, the same can be said for me."

His brow wrinkled. "You're your own best friend?"

She laughed, her hair fanning out around her head as she repositioned her head on the pillow and looked back up. "No. I mean that you're my best friend, too."

"Is that weird?"

"A little. But I don't care."

"I consider it a bonus to the nightmare we went through with Erin."

"You know what I sometimes wish?"

"No."

"Sometimes, and I'm only admitting to this because we're both too blasted to care right now, but sometimes I wish you and I would have met first."

"Why?" he asked, genuinely perplexed.

"Because then maybe you would have asked me out, instead of her."

"Huh," he said, turning his head to the ceiling, to think about it. "And I might have, too. You both have the same energy, the same sense of humor. The packaging isn't all that different…"

She pulled the pillow out from under her head and slammed it down onto his stomach.

"Ow! Damn," he said through laughter.

"But then I feel guilty, because then Erin wouldn't have had you through treatment."

"Oh, please. If I'd have been dating you, and your sister was going through all that, I'd still have helped."

"But not in the same way. And you know it. How you were with her is something I'd never take away from my sister."

He glanced at her before looking back up at the ceiling. "Sometimes I wish someone could take it away from me."

Stephanie deflated, "Of course I wish she'd have never gotten the cancer, or that it was found sooner."

"No, I know what you mean. It's just that sometimes I wish someone else would have seen her through it all. There's a price to pay for being the good guy. The emotional scars hurt like hell."

She let out a half-chuckle, "Yeah. Same. Sometimes I wish one of us would have moved away from here. Like maybe she could have moved to Florida with Mom and Dad, and they could have seen her through it. But then I'd feel as guilty as they do, for not being there for her."

"It was a no-win situation, for all of us."

"And so," she said, pausing to bend the straw down to her lips and suck down some more margarita, "here we are."

He chuckled, sucking down some more of his margarita. "Yeah, here we are."

"You're saving the lives of famous and important people, and I'm getting them back on their feet so they can go back to their famous and important lives."

He laughed, "We're drunk on my living room floor on a Friday night."

"Hey, we could have been drunk in a bar. You're the one that determined we'd stay here."

He lifted his legs up in the air, then let them drop to the floor as he used the momentum to sit up. "Alright, enough of the depression. Time to break the mood." He picked up his glass, then moved to grab hers. "I'm going to refill our glasses. You put on some music. We'll dance it out." Then he disappeared into the kitchen.

She rolled to her side, and onto her stomach, before successfully defying gravity by standing upright without falling on her face. She bent down to move the pillows but missed. So, she kicked the pillows out of the way, instead. They didn't move very far with one kick, but the job got done.

He rounded the corner. "Where's the music?"

She looked up at him, "Why is your shirt all wet?"

"I might have spilled some tequila. It'll dry."

"And I was clearing the dance floor. It took some effort."

"Well, pull up that dance playlist you have for your workouts."

"Oh, great," she said, focusing her eyes on her phone screen, "we'll sweat out all the alcohol we're drinking." She managed to connect her phone to his Bluetooth speakers, hit play, and put the phone on the coffee table.

"A slow song?" he asked, handing her drink to her.

She grabbed the glass. "It's my warmup song."

He stepped up to her, wrapping his hand around the back of her waist before he began to sway with her. "I could imagine stretching to this."

She wrapped a hand around the back of his neck. "You should hear my yoga playlist." She smiled as she brought her glass to her lips.

"Do you ever fall asleep doing your stretches?"

She smiled. "Oh, shut up, it's one song."

The song ended, the music changed, and for forty-five minutes they danced and drank, joked and laughed, fell and giggled, got back up and danced some more.

A haunting, woodwind instrumental piece began to play. They froze in their dance moves, eyes flying to the other's, and they burst into laughter. He put his empty glass down and lifted his arms. She put hers down, ignoring when it fell off the edge of the table, and walked straight into his arms.

His arms went around her waist, her hands came to rest at the nape of his neck, and she smiled up at him as they once again began to sway. His head tilted down, about to make a remark on her taste in cooldown music. But she raised on tiptoe, pretending she was wearing heels, and he suddenly got distracted by her lips. Once his gaze shifted, her own gaze drew to his lips.

Before either of them realized what was about to happen, he lowered his lips to hers, softly at first. But then she began to kiss him back. He pulled her closer to him, to settle into the kiss. But then she nipped his bottom lip, eliciting a groan from him. He deepened the kiss in response. Tongues twined and hands began to roam, as the song ended, and the speakers went silent.

They froze in the sudden silence. Then she lowered to her natural height, and he withdrew his hands from her, just before she pulled hers away and they stared at each other.

"What the hell was that?" he whispered.

"I have no damned idea."

"You're, like, my sister."

"Kissing me was like kissing your sister?" she asked, drawing her hands to her mouth. "Oh, my God!"

"No! That's not what I meant."

"You mean it was like kissing *my* sister?" she whisper-yelled. "I don't even know how to take that!"

"No! That was nothing like kissing either one of our sisters. I'm just saying, we don't do that. We don't kiss."

"Agreed. But was it better or worse than kissing my sister?"

He zeroed his gaze in on her, "Are you freaking kidding me with this?"

She shook her head to clear it. "Let's just call it an enjoyable mistake."

"You enjoyed it?"

"You didn't?"

"Of course, I did!" he paused to sigh and get his thoughts together. "Fine. Agreed. Enjoyable mistake."

"Now let's clean up and retreat to our separate bedrooms. Or do I need to order a ride?"

He looked up to the ceiling and let out a long breath. "No, of course you don't have to get a ride. It was a drunken kiss. It's not like anyone's waking up naked in the morning." He brought his head down, took in her annoyed expression, and shook his head. "I'm sorry. I heard the words coming out of my mouth and realized I was sounding dismissive."

She nodded. "Yeah, you were."

"I'm not saying it was nothing. I'm saying, let's not blow it out of proportion. That's all. We kissed, we stopped, let's not let it change things between us."

She sighed and started picking up trash.

"What?"

"Nothing. You're right. Let's forget it."

18 CALL IT OFF

"My husband said you needed to talk to me," Joy said from an office setting at the North Pole, on Monday afternoon. "Is there something more wrong with him? Something you couldn't tell him yourself?"

"No," Jacob said, rocking back in his office chair. "Santa is progressing nicely, all things considered."

"Then what did you need to speak with me about?"

"I want you to call it off."

Her head tilted. "Call what off?"

"The spell."

The tilt inclined further. "The spell? What spell?"

"The curse, the hex, whatever you want to call it."

"I didn't cast any spell," she said, her neck straightening. "I have no idea what you're talking about. What happened?"

"You got into our heads, that's what happened."

"*Our* heads? You mean you and Stephanie?"

"Yes!" he said, rocking forward and stopping.

"Jacob, what happened?"

"Something that never would have happened, if you hadn't started putting ideas into our thoughts."

"Sweetheart, use your words. Tell me what happened."

"I saved a future Sultan."

"Well, that's fantastic news."

"And Stephanie's been promoted to the head of her department."

"That's amazing! What's the problem?"

"We got together last night to celebrate."

Her head tiled up as she fought off a smile. "Aha."

"Dinner, drinks, a movie, some dancing… and then it happened."

"Did you two wake up naked?" she asked, her eyes narrowed at him.

135

"No! We shared a drunken kiss. And now things are weird between us."

She folded her hands and rested her chin on them, thinking. "And this is somehow my fault?"

"Yes, it has to be."

"Let me ask you this, why is it that you two somehow seem to spend time together every weekend?"

He rocked back in his chair again. "To screw with your head."

She sat up straight in her chair, "Excuse me?"

"We came up with reasons to spend time together, to be able to report it back to you the next week, just to let you think that you were making progress with getting us together."

"But I wasn't in town last week. Why would you two get together this weekend?"

"To celebrate last week's victories. It's something we would have gotten together for, regardless of your interference."

"So, you two got together, with it having nothing to do with me, and that's when you two kissed?"

"It was a drunken kiss."

"You know, it's said, 'In wine, there is truth.'"

"No wine, no truth. Just an enjoyable mistake."

That gave her pause. "She's going to be annoyed if you call it that."

He shook his head. "She's the one calling it that."

"So, you both agree that it was enjoyable."

"And we both agree that it was a mistake."

"So, ride out the weirdness. Things will resettle between the two of you."

"But the spell…"

She paused to smile. "There is no spell. I don't have that kind of power. I'm just able to see the similarities and complimenting personality traits between two people. I can see the potential between the two of you and then I set out to draw attention to it. That's all."

He stared the camera down until he heard her sigh.

"I mean, I can affect emotions in my immediate vicinity, if I choose to. But neither one of you were in my vicinity while you two were drunk."

"But you must have gotten into our heads. I mean, it's not the first time we were ever drunk together, and nothing like this ever happened before."

"Honestly, what's so wrong with it?"

"I can't lose her."

"You mean as a friend?"

He looked at a point somewhere above the camera, going quiet for a moment, "I can't watch another one die."

She started to chuckle.

"Do not scoff! I have watched two women, that I loved and wanted to spend my life with, die. I cannot do it again."

Joy's lips drew back in a straight line as she regarded him. "I'm sorry. Laughter should not have been my reaction."

"I'm cursed."

"You are not."

"And you're an authority on curses?"

That gave her pause. "Well, no."

"Then don't dismiss me when I tell you that I believe there's some sort of curse on me. Call it bad luck, if you want, I don't care. But don't try to convince me I'm wrong when you don't know."

She sighed and tilted her head from side to side, stretching the muscles. "Okay. You're right. Maybe you are cursed in the area of love. And maybe any woman you fall in love with is doomed to die in your arms, long before her time."

"Exactly."

She steepled her hands, resting her chin on her lowered thumbs, as she bit back her retort, determined to take him seriously. "Okay. I've been insanely busy this past week, but I'm going to make a call on your behalf and see if I can't get to the bottom of why you seemed so cursed."

He sat up in his chair and leaned in on his elbows. "You mean there's an actual authority on this?"

"Yes. At least for when it comes to love, there is."

"Well... Okay then."

"And if I'm right and you aren't cursed?"

He put up a hand. "One potential revelation at a time."

She smiled.

He rocked back in his chair. "What's had you so busy this week? Things should be calmer now, with no ride coming up."

She let out a soft chuckle. "One would think so."

"What are you up to?"

"Oh, not much. Just stretching the power of the elves, seeing how far it can extend."

"That sounds... kind of fun."

She smiled. "It is."

Joy disconnected the call and left Santa's office, which seemed more her office than his lately, and headed into the living room.

"So, what was so important for the good doctor to discuss with you and not me?" Santa asked.

She smiled at him and moved to the couch, to plop herself down beside him and cuddle into his side. "He thinks I casted a love spell on him and Stephanie."

He tilted his head back against the couch cushion and burst with laughter. "What happened?"

"They kissed."

"And a kiss means there's some sort of spell?"

"Yep."

"I thought he said he was cursed."

"Yes. Now he thinks he's doubly screwed. Spelled to love, cursed to watch that love die. Rinse and repeat."

"Well, he has been through a lot."

"I know he has. I could smell his fear through the computer screen." She pulled out her phone and started typing.

"What now?"

"I told him that I'd find out for sure if he was cursed."

"Seriously?"

"I'm a woman of my word, am I not?"

"Yes. Yes, you most certainly are."

She put her phone down and snuggled a bit closer as he squeezed his arm around her shoulders. "So, how's your special project coming along? Is it going to happen?" he asked.

She sighed. "It's coming along."

"And when are you going to let me in on the plan?"

"When I know for sure that I can pull it off."

"What I can't understand is why you're bending over backwards to come up with another plan when we already had everything set up to postpone. You're barely sleeping, you're gone for hours on end, and your mood has not always been the best lately. You're stressed, and I don't like it."

Joy shifted to pull a letter out of her pocket. Unfolding the paper, she cleared her throat.

> *"Dear Santa,*
> *I cried when I heard about your heart attack. Mommy says a heart attack is not good. She says that you're lucky to be alive.*
> *I want you to live for a long time. And mommy says that it takes a lot of time to get better from a heart attack. I want you to take all the time you need to get better. If you aren't ready by Valentine's Day, maybe you can ask the Easter Bunny to deliver your gifts, when he comes to hide all the eggs.*
> *I know a lot of people are mad at you. I yell at anybody who says you should still find a way to deliver. They say you should find a substitute, and I said you're not a teacher. I said that there's only one Santa Claus. They say you only work one day a year, and I said that Mommy said that you can't schedule a heart attack.*
> *I'm not mad at you. I know what it's like to be sick and you can't do the*

things you want to do. I know that you have to do what the doctors say, so that you can get better.

My Mommy is a nurse and she said if you need one at the North Pole, that she can help. And my Daddy owns a cleaning business, so if you need someone to help clean up anything, he can help you. And Daddy taught me to use some power tools, so, if you need help making some toys, I'm your girl. And my brother wants to be a vet, so if you need help taking care of all the puppies that some kids get for Christmas, but now they have to stay up there longer, he can help. My whole family can come help out, if you need it.

For real, one call and we can all be there,
Julianna Daniels, age 9"

"Just so you know," Santa said, "she never had any sort of dread disease. She had a nasty stomach bug on a trip to Disney. The girl threw up all over Tinkerbell."

"I know."

"Tinkerbell cried while the handlers pulled her into the back."

"I know."

"They sent Peter Pan over to try and calm the line of kids down, but he was sure to keep his distance from Julianna."

"I know."

"You know?" he asked, cocking his head, and looking her over. "How do you know?"

She winked at him. "I have my ways." She kissed his cheek and got up, heading for the door.

"You never used to have ways," he called after her.

She purposely left a trail of giggles behind her as she exited through the front door.

His head tilted in the opposite direction as his mind's eye searched for an answer as to exactly what his wife was up to.

"Come in, come in!" Penelope, the oldest elf and therefore the one in charge of all magical distribution matters, called out when Joy knocked on the door.

"My apologies for being late," Joy said. "Santa's doctor requested a conference at the last minute."

"Is everything alright?" Penelope asked.

"It is. He actually had a personal crisis going on. One that he confided in me about, when I was down there." Joy grinned. "He thinks he's cursed."

Penelope grinned. "Did you convince him otherwise?"

Joy shook her head. "I'm not an authority on love curses. So, I promised to consult an expert on the matter."

Penelope laughed. "Oh, I know who's going to love that."

"Oh, yeah, he already texted me back, on my walk over here, asking me what it was that I thought he could do about the doctor."

Shaking her head, Penelope raised her eyebrows, "Ready to get started?"

Joy took in a fortifying breath and nodded. "These rapid-fire sessions are exhausting."

"Because you aren't sleeping," Penelope said on a sigh.

"Who can sleep? My mind reels from all the information, all night long." She sat on the upholstered chair in the center of the room.

"You must stop insisting on examining everything that comes into your mind. Just let it enter and take root."

"I can't help it."

Penelope settled a look on Joy, "I understand that you've been in 'taking care of business' mode, ever since Santa took ill. But you must let go of the control, if our attempt at this is going to be successful."

"What if I drank some alcohol to relax me?"

Penelope shook her head. "We can't risk the alcohol muddying the waters. Things mustn't get jumbled in your mind, or the whole thing is going to backfire."

"Alright," Joy said, relaxing back into the chair, "give me a couple moments to meditate and clear my head, then have at it."

Penelope took a calming breath and moved to her office door, looking inside, and waving the awaiting elves into the main room.

As Joy sat with her eyes closed, softly humming to herself, the seven elder elves took their positions around the chair, preparing to resume imbuing their magic.

19 JOY SENT ME

Jacob walked past his guards and into his office, to find the subject of his eleven o'clock meeting already seated and waiting for him. "Hello, Mr. Smythe. How are you doing today?" Jacob asked, extending his hand.

"I'm slightly annoyed, but I've had worse days," the man said, returning the handshake.

Jacob's smile was genuine. "Yeah, me too," he said, taking his seat at the desk. "I'm afraid the reason for this meeting was left off my schedule. So, I have no idea why you're here, how can I help you?"

The stranger's laugh was full and hearty. "Oh, that's hilarious. I'm not here for you to help me. Don't be ridiculous."

"...Okay. Then why is it that you're here?"

"Because a mutual friend called in a favor. Even though if anyone owes anyone a favor, right about now, it's her owing me."

"Um, okay," Jacob said, taking in the slightly annoyed manner the man carried himself in. "I have no idea who or what you're talking about. So, if you could cut to the chase…"

The man looked at Jacob long enough to make Jacob uncomfortable, raised an eyebrow, then let 'er rip. "You're not cursed. You're a blessing. Without you, two young women would have died without ever having experienced true romantic love. You blessed their short lives, making them richer, fuller, more worth having taken the human journey. So, change your thinking because those experiences weren't all about you."

If ever Jacob felt like he was left sputtering, now was that moment. "I'm not cursed for having loved them. I'm cursed for having them both die on me."

"So, you'd rather they both died without ever knowing love?"

Jacob's head tilted at the question. "Well, no. I just wish at least one of them hadn't died. I'd like to love someone for more than a couple of years.

I'd like to build a life and a family with someone."

"And that will happen. But let me ask you this…" the man slouched back in his chair. "Would you have rather just been alone these past seven years?"

"What? No! I wanted to have already been building a family!"

The man's head started shaking, annoyed even further. "But that wasn't in the cards for you, not that early in life. You had an important career to build and lives to save. In fact, without the experiences you've had, you'd have never met the woman you'll be building your dream of a life with."

"What do you mean?"

The man rolled his eyes in an exaggerated way. "I mean you have a big, important life. You're the kind of person who affects those around him. And because of that, your personal life has had to happen slowly. It has to follow a certain order, a chain of events, so that you can do all the things you're needed to do. So that you could be the man those two women needed you to be."

Jacob's entire forehead wrinkled in confusion. "Who the hell are you?"

The man *harrumphed* at him. "Joy sent me to talk to you. I'm here to tell you that you already know the woman you're meant to spend the rest of your life with. But you're too stubborn over the hurts you've suffered to accept the love that could be present in your life right now."

Jacob's brow was growing increasingly furrowed the deeper into the conversation the two of them got. "What are you talking about?"

"I'm saying the only thing holding you back from the life you want, is you. Because now? Now it's your turn. It's your turn to get what you want. What you've been waiting for. Your time, is now."

Jacob tried to take a mental step back. "…Joy sent you."

The man rolled his eyes at having to repeat himself. "Yes."

Jacob's eyes narrowed. "And this is now when you tell me that I should be dating Stephanie?"

The man drew his lips together and regarded the doctor. "If you already know who you should be pursuing at this point, why did Joy feel the need to send me?"

"Joy wants to see me with Stephanie. That doesn't mean she's right."

"Joy has very good instincts about these things. If you would have listened to her, I wouldn't need to be here now."

Jacob's eyes rolled. "She's Mrs. Claus, she isn't Cupid."

"No, she isn't. I am, though."

Jacob's chin tilted upward. "…What?"

A condescending grin passed over the man's features. "I am Cupid. I've put your future wife in your path. Actually, right under your nose, most days. All you have to do is open your heart and accept love. Oh, and give it in return."

"Stephanie."

"Yeah."

"I'd have met her without knowing Erin. Our paths would have crossed."

"But you wouldn't have gotten to know her on a personal level."

"She's who I'm going to build a life and a family with? Really?"

"Yeah. What part of this is so unbelievable for you?"

Jacob let his office chair rock upright. "The part where I don't feel that way about her."

"Nor her, about you. But if you'll unblock your heart, take the walls down from around it, and let her in, you'll both sense the shift in feelings for one another."

Jacob began to question how serious he should be taking this guy. Like, really? Was this annoyed guy actually Cupid? "...And she won't die if I let her in?"

"No. I mean, eventually, one of you has to die first. But I can promise, you and she will make it well past a silver anniversary together."

Jacob was still having a hard time processing what was transpiring in his office. "With Stephanie?"

"Yes. Are you always so dense?"

"She's like—"

"She's your dead fiancé's sister. She's not your sister. Wrap your head around it and start embracing it. Otherwise, you're both going to be lonely for an awfully long time."

Jacob wasn't sure what to say to that.

The man sighed and looked at his phone, before standing.

"You're really Cupid?"

"Yes. What part of this are you not understanding?"

"Knock, knock!" Stephanie said from the doorway. "I don't mean to interrupt. I'm just here to drop Doctor Hershey's lunch off." She dodged into the room to place the plastic container on the desk.

The man moved to block the door before Stephanie could spin around and beat a hasty retreat.

And when she did spin around, she came face to face with a disconcerted looking man. "You two can continue discussing whatever matters you were talking about," she said, waiting for the man to move.

"Is that what you want?" the man asked her.

"What?" Stephanie asked, flustered.

"Do you want to rush off and eat your lunch alone? Just because you two haven't worked through your awkwardness, yet? How long do you think this is going to keep going on?"

She turned her head to Jacob, "What?"

Jacob sighed, tilted his head down, and began massaging his forehead.

"Joy sent me," the man said.

Stephanie whipped her head back to the man. "Oh, dear Lord."

"I'm Cupid."

"The hell you are."

Jacob's soft laughter broke the silence.

The stranger raised an eyebrow at her. "Do you want me to begin a recitation of every date and ill-fated relationship you've ever had, including your current mess of an arrangement with Roger, to prove it?"

"No, I really don't."

"I didn't think so."

She let out a sigh and gave him a look of such consternation that he started to get irritated with her.

"Look, I'm just going to bottom-line this for you. I'm Cupid. That guy over there is the love of your life. The timing for you two to shift from friends to life partners is now."

Her head turned to look at Jacob again.

All Jacob could do was to blink rapidly, shake his head, and hold his hands up in front of him. "I don't know."

The man looked at his phone again before pocketing it. "The two of you are way too educated to be this stupid." He looked at Jacob, "She's not going to die. She's safe. Go ahead and love her." Then he turned to Stephanie, "Loving him is not betraying your sister. She's not here anymore, she's dead. And she wouldn't want him to spend his life alone. And you? She'd be the first person to say that you deserve a catch like him. She'd bless this union, and you both know it." He paused to look from one to the other and back again, "Time to move forward." He turned to leave, but then turned back, "With each other, just to be clear." He turned back around and left.

Stephanie slowly moved to sit in her usual seat. "…That's …not …how I pictured Cupid. …You?"

Jacob slowly shook his head. "Not at all."

She looked up and stared at him.

He glanced at her, looked to the floor, and rocked back in his seat. He sighed, trying to shake off the feeling of the room, and looked back up at her, only to find her staring. So, he stared back.

She shook her head. "What are we supposed to do, now?"

He lifted an eyebrow at her, before looking away and shaking his head, ending the show of movement with a shrug, and then landing his gaze on her once again. "How the hell am I supposed to know what we're supposed to do with that?"

"I have a date tonight. Am I supposed to go on it?"

"You have a date? With whom?"

"Roger."

"Roger?!"

"Well, yeah."

"Your friends with benefits, reporter buddy," he spat out.

She didn't even flinch. "His plane lands in an hour."

"Sure," he said with a nod. "Just in time to bang you, before settling in with his family for the holiday."

"That's our understanding with one another, yes."

"Why aren't you flying out to spend the holiday with family?"

"Why aren't you?"

"I can't. I have patients I need to be close by for."

"Convenient excuse to avoid family."

"What's your excuse?"

"No excuse. Erin left too big a hole. The family is incomplete without her. If I stay here, it hurts less."

He let out a sigh. "Don't go out with Roger."

She slumped back in her chair. "There goes my lobster dinner."

"I can buy you a lobster."

"You can't stand the smell of seafood."

"I'll sit under an air vent, or something."

She tilted her head, "Jake."

His gaze softened and his voice lowered, "Don't go out with Roger."

She took in a shaky breath, nodded, and whispered, "Okay."

His whisper matched hers, "Don't spend Christmas alone."

She leaned forward in her chair. "You want me to go to Florida?"

He shook his head. "Spend it with me."

Their eyes held for a few breathless seconds before his cell phone buzzed. With a sigh, he looked down and quickly read the text. "I gotta go. Eat lunch without me. There's a senator's mom, down in the ER, with a probable heart attack."

She nodded as he stood and put his lunch in his small office fridge and grabbed a bottle of water.

He straightened and turned to look back at her. "I hate leaving in the middle of this."

She shook her head, "Don't worry about it. We should take some time to process."

He let out a breath, "You'll think about Christmas?"

She nodded.

He looked like he wanted to say something else but couldn't figure out what. In the end, he softly grunted and left the room.

Stephanie slumped and took a few breaths, alternating between disbelief and trying to wrap her mind around all the ramifications. In the end, she pulled her phone out of her pocket and texted Roger about her mountain of paperwork. It was truthful in that she did have a ton of administrative work to deal with. The lie was in using it as an excuse to beg off for the night.

20 BENJAMIN FROM OT

"What is she up to?" Santa muttered to himself.

"Who?" Chip asked from the doorway.

Santa turned to the elf in charge of the barn. "Mrs. Claus. For a woman who was up my butt, throughout my entire recovery, she sure has been missing a lot this past week."

He nodded. "She's been in a lot of lengthy meetings."

"I don't understand how much coordination there could possibly be left to do with the Present Makers Guild."

Chip lifted an eyebrow. "She hasn't been meeting with the Guild Board Members."

"Well, then the UN over trying to secure air space for Valentine's."

Chip went silent.

It was the silence that alerted Santa to the idea that he no longer knew all the North Pole happenings. Santa straightened and turned to Chip more fully. "Who has she been meeting with?"

Chip cleared his throat. "I can't be sure of all the names on the list, but I can tell you what it looks like."

"Tell me."

"It appears, to those keeping track of certain comings and goings, that she's been meeting with the Council."

"The Council of Elders? For hours on end?"

"So it would seem."

Santa's mind reeled. "Why?"

Chip shook his head. "No one knows."

Santa narrowed his eyes, "Why are you here?"

"For clarification on an order Toot passed onto me."

"What was the order?"

"To prepare all the reindeer."

"For?"

"Flight."

"And why did it come through Toot?"

"Because he was ordered to ready the sleigh."

Santa could feel his blood pressure rising. "Which sleigh?"

"The big one."

"And what clarification are you looking for?"

"Are we prepping for a trip, or are we prepping for *the* trip? Toot needs to know whether or not to take out the extra bench seats to make room for the bag. And I need to know if I should add the Christmas blend to the reindeer feed, because of the weight they'll pull and the length of the journey."

Santa shook his head, set a line to his jaw, and headed straight for the front door.

"Where are you going?" Chip asked, falling into footstep behind Santa.

"To Penelope's office."

Chip's brow line rose to mid-forehead and promptly fell out of step, veering back towards the barn. He had no desire to watch the Claus' get into an argument. His clarification could wait.

Santa walked a determined path, as curious eyes followed him as he walked. And as soon as it became clear that he was headed for Penelope's office, and them having seen the comings and goings from the office as of late, and seeing the look on Santa's face, they all promptly turned away, hurrying back to their tasks.

Santa paused at the door and decided to look in through a window. The sight he spied on had his blood boiling.

He huffed, moved back to the door, pounded on it twice, and threw it open. "What, in the jingle hells, do you all think you are doing?!" he bellowed.

In the center of the circle of elders sat Joy, on a chair, with her eyes closed.

To their credit, their concentration was so thick, not a single one of them flinched.

Penelope's incantation recitations did halt, while the others continued. She made eye contact with Santa and silently stepped back from the circle. Others closed the gap by tightening the encirclement around Joy.

Penelope's own jaw set a firm line as she walked around the circle, across to Santa, enclosed her hand around his wrist, and pulled him into her inner office. She sat him in a chair and shut the door firmly behind them. She moved behind her desk and took her seat, meeting his glare head-on, "How may I be of service to you?"

He maintained eye contact as he tilted his head downward, the fires of fury entering his gaze. "Make it stop, right now."

"If you do not calm your human frailties, right this moment, this argument will end with you back in the Sniffles Ward, waiting on another rescue helicopter. And, this time, you won't survive. So, you're going to calm your breathing, and your heart rate. And, when you are ready, you and I are going to have a *civil* conversation."

He picked a focus point on her desk to stare at, and focused on his breathing, even as he was determined to maintain his fury. After a moment, his gaze rose to glare at her once more. "Penelope. Make. It. Stop."

"I cannot. We're far past that point," she said, maintaining an implacable, eerie calm born of a woman who knew the man sitting across from him could huff and puff all he wanted, but he would not be able to blow her down.

Santa took in her façade and felt a fresh red flush of fury spread across his face and idly wondered if his cheeks would start steaming. "I won't have it."

"You put her in charge, in your stead. This was her decision."

"This was not the deal."

"That deal is eight hundred years old. And it has served its purpose."

"There was no time-limit on it."

"The deal never allowed for you to put her in charge of anything."

"What was I supposed to do?"

"What was I supposed to do?" she asked, turning his words back on him.

"Whose idea was it?"

"Hers."

"I doubt that."

"Do you? Really? Because I would say it is merely par for the course."

"The course? She's never shown one sign of jealousy!"

"I was referring to the course of being a woman."

"What?"

"When men fail, women learn to take it and do it all for themselves."

He let out a long sigh. "I merely need a respite. Not a replacement."

"She's not replacing you. And as soon as you're healed, the task is yours again."

"I do not need a substitute."

"She seems to think you do. The humans of the world think you do. And the other elders agreed."

"I don't want her to be burdened with neither the responsibility, nor the knowledge."

"She chose this."

"Only because she can't stand for so many around the world to be disappointed."

"A disappointment that she feels deeply."

"I know—"

"I don't think you do."

He paused long enough to listen.

"You don't know what it's like to absorb that much sadness and disappointment. She does. And it's something she does not wish to suffer for the next several weeks. She prefers to endure an intense and lengthy rapid-fire imbuement, rather than have to walk through the emotional turmoil headed her way."

He let out a long sigh.

"I know her ability is why you agreed to take on the task of being Santa, to begin with."

He shook his head. "At the time, she only seemed to absorb the feelings of those around her. If I would have known that by becoming Santa, her absorption would expand to the world, I'd have denied the task."

"No, you wouldn't have. You understand her unique ability to focus on the positive emotions people feel, letting their light outshine the negative ones. So, you know the joy she feels in the wake of your yearly flight has her flying happy and centered for quite a long while, afterwards."

"Can you undo it, after she gets back?"

"Unfortunately, no."

"And what do you think all that knowledge is going to do to her sensibilities? The amount of sadness, grief, and depression in the world is overwhelming. The exposure to it that she'll suffer through will bond her more closely to it."

"So will the joy, wonderment, and peace in the world, if one chooses to focus on it, as we both know she will."

"She can't be in the same room with two lonely hearts, without trying to push them into each other's arms. How can she deal with knowing who's suffering the most in the world, and knowing that it's their fate? To know a person's pain and know there's nothing you can do... it's the downfall to knowing what everyone desires most in the world. All she can do for those people is to throw a present at it and hope it brings them a modicum of joy, for no matter how fleeting a moment."

"And she'll know she was responsible for that fleeting moment. She'll learn to soak in those moments, and fuel herself on the direct difference she made. She'll learn to line those moments up, and pace her absorption, rather than have it hit her all in waves."

Santa shook his head. "She doesn't work that way."

"But she will. We've made it a part of the imbuement."

His head came up with that. "Can you imbue a filter?"

"No. But I will counsel her on how to target her focus and pick out the pieces that are most beneficial to focus on, for her own wellbeing."

"And how long is that going to take?"

"Not long, once I get her to understand that she can cheat the system by using her own mood manipulating abilities on herself."

"She can?"

Penelope nodded, "She always has, she just never realized it. Previously, it was a subconscious habit she's used to protect herself. I've been teaching her how to do it purposefully. She's already started doing it by meditating before we start each session. She clears her mind and allows calm to enter. She'll be all right. The council and I will make sure she is."

"I still don't like it."

"None of us expected you to."

"Is that why she's been lying to me about it?"

Penelope raised her hand. "She never lied, she merely omitted."

"Well, that's par for the course, as well."

Penelope smiled, "Of being a woman?"

"Well, yes, but no. Of being a Claus. I've been omitting things to her since the day I started this task."

"You worry that she can't handle it. But have you known her, ever, to take on a task she couldn't handle?"

"No. But she has no idea what she's signing herself up for. It's not that I think she can't handle it. It's that I don't think it's what's best for her own mental health. It's a battle I never wanted her to suffer fighting her way through."

"She won't have to suffer in silence. She'll have something that you've never had."

"What's that?"

"A counterpart to talk it over with. Someone who knows exactly what she's gotten herself into. She'll have you."

He sighed.

"And, the real reason we've all allowed this to happen, you'll have her. You will have someone to share the burden with."

"She shouldn't—"

"She's been feeling aimless, up here."

"Since when?"

"Since always. She came here for you, so you could do this. Her empath abilities sharpened, with no purpose for it. Maybe with the knowledge floodgates opened, it's possible that she can find a purpose for herself."

"Like what?"

"Like, we don't know what. But we're giving her the ability to expand her role and figure it out."

He sighed, then shook his head.

Penelope stood, sensing he'd finished with his rantings. "I really should get back in there. The more we have involved, then more likely we can have her prepared in time."

"I've never felt so powerless in my life," he muttered, standing to leave the room.

"Funnily enough, I've felt that way ever since you arrived. Some human coming in, running gift distribution, infiltrating our domain, and bringing his mate with him. But after I accepted the changes, I came to realize that you enhanced our village. We slowly lost enemies because we had you to liaise with the humans on our behalf. I slowly came to value your place in our world."

"And so, you imagine that I'll find my peace with this new norm, after the dust settles."

"I imagine that you both will."

Penelope opened the office door and held it. Santa took the hint and exited the room, taking another peek into the meeting room, and seeing the calm expression on his wife's face. He gave a sigh and another shake of his head, before moving for the main door and letting himself out.

"I'm not buying it," a voice said from the hallway that Jacob was about to round the corner into.

It was later into the evening, and occupants in the hallway full of offices had dwindled. Jacob slowed his pace and peeked around the corner, to see a man peering into Stephanie's open-doored office.

"Roger?" he heard Stephanie's voice ask. "What are you doing here?"

"We had a date," Roger replied.

"But I texted to cancel."

"I'm not buying it."

"What?"

"You never cancel on me."

She let out a short chuckle. "I've never delt with this kind of paperwork before."

Roger stepped into the doorway, leaning against the doorjamb, causing Jacob to strain harder to hear. "You're really that swamped?"

A helpless noise came from her, "I had no idea how much of an adjustment this position was going to require. I'm sure, once I'm used to doing it all, it'll go faster. But I'm still learning how to do everything."

"Okay, I'll give you that. But you know you could have begged off spending the whole evening with me and just taken an hour or two off for some fun."

She sighed. "I was afraid that if I stepped away, I'd never come back in to deal with it."

"I could bend you over that desk and take no more than fifteen minutes of your time."

She giggled, and Jacob felt the nearly overwhelming urge to punch a hole in the wall.

"I'm not buying the idea that you don't have fifteen minutes," Roger said, his tone still light.

Stephanie's sigh was heavy.

"Steph," Roger said, "this is me. Whatever it is, just say it."

"There... There may be someone else."

"Why wouldn't you just tell me that?"

There was silence.

Roger shook his head. "We've been doing this for about five years now, and we always hit pause when one of us is dating someone. Why accept the date if there's somebody else?"

"Because there wasn't anyone else when we made our plans."

"So, this is new?"

"Yeah, if it's anything."

"Okay, we've known each other since we were fifteen, and I know that look on your face. Spill it. What's the part you're not saying."

Jacob rolled his eyes, even as he settled himself against the wall. He couldn't wait to hear how much of the full story she was willing to try to get him to understand.

"It's... It's Jacob."

"Wait," Roger said, shifting his balance around as he processed. "Erin's Jacob?"

"Yes."

"Mr. Off-Limits, because you don't share men with your sister, Jacob?"

"Yes."

Roger started snickering.

"Shut up," she told him.

"I would, but I have to say it."

"Shut up."

"I'd like to, but I can't help it. I can feel it rising within me."

"I really don't want to hear it."

"I'm sorry. I am. But it's still coming."

"Don't be an ass."

"Here it comes," he warned.

"Shut up."

Roger took a deep breath. "I... Told..."

"Please stop."

"You... So."

"Are you done?"

"I told you so. I told you so. I told you so."

"Yes, you did. Good for you."

"Now, you have to say it."

"No, I don't."

"Yes, you do. I won't be able to sleep tonight until I hear you say it."

"Then you're going to have a very sleepless night."

"Say it."

"I'm not going to tell you that you were right until I know whether the whole thing is about to be a monumental mistake."

"I only heard three of those words."

"Out of context."

"I don't care. I still heard them."

"Roger," she warned.

"No, Steph, I get it. Okay? You need this not to blow up in your face. You need a win."

"I'm still swimming in the paperwork of my last win. I'd settle for being able to salvage my friendship with him."

Roger moved to go sit down in her office.

Jacob slowly moved around the corner and took a spot outside her office, to continue eavesdropping.

"I was Erin's friend, too. I saw what she was going through. And Jacob? He's a good guy, Steph. You deserve a guy like him."

"He's hers."

"No. He *was* hers."

"We don't share men."

"How long are you going to cling to that?"

There was a pause, and Jacob could only imagine the look on her face in response. "It's the only thing I have left that I can do for her. I'll never talk to her again. I'll never do her a favor, or warm Mom and Dad up on a subject for her, ever again. And she'll never be able to do anything for me. This is it. Adhering to a pact is all that I have left."

"*Yeesh.* You make it hard to be reasoned with."

"Yeah, well, welcome to my world."

"Except…"

"Except what?"

"Except that you wouldn't be sharing him."

"What do you mean?"

"I mean that in order to share, both have to be around to participate."

Steph said nothing in response.

"She's gone. That's not sharing that's a…"

"A what? A hand-me-down? I'm twenty-eight years old and still getting my sister's hand-me-downs?"

"You've said yourself that some of her hand-me-downs were damned good."

She snorted, and there was a long pause before Jacob heard Stephanie speak again, "You know that Santa was here, right?"

"I'm a reporter. Of course, I've heard. Were you his therapist?"

"Yes."

"And Jacob his surgeon?"

"Yes."

"Okay."

"Mrs. Claus came to town with him. She was here."

"Okay."

"She kept trying to push Jake and me together."

"Oh, geez."

"She talked to Cupid."

"…And?"

"Cupid freaking showed up here this morning and told the two of us that we're meant to be together."

Jacob could only imagine Roger's face contort as he mentally stumbled around with that tidbit of information. "…I don't have an appropriate response for that," Roger said as Jacob edged closer to the doorway.

"It's the only reason I'm considering a relationship with him."

Jacob heard Roger shift around in his seat, trying to come up with something he could say, that wouldn't imply that he wondered if his buddy was off her rocker, given that he knew Santa had actually been here. "Didn't Erin used to say that Jacob was her favorite thing on this planet?"

She sighed with reluctance. "Yeah."

"Then maybe don't think of him as a hand-me-down. Think of him as an inheritance. She's left behind her most very favorite thing, and she's left him here just for you."

Jacob figured that was just as good a moment to interrupt as he was going to get. He moved into the doorway, holding up his bags of takeout containers.

Both Stephanie and Roger turned toward him. "Speak of the devil bearing gifts," Roger said.

Jacob raised an eyebrow, pretending he hadn't just overheard their whole exchange while the food in the bags grew cool.

"What'cha got there?" Stephanie asked.

"You told me I owed you a lobster. I'm making good on my debt."

Roger started chuckling. "You're going to owe her more than that, by the end of the night," he said, standing.

"The lobster will suffice," Stephanie blurted.

Roger clapped a hand on Jacob's shoulder, "Best of luck to you, you're going to need it." He turned to Stephanie. "If you need me, call me."

"Okay. Right back at 'cha."

He left the room, but then turned back. "Hey, you don't happen to have the number of the escort service some of the big guys in town use, would you?"

She picked up a stress ball from her desk and chucked it at him.

He dodged it, leaving a trail of his laughter as he headed down the hall.

Jacob turned to Stephanie, "I take it that was Roger?"

She nodded. "He knew something had to be up, for me to cancel on him, since I never have before."

"Because you're such a planner, and he was on your calendar."

"Yeah. That, and I made no offer to reschedule. So, he wanted to check in on me."

"And knows you well enough to know that if you said you'd be doing paperwork, that he'd find you here."

"He's my friend."

"With benefits."

"He was my friend long before there were any benefits. Get to your point."

"He's not going to be jealous?"

"No. Look, we tried a relationship when we were teens. It didn't work."

"And yet, you maintained that friendship, regardless of the romantic relationship not working."

"That's the exception to the rule, and you know it."

He shook his head. "I'm just pointing out that it's possible."

She rocked back in her chair. "It only worked because the sex was that good."

He rolled his eyes. "Even I know that's not true."

"It's sort of true."

"It worked out because you both were married to building your careers and served a convenient purpose for each other."

"What, exactly, is your point?"

"That the friendship between us will remain."

"I don't need two friends with benefits."

"No, I mean you'll still need a work-husband." And then he flashed her a smile. "I make an excellent work-husband."

"Great, so if it does work out, I'm going to have to find a new work-husband."

"I'll be both."

"You can't be both."

"Why not?"

"Because that's not how it works."

"We could make it work."

She shook her head. "I'm going to have to befriend Benjamin."

"Benjamin from neuro?"

"No. Benjamin from OT."

"Benjamin from OT is gay."

"That's what would make him so perfect."

"How?"

"Because there's no chance of a real-life crossover."

He pursed his lips and gave a nod. "Suddenly I'm liking the idea of Benjamin from OT a whole lot more now."

She took the bag from his hands to start unpacking it. She opened her lobster, felt the lack of steam pouring from the Styrofoam container and glanced up at him. "So, how long were you listening to my talk with Roger?"

"Pretty much from the moment he started talking."

She shook her head. "This is why work-husband and real-husband can't be the same person."

"How many rings are on your finger?" he asked, sitting down, and grabbing his dinner container.

She smirked. "None."

"Then stop threatening me with Benjamin from OT."

21 CHRISTMAS EVE

"Annie," the President said in a tired tone, entering the living room of the White House residence.

"Yes, Daddy?" Annie answered, looking up from her poster-sized, Christmas coloring book.

"Why is there a driver at the gate, trying to deliver a bale of hay?"

"It's for my pony. She has to eat something, Daddy."

"Andrea, you do not have a pony."

"I know. It's coming tonight. I just want to be prepared. I'm going to leave the hay by the tree in case the pony is hungry after her trip."

The President massaged his forehead. "Sweetheart, we've been through this. The White House does not have a barn."

"It's just one pony. And we have extra bedrooms. We can just put her in one of those. I vote for the room next to mine."

"Housekeeping is never going to agree to letting you keep a pony in a bedroom."

"But you're the president. You can order them to agree to it, can't you, Daddy?" And then she flashed him her big, round, brown, puppy dog eyes at him.

"Don't you do it," his wife said from behind him, coming into the room.

"Don't do what?" he asked.

"Don't you fall victim to her. She flashes those eyes, you melt, and then you cave."

"I can't cave. The housekeeping department would go on strike."

Andrea got up and ran over to the window, pointing, "We could put in a little barn, over there, Daddy."

"I'm not putting a barn in the Rose Garden," he replied.

"It'd just be like a large doghouse." She ran over to her daddy, hugged his leg, and looked up at him, big, brown eyes pleading.

His wife leaned over his shoulder, whispering in his ear. "Now that's a politician's daughter, if ever I saw one."

"My fiercest foe," he grumbled.

"Annie, honey, your mother and I both agree on this one. No pony."

"But I asked Santa for one. If he brings me one, I can't kick it out."

"He's not going to bring you one. No animals. It's a rule. I even asked him not to bring you a pony."

"Why?"

"Because little kids can't be trusted to clean up after an animal."

"But we have housekeeping."

"Exactly, my point. Your gift will make their jobs harder, because you expect them to do the cleaning up after a non-housebroken pony."

"But my friend, Trisha, got a puppy last Christmas."

He turned to his wife, "I can't have this argument again."

"Well, I don't want to have it with her, either."

"Think I could staff it out?"

"I think it makes you no better than her. But if you could find someone willing, go for it."

"It doesn't matter if you asked him not to bring one. I'm the kid. I get the wish," Annie said.

"I'm the President. And I've done a lot of favors for that man, lately. I'm the one he owes a favor to."

"You said that when you do a favor for someone, you aren't supposed to expect some sort of repayment."

"But I'm a politician. Favors are like money in my world."

"Huh?"

"Somebody always owes somebody something."

"Then what you did was repayment for your presents you got when you were a kid."

He ignored the validity of that point. "Annie. No pony."

"Well, I guess we'll know soon enough. The sleigh must be packed by now."

"Annie, honey, we've been over this. He can't deliver tonight."

Annie held up her phone. "NORAD's tracking the sleigh. They said it's loaded and ready to fly."

He took hold of the phone that made it easier for the Secret Service to keep track of his daughter and looked to see if she was looking at the real site, and not some knock-off. Then he held the phone up for his wife to see.

She looked at it, "Did you revoke their clearance?"

"No, Christmas Eve is always reserved for him. It's in the treaty that we never take it away on this date, every year, in perpetuity."

159

"So, are they just going to show the tracker at the North Pole all night? Or have they found a way to deliver?"

"I don't know." He handed the phone back to Annie. "Daddy's gotta go make a few phone calls, now."

Annie watched her Daddy leave the room, before looking up at her Mommy. "It's still too late to get the pony off the sleigh though, right?"

The First Lady looked down at her daughter and hard, open-mouthed sigh.

"Now, remember," Santa told Joy, "you don't have to rush. It's more important that you get the right gifts to the right houses."

She glanced around, taking in the sea of faces gathered around them. "I know, dear."

"But you can't lolly-gag, either. Time is merely slowed, not stopped."

She was careful to note the familiar change in the energy around her, that only seemed to happen on Christmas Eve. She let out a happy sigh, reveling in the knowledge that they were all gathered for her this time. "I know, dear."

"And go with your instincts. If you start second-guessing yourself, things will start to get jumbled in your head."

It all felt so surreal. "I know, dear."

"One last instruction, and then I'll stop telling you things you already know."

She smiled, turning to give him her full attention. "Okay. Shoot."

"It's your first trip, and you only get one first. Don't get so caught up in it that you forget to enjoy the ride. Eat a cookie, appreciate the holiday lights, leave a note on the coloring book pages, and soak in the spirit of the night. It goes a long way in turning the overwhelming responsibility into a very humbling blessing."

She took in a cleansing and calming breath. "Thank you."

He smiled and kissed her on the forehead. "You ready?"

She nodded and started making her way to the sleigh, pausing to whisper something to each of the reindeer, encouraging them and asking for a bit of latitude in understanding with her, tonight.

Santa waited until she was in the sleigh, seated, and turned to him. "I have faith in your abilities. You're ready. You've got this."

She nodded, taking a good look around the sleigh, seeing if the elves had put in all the supplies she'd requested. Then, suddenly, she pointed to the dash and turned to look at him. "Is that a GoPro?"

He shrugged a bit sheepishly. "I wanted to live vicariously. I'm a bit jealous that I'm missing out."

"No criticisms."

His hand moved to make a cross over his heart. "None."

"No texting me about how I'm doing it wrong."

"It only functions as a dash cam. It's not like it's hovering above you, watching your every move."

"You promise? Because if you say you're going to trust me, then you have to actually trust me."

"I trust you more than I trusted myself on my first delivery run."

"You were a nervous wreck on your first run!"

"Hence my telling you to take time to enjoy it."

She rolled her eyes and sighed at him.

"I love you."

She smiled, "I love you, too. Thank you for not arguing with me about this."

He gave her a wink, still refusing to admit that Penelope had run interference for her. "You've got this. Now, get out there."

She nodded, resolved and encouraged.

Santa turned and bellowed, "Light the runway!"

In the small tower, Elvin hit the runway light buttons.

Standing beside him, Penelope looked on, watching as Joy lifted the reins and gave the command. She watched as Dasher and Dancer started running, and the others lined up behind them followed suit. She watched the running start and the lift off, as the sleigh then circled around the village, climbing higher, before disappearing from sight.

"How do you think she's going to fare?" Elvin asked.

"I think she's going to handle the flight just fine."

"What about the aftermath?"

"I think, if Santa can find it in himself to support her, for a change, she'll find her way."

"After eight hundred years, you don't think it's going to change the balance between them?"

"I think that after eight hundred years, their balance needs a little shaking up."

"And the heart attack didn't accomplish that?"

"Everyone needs some adventure in their lives. And this will certainly be that, for her."

"And for him?"

"If you think tonight won't be a new experience for him, then you haven't been paying attention. A little role reversal will do them both some good, just you wait and see."

Brr! It's cold out there," Jacob said, coming through the back door, into the kitchen, of Stephanie's house. He gave a shiver even as he stripped off his gloves and unbuttoned his coat.

Stephanie smiled at him. "At least you got here before the roads turn to ice."

He nodded as he hung his things on one of the pegs by the door. "Let's hope I don't get called back to the hospital, tonight."

"You're on call?"

He let out a sigh. "I'm the only one without kids."

"Are you on call all day tomorrow, as well?"

"No. Eric will take over on call service at five a.m. He's divorced, and his ex has the kids for Christmas Day, he's got them now. So, he's splitting the time with me. Margaret says her family's festivities are done by midday, so she's taking over the service at five, tomorrow evening."

"Nice! Eric will be on for rounds, and you might get away with not having to go back in, at all."

"I'd imagine they'll be a few phone calls, at least. But other than that, I'm all yours." He watched for her reaction to his last comment.

Her smirk was in full view for him. A rueful smirk that told him she was still trying to make the transition in her mind. It also told him that she'd thought of a biting comeback for him, but was putting it on reserve for possible use later. She looked up at him. "I'm used to there being parameters on your time. You don't have to put me through any kind of test to see if I can handle dating a doctor. I've been spending time in your presence for years now, remember?"

He looked down with a frown. "Sorry. I think it's a defense mechanism."

"To try and talk someone out of growing too attached to you, I'm sure. I think we've both tried that. So, why don't we put down the defenses and realize that we both already know each other's quirks? We'll save each other the grief of thinking we're breaking someone new in."

He nodded and looked back up at her. "It's hard not to think that we're starting over with each other."

She laughed at that. "No way in hell are we starting over. We've been through way too much, and I'm in no mood to repeat it."

He chuckled. "True and agreed." He looked around the room, taking in how many preparations she'd gone through. "You're still doing your family's traditional Christmas Eve and Day meals?"

"Well…" she said, looking around the countertops, "Yeah." Her eyes wandered back around to him. "Why wouldn't I?"

He shrugged his shoulders. "I guess I thought you were trying to avoid the traditions."

"No, I was trying to avoid the sad looks around the room. I miss my sister, but I have made my peace with it. My Mom, though, she hasn't. At least not when we gather. It's like the loss is glaring her in the face to see me without Erin. Tears form in the corners of her eyes, and once they start falling Dad and I both start crying, too. That's the part I can't deal with."

"Well, that's a plan I can get onboard with. Because that means we'll be feasting on lasagna and cheesecake, tonight."

"I think you like my family's Christmas Eve dinner more than you do the much more involved Christmas Day dinner."

"Okay, let it be said that I highly enjoy both. But, yes, it's true. I favor lasagna over turkey, and so do you."

She grinned. "I think we all do."

He laughed. "It's like having Thanksgiving dinner all over again."

"Which no one should mind, they're over a month apart."

"Except that they're the only two times a year that most people eat a turkey. It's just not a fan favorite."

She took a deep breath, ready to shake of the vestiges of whatever awkwardness it was that had them analyzing a shared lack of turkey enthusiasm. "At any rate, I fixed up a bedroom for you. Fresh sheets and whatnot."

He raised an eyebrow. "Are we drinking? Because I can't. I'm on call."

She shrugged. "I saw the weather report calling for black ice. So, I'm just returning the favor."

"I appreciate the effort, but there's no way I want to sleep in Erin's old room. I'd rather couch it."

"*Pfft.* Do you think I'd put you in her room, when you and I are trying to tentatively start up whatever in the hell you would call this debacle of a quasi-relationship we've gotten ourselves into?"

"Okay… then where have you put me? In your parents' room?"

"Nope. I put you in my room." She turned and bent to open the oven door, fully aware of the thoughts flowing through his head. She pulled out the cheesecake, took a slow sniff of it and declared, "This is done." She moved to put the cake on a cooling rack.

"Uh, I didn't pack for the night. I don't have… I'm not quite prepared to…"

"You can stop your sputtering. Mom and Dad have no use for this house. So, I've taken over the master bedroom. If you need clothes, I've stuffed Dad's things he left behind into the closet of Erin's room. As for anything else you might need," she said with a wink, "I'm pretty sure I'm prepared with a supply of my own." She bent back down, pulling the lasagna out of the oven, and straightening to set it on top of the stove, before shutting the oven door.

"I don't know how to act around you," he whispered.

She turned back to face him.

"I don't know what you expect from me."

She nodded. "I feel the same way about you. I don't know what the rules are for what we're doing."

"Did you say you were bedding me down in your bedroom specifically to mess with me?"

"Yes."

He narrowed his gaze and sighed. "Why?"

"Because I wanted to hear how you'd respond."

"What did you want me to say?"

"I don't know what I wanted you to say. I have zero clue where I stand on the sex issue between us."

"Okay, well, for tonight anyway, you should know that I never expect sex on a first date."

"But is this a date? I mean, it's Christmas Eve. Literally no one has a first date on December twenty-fourth. Isn't this two friends getting together due to a distinct lack of familial presence?"

"Is it?"

"If it isn't, then what is this?"

"Shouldn't something shift between us? I mean, yes, we're two friends getting together for the holiday. But aren't we two people who are trying to shift into something more?"

"What more should there be tonight?"

He let out a sigh and glanced around, seeing the light on in the dining room. "Did you set a formal table?"

"Yes."

"Why?"

She bounced on her feet, showing her first sign of visible frustration. "Because it's Christmas Eve!"

He walked over to her and put his hands on her shoulders. "Okay. Guideline number one, we're still us. Holiday or not, we are still us." His hands fell from her shoulders, and he took off for the dining room.

Her eyebrows crashed together as her gaze followed his path. "What does that even mean?"

He came back out of the dining room with plates and utensils. "It means that when we're alone in a house, we still sit on the living room floor and eat at the coffee table, with the television on. It's our thing because we both enjoy it. So, we're keeping it. It's one of the things that makes us, us."

Her shoulders dropped as she felt a layer of tension leave her body. "Thank God."

He grinned, stepped over to her, his hands still full, and drew close. "We're going to figure this out," he whispered, and kissed her cheek, before turning and heading into the living room.

She let out a long breath, trying to gather her thoughts, so she could see if she needed to do anything else before she sat down to eat.

His head appeared back in the doorway. "Did you find yourself thinking

I was going to kiss you?"

She released a breath with a smile drifting across her features. "Yes."

"And were you at least a little disappointed when I didn't, or were you relieved?"

A soft chuckle passed through her lips. "I felt let down."

"Anticipation."

"What?"

"We need to work on building anticipation. We're not going to kiss merely because we think we should, to give a romance between us a go. We're going to let it come about when it comes about. For now, we're going to act normal and open our minds to the idea of touching one another."

"Relaxing our ideals on propriety."

"Exactly."

She nodded as she took a moment to process. "Well, Christmas Eve dinner at the coffee table ought to give us a jumpstart on that."

"That's the idea."

"Except…"

"What?"

"The only thing I have to do to build anticipation is to think back to when we last kissed. The minute I do that, I immediately wonder when you'll kiss me again."

His breath caught and his eyes moved to her lips, his own thoughts traveling back to that night, as she drifted across the room, drawing nearer. She stopped when she was a breath away and murmured, "It's how I knew to be disappointed when you turned away." And then she let out a dreamy sigh, before she turned abruptly, went back to the counter, and picked up two hot pads to grab the lasagna with.

He cleared his throat and blinked a few times, staring after her. And then he saw the faintest smirk come across her features. "Smartass."

Giggles bubbled up, out of her. "And were you disappointed, or relieved?"

His voice softened, yet still reached her, "Damn near devastated."

22 MIDNIGHT IN DC

One would think, they just would, one would just simply think that after millions of homes, Mrs. Claus would have learned to only let a gift expand after placing it where she wanted it.

Honestly, she was ticking herself off with each heavy delivery.

It's not like she didn't know what she was delivering, beforehand.

And that one person who would think such things was Joy, herself, as she pushed the damned giftbox containing Annie's pony across the living room floor of the White House residence.

The whole experience was proving to her just how out of shape she'd grown in the last eight hundred years.

"Heavy, is it?" a familiar voice asked from the doorway, just before a light switch was flipped on.

Joy blinked at the change in lighting. "Just a bit."

The President eyed the rather large box down. "Please tell me that's not a pony."

Joy let out a grunt as she continued pushing it towards the tree. "The girl wants what she wants. How you deal with the ramifications is up to you."

He walked around the box once Joy had it placed where she wanted it. "I'm encouraged to see there're no airholes."

"Are you in here to reject the pony, or to admonish me about how I've handled this whole mess?"

"Neither. Annie left out milk and cookies. But I came in to put out a shot of whiskey, knowing that whoever showed up was sure to be having a trying night."

"I shouldn't," she said.

"Are you doing all the deliveries, yourself?"

"I am."

"Then I don't think it's a matter of whether you should or shouldn't.

I'm thinking it's crossed into a matter of need."

A half-chuckle escaped her lips.

He nodded and moved to pour a shot for each of them. "I'm not about to admonish you when I have no idea how else you should have handled all this. But why didn't you just go with this plan from the beginning?" He turned and handed her a glass with a three-finger pour in it and nodded to a pair of chairs in the corner of the room.

"This is far more than a shot," she said, taking a seat and sighing at the comfort of the chair.

"You're a grown woman. Drink as much as you can handle, no more, no less.

She took a rather healthy sip, enjoying the warmth seeping from her throat to her chest, to her shoulders, then down her arms. Her sigh was long as she sank back into the cushioning. "The process of making a new Santa from scratch is arduous and takes quite a bit of time."

"And you didn't have enough time to work the process, so you didn't think it was an option?"

"Yes."

"So how do you explain your sudden abilities?"

"The Council of Elders decided to do a magical reading on me."

"And they discovered what?"

"That I'd been soaking up more magic than originally intended, just through osmosis, after having spent centuries with Santa. It reduced the amount of magical transference they'd need to do, to give me his same abilities. So, I spent several very long, very intense sessions with the elders, to get me ready for tonight."

"Are you like a second Santa, now?"

She shrugged. "More or less."

"Is Santa his name, his title, or a label for what he is?"

"Yes, to all."

"What did you call him before he was Santa?"

"Nicholas."

"Yet you don't call him Nick, or maybe even Nicky?" he asked with a wry smile.

She grinned. "I did, for a long time. But after you hear everyone else around you refer to him only as Santa, you tend to adopt it along with everyone else. Honestly, now whenever one of us refers to the name, we're often thinking about our lives from before the North Pole."

The air of silence fell around them for a brief moment.

"I'd like to thank you for allowing me to see you tonight," he said.

"I felt like I owed you that much."

The conversation flowed back and forth, congenially enough, between the two, as they sipped their drinks. Both aware that the small gesture of sharing a drink was serving to bond and repair their political relationship.

"The theories and rumors as to who is making tonight's trip, or even if the trip is happening and not just some sort of hoax, are rampant," he remarked.

"I've refused to look at any of it. This is the first break I've taken since I left the North Pole. And now," she said, putting the glass down on the side table and standing, "I should get going. Thank you for the respite."

"You're quite welcome. I didn't suppose you'd be able to stop and sit at all. I hope the last fifteen minutes haven't put you behind."

"Fifteen minutes? Are you sure?" she asked with a raised brow.

The President looked from her to his watch and scrunched his eyebrows together.

She smiled. "It's only been about two seconds."

He shook his head. "My dealings with you are never boring."

"Nor mine with you. Merry Christmas, Mr. President."

"Merry Christmas, Mrs. Claus."

She winked at him, laid a finger aside her nose, and disappeared before his eyes.

He found himself smiling as he suddenly became aware that the ticking of the grandfather clock had resumed, in the quiet of the night. He turned to pick up the glasses but forgot all about them as his eyes landed on the monstrosity of the box she left behind. He gave it one last look of frustration before he headed off to bed.

Jacob was enjoying a cup of tea, while staring at the logs burning in the fireplace, soaking up the quiet of the moment, contemplating the twists and turns his life had seen as of late.

"Can't sleep?" a familiar voice asked from the doorway behind him.

He smiled but didn't turn to face her. "There's a cardiac patient struggling at the hospital. I'm waiting for an update on how well the medication I ordered for her is working before I go to bed."

Joy came to sit on the couch with him, taking up a position to stare at the fire. "Isn't this Stephanie's house?"

"Yeah."

"Where is she?"

"She went to bed an hour ago."

"And you started a fire in her house?"

He grinned. "No. We started the fire, earlier in the evening. I just figured to wait for the update while staring at it, instead of my phone. So, I told her I'd make sure it was out before I laid down in the guest room."

"I've got to say, I kind of thought that if I found you two in the same house, that I'd find you two in the same bed."

"And I've got to say, I expected you to be a bit more traditional in your values."

"Well, I am, but every culture is different. Besides, even I'm aware that the world has evolved. Values have shifted and changed, for everyone. I've also found they tend to swing from one extreme to the other like a pendulum on a clock. Besides, my values are mine. I'm not about to impose them on someone else. If you're not bringing harm to anyone else, I'll respect that it's none of my business."

"Well, you might be surprised to find us at a point where we didn't even kiss tonight."

She let out a sigh of indecision, as she stared at the flames. "You know, I've never understood why my husband always keeps himself so tight-lipped when he knew so much, until now."

"Oh, yeah? How's that?"

"Because, after spending my last several days gaining his abilities, my intent was to come in here and tell you all about the good times coming to you both. But I also know that both of you are having a difficult time trusting that there's a path forward for the two of you. You're both being so careful to pick and choose each tentative step you take with each other. And if I tell you all about it, you might not be careful enough and the whole thing might fall apart. And yet, if you keep moving so slowly, you might never get there. So now I struggle with what to tell you and what not to tell you. And, I must admit, silence seems like the most intelligent option."

He fought off a chuckle. "Maybe it's enough to know that it's going to work out and we're going to be happy."

She turned to him. "It bugs me to know that you view it as a form of cheating."

His eyes flew to her face, "She's Erin's sister. It's not cheating so much as… incest."

Joy's eyes rolled. "She's not your sister. And if death has the power to end a marriage, then it also ended your engagement. It's not cheating, incest, betrayal, or wrong in any way. It's not like you jumped each other's bones before the ground settled on Erin's grave. It's been years."

"I think I use guilt as a defense mechanism."

"To protect yourself from her."

"Yes."

"Which means you've held an interest in her for a bit of a while, haven't you?"

He winced. "I feel like I shouldn't notice her, like I have no right to notice her. And that's on top of being scared out of my mind to lose another one."

"And the longer you deny your romantic feelings towards her, the longer you can keep your hands to yourself, the longer you can single-handedly keep her alive and in your life."

He shot her a warning look.

"Go ahead," she said. "Tell me I'm wrong."

"It's not that I don't know they would have died whether I was with them or not."

"Well, no. It's that they didn't get on with the dying until you were right by their sides."

"No. It's that I need women to come with warning labels. Caution: Expiration date is earlier than assumed."

She chuckled.

"You think I'm nuts."

"No," she said, still laughing. "I'm just trying to picture the warning labels my husband would have come with."

He started laughing with her.

Their laughter faded after a moment, and she focused on him. "What if you took the guilt and the fear out of the equation?"

He let out a sigh and refocused on the flames. "Then there's no one else I'd rather try and make a go of it with."

"Once you get past this initial shift, things will fall into place for the two of you."

"You can't promise a lifetime of happiness. Bad things happen, they always do."

"Yes, but you'll be happy that if you have to weather them, you'll get to weather them with her."

"And will we have kids?"

"Yes."

"And will I have to watch any of them die?"

There was a slight hesitation as she debated how much to tell him, "There'll be a miscarriage."

He was silent for a moment. "But then that's it?"

"Yes. Your children will bury their parents, not the other way around."

He took in a long, fortifying breath. "Alright then."

She smiled, "Well, then, I should be on my way."

He shook his head. "Can I ask why you smell like strong whiskey?"

Her grin was wicked, "Because I've just come from the White House."

"Little Annie left out whiskey for Santa?"

Her grin broadened. "No, it was the President looking to fortify whatever poor unfortunate soul had been saddled with this trip."

"And did you stop by here just to chat?"

"I stopped by to say I told you so, but you were contemplative, so I set out to stop you from talking yourself out of giving this relationship a chance."

"I was sitting here, trying to talk myself into giving it a chance. Just because I wanted Cupid to be wrong doesn't mean I have the idiocy to try and deny a future that's set to be happy."

She chuckled. "Well, did I help you achieve that goal?"

"You did."

Jacob's phone began an odd, unending *buzz*, that couldn't even be described as an actual buzz. "What is wrong with my phone?" he asked, picking it up.

She giggled. "Time is slowed for me tonight, and you're in my immediate bubble. It's not buzzing strangely. We're just experiencing it in extreme slow motion. Your update is coming through."

He looked up at her, "Thanks for coming to check up on us."

"Seems the least I could do, after instigating this whole mess." She winked at him, laid her finger aside her nose, and vanished.

The phone ended the first *buzz*, then gave a normal second *buzz*, and *ding*ed.

He turned it over in his hand, woke it, and read the update. It seemed that the patient was now stable, and he was cleared to put out the fire and go to bed.

23 MERRY CHRISTMAS

Stephanie's eyes opened to early morning sunlight streaming in through the windows and onto her face. Feeling a bit toasty, she flung the blankets behind her, hitting something large on the bed, beside her. She froze, remembering the events of the night, remembering that while she had invited him to stay, she had not invited him into her bed...

Tentatively, she turned to face whatever it was that had infiltrated her bedroom and found huge, black eyes staring back at her. With a black mane and short gray fur, a rather floppy, thirty-six-inch, stuffed Eeyore was sitting there, waiting to be discovered.

She squealed and sat up just enough to snatch him up and cuddle him to her torso. He came without a gift tag, and that thought left her a little befuddled. She laid back, enjoying the quiet of the moment, when her nose alerted her that Jacob was very obviously awake and had put the cinnamon sticky buns into the oven. She hugged Eeyore one last time and got up to get dressed and start her day.

He saw Eeyore's backside descending the stairs before he spotted her holding it. He shook his head with a smile on his face just as he was placing the plated sticky buns and glasses of orange juice on the coffee table. "I see you have a friend, this morning."

She nodded and sat at her spot on the floor, placing the stuffed animal at the table, next to her.

He grinned and left the room, returning after a moment with three mugs of coffee, placing one in front of Eeyore.

She giggled like a little girl, in response. "And do I have you to thank for our friend, this morning, or did whoever made the deliveries last night bring him?"

"Mrs. Claus made the deliveries."

Her head came up, "Really?"

"Yes. She and I talked for what felt like a few moments."

"How was she? I mean, did she look tired? Was she handling it, all right?"

He chuckled. "She seemed tired yet refreshed."

"Refreshed?"

"It seems she stopped by just after drinks with the President."

She deadpanned a look at him.

He held up his hands. "I was just as surprised as you are. I'm guessing she had some political smoothing over to do and they used whiskey to calm any ire. She seemed perfectly sober, if not a little on the relaxed side."

"And she let you see her? What did she want? Is Santa progressing well?"

"She wanted to reassure us. Actually, it was more like she wanted to say something along the lines of she told us so."

Stephanie rolled her eyes, "Of course she did."

"She's yet one more person telling us to get over ourselves and give in to this relationship."

"It's not that I don't want to," she whispered.

His eyes landed on hers, with the spinning swing she took within the topic. "Same."

She took a breath, letting her gaze shift to the stuffed animal. "Did she drop off Eeyore, because it's been a very long time since I've gotten a gift from Santa."

He smiled with a shake of his head. "I had him in my car. I was going to put him under the tree, but I thought you'd have more fun if he greeted you when you woke up. And I take it from the squeal and laughter I heard, earlier, that he was well-received."

"You snuck into my room?"

"I did."

She let a small smile cross her lips. "He was a wonderful surprise, thank you."

He nodded. "I thought you'd like him. He's a bit larger and floppier than I thought he'd be."

"He's perfect for cuddling."

"Which is why I thought of it. With all the new responsibilities of your promotion, I thought you might appreciate something to remind you to take care of your inner child."

"Well, thank you. It's perfect."

"You're welcome." And then he gave her an expectant look.

She scrunched her nose at him. "I'm afraid your gift isn't here."

"Oh. They didn't ship it in time?"

"They shipped it to the hospital."

"And you forgot to bring it home?" He shrugged, "I can get it tomorrow."

The smile that broke across her face had started as a small smirk, but she failed in containing it. It grew so huge that she ended up biting her bottom lip.

He leaned forward. "What have you done?"

"I think the correct question is, what am I helping to have done?"

"I'm scared."

"As well you should be."

"What the hell—?"

"Margaret wasn't really happy to have to pull a shift this evening, and her husband is an engineer, and her three teenagers are incredibly creative. And, while it's true that I took on the job of coordinating the purchasing and setup efforts, you should know that many you work with, and alongside of, have pooled their money to get you a gift. Well, several gifts that you will never forget. A lot of strings were pulled to make this happen."

He was struck silent, watching her warily.

"You should be afraid, very afraid. While you won't find much evidence of anything right now, you will tomorrow morning."

"Margaret's whole family is coming in with her tonight, aren't they?"

She nodded, so satisfied it was frightening.

"I'm torn."

"I know."

"I really want to make a few phone calls and stop it."

"You can try, but they'll find a way around it. Everyone's too invested."

He sighed, agitation starting to take over.

"It's nothing harmful. You know I'd never be a part of anything that would make things more difficult for you."

"Then why warn me now?"

"Because I'm going to be giggling quite a bit throughout the day, every time I think about it or get a text about it. I figured it would be easier to let you know why."

"Great," he muttered.

"It's all in good fun. If you think it's escaped anyone's attention how stressful the last few weeks have been for you, it hasn't. You might take it all in stride and let the media attention roll off your back, but we know it's been hard. And you aren't arrogant in your confidence. You just calmly stroll on through life, acting as if there's nothing to worry about, acting as though none of it gets to you. And you do it in a manner that everyone appreciates because you aren't letting it change you. People admire what you're able to shake off."

"The media attention will pass. It always does. There's no point in letting it affect how I act towards others. And who I treat and save stops mattering the moment the next high-profile patient comes in. Because all everyone will talk about, going forward, is whether I was able to save whoever is on my operating table in that moment, at least until the next one after that rolls in."

"And that, right there, is the attitude that everyone appreciates."

"Do you know what keeps me humble? How I'm able not to let it affect me?"

"No."

"First of all, I know what it means to the family if I fail. So, it's part in knowing that for many of those coming to me, I am their last hope, and that's a great weight to bear. Some would adopt a cloak of arrogance to hide their insecurities behind. But I'm too close to failure, way too often, for me to react that way. But the other part..."

"What?"

"I was allowed entrance to the North Pole. And then, just a few hours later, I held Santa Claus' heart in my hand. It was the most intensely thrilling and singularly scariest moment of my life. And when it was done, I had no idea if I wanted to crack one open to celebrate, or if I should go puke somewhere. Those are the moments in my job that keep me humble, intrigued, and excited to keep going."

"And yet, it's taxing on a person. Walking the line between thrilled and burnt out can be a tightrope. And what they're working on, it's meant to keep you on your toes and be a bit of a thrill. So let it be."

He nodded. "Very well. The food's getting cold."

She bit the inside corner of her mouth, to keep herself from smiling, both over her win, and over the newfound confidence he'd just given her about the gift she'd had made for him. She picked up her fork and began eating her breakfast.

The drapes were still drawn throughout the White House residence, when a shrill scream rent the air.

Secret Service and military guards flooded the living room. The President and First Lady fairly flew into the room before agents could get to them to hold them back.

And in the middle of it all stood one very outraged six-year-old. "He can't breathe!" she bellowed, clawing at the wrapping paper.

The President turned and gave a nod to the guards and agents. "I think it's best if I take it from here," he told them.

The First Lady lunged for her distraught daughter, pulling her away from the box. "Santa would not send you a pony in a box. Now sit down and calm yourself," she said, pushing the child onto the couch and sitting beside her.

"But I asked for a pony and it's big enough for a small pony!" she continued yelling at volumes not heard in the White House since the 1812 burning. "It might be a baby!"

"Even a baby would have kicked its way through cardboard," the President muttered.

"But maybe it was sleeping, and it needs a bottle!" Annie screeched, tears cascading down her sweet, heathen face.

The President and his wife shared a look.

The First Lady hugged her daughter close.

"No one from the North Pole would send out a live animal and let it suffocate before the child has the opportunity to abuse it," the President said, right before his wife slapped his knee to get him to stop talking.

"But Santa didn't deliver it," Annie said, tears still streaming. "Someone who didn't know what they were doing brought it and killed it!"

The President's eyes shot to the ceiling in a bid to hold on to his patience. "Mrs. Claus did the deliveries, and the elves still did the packaging. They wouldn't have let an animal die in transport. If you would just open it, you could see what it really is—"

Annie clutched closer into her mother's side, "I don't want to see a dead pony!" she bellowed more in anger, this time.

The President gave a sigh. "Fine. I'll open the box. I'll see what it is that she brought."

Little Annie hid her eyes as the President finished pulling off the paper from the top of the box, and then pulled on the flaps of the cardboard with enough force to get the glue to give way. He pulled out a bag holding a remote control and an instruction manual. He quickly scanned the front of the manual and broke out in chuckles.

"What is it?" his wife asked.

"It's very political, actually," he answered.

"What?"

"It's a political compromise, I'm afraid."

"What does that mean?" Annie asked warily.

"It means Mrs. Claus brought you exactly what you asked for, while not giving you anything near what you really wanted."

Annie's expression looked downright perplexed. "Does that mean it's a pony, or that it's not a pony?"

"Oh, it's a pony," he said with a smile, and gave his wife a wink.

Annie pulled herself out of her mother's grasp, slid off the couch, went to the box, grabbed the flap closest to her and started pulling on it with all her little might. As the cardboard gave way and was pulled outwards, Styrofoam peanuts began falling out and onto the floor. And with one more, great yank, the whole front panel opened, more Styrofoam fell, and a pony was revealed. "It's stuffed!"

"Not quite," her father said, kneeling and handing her the remote. "It's a robotic pony. You can pretend to feed it, have it trot around the room, ride it, keep it in a bedroom. All the things you wanted a pony to do, without it doing any of the things your mother and I didn't want it to do."

Annie was visibly fighting her outrage.

"No one will give you a hard time if you forget to feed it. No one will be handing you a shovel, telling you to clean up its poop. No one will mind if you stick it in a closet and don't walk it for a few days. This is the best option for you."

Her mother reached out and grasped Annie's arm. "I think it's perfect for you to practice taking care of a pet with. Prove that you really would pay attention to a pony and enjoy it every day, to see if you're truly ready for the responsibility of a real one. And in the meantime, you got all the good parts, with none of the bad."

In true six-year-old who just lost a battle fashion, little Annie turned to her mother and asked, "Can we open the other presents now?"

There was a knock on the front door and Santa stood to answer it. He turned the knob and pulled open the door. "Afternoon, Penelope."

"How is she?" the elder asked.

"She's asleep."

"Is it a calm sleep, or fitful?"

"It's deep."

"What do you mean?"

"She's so far gone into the depths of sleep that if you stand here in silence, you'll be able to hear her snore."

Penelope was taken aback. "She snores?"

"Not usually, no. But when she's exhausted, she does. I could throw a party out here, with deafening music, and she'd be none the wiser."

"Would you mind if I checked on her?"

"Well, no, but why? Should I be worried?"

"If she's sleeping that soundly, I'd like to make sure she isn't trapped in a nightmare from some of the things she saw last night."

Santa's expression turned grim and nodded. "She came in more subdued than I expected. I think I preferred to believe it was because of how exhausting the night was."

"But you and I both know how a number of humans are heartbreakingly forced to live. And to see what some children are surviving, well it's not something any of our warnings could prepare her for. I just want to weave a calmness spell on the room, so she can rest peacefully."

He nodded. "Of course." He stepped back to let her inside. "How long do you think she'll sleep?"

"Well, as I recall, you slept for three full days, after your first trip. And there were far fewer people, back in those days."

"Santa?" Toot said, from the still opened doorway.

Santa gave Penelope a nod, "Go on ahead inside," he said, pointing towards the bedroom door. He turned to Toot and went back to the doorway. "I can tell by the look on your face that trouble is brewing."

"It's Comet," Toot said, looking grim.

"I know she was limping when they landed. Joy said she took a misstep on the roof of a high rise."

"The area above the hoof is greatly swollen. And it's bothering her enough that she isn't sleeping. She won't stand on it, and I can see it in her eyes that she's hurting."

"Can you get her moved to the Sniffles Ward? We have an x-ray machine. Let's get a closer look."

"It's just that, if something's broken, I'm afraid I'm a bit out of my depth. I don't want to chance making a wrong call with a broken leg."

Santa nodded. "Do we have two reindeer we can wake and get them to fly a quick trip?"

"Why?" a voice asked when Stephanie answered her phone.

"Why, what, Roger?" she asked, drawing Jacob's attention.

"Why would you send me that, and how did you get it under the tree?"

Stephanie shook her head, even as she put the phone on speaker so Jacob could hear. "I didn't send you anything. We aren't in the habit of exchanging gifts."

"Well, then, did Jacob develop a twisted sense of humor and send it to me?"

Jacob cleared his throat by way of alerting Roger that he was listening and said, "I didn't send you anything, either."

"Look, I'm not mad about it," Roger said. "I'd just rather that I wasn't set up to open it in front of my entire family, this morning."

Stephanie shook her head again. "I promise, I didn't send you anything, but now I've got to know what the gift was."

Roger hesitated a moment. "It was a doll."

"A doll?" Stephanie asked. "What sort of doll?"

"It was a doll. You know… a doll."

Jacob and Stephanie exchanged questioning looks, before she looked back at the phone, "We're not following."

"Steph," Roger said in a harsh whisper. "It was a doll to replace you!"

Jacob snorted, trying to contain his laughter.

"Well," Stephanie said, not sure what to say. "That must have been…

awkward."

"Awkward?" Roger repeated, his volume coming back to normal. "My grandmother choked on her coffee and turned damned near purple. My mother is still shaking her head, repeatedly asking what it was that I did that instigated someone into sending this thing to me. My brothers cannot stop cracking jokes about it and then they tried to set her a place at the breakfast table! And my nieces are so confused as to why Santa would send me a life-sized doll, while at the same time trying to convince me that I should give it to them to play with. And I cannot begin to tell you how pissed my sister-in-law is about that, because she refuses to explain to them the real reason they can't have it."

It was at the mention of Santa that Stephanie's eyes flew to Jacob's and her mouth dropped open. "Well, that sounds... Joyful," she said, not knowing quite what to say.

Jacob shook his head, fighting another bout of laughter.

"Joyful is not the word I'd use," Roger said, nonplused.

"Hey, man," Jacob said, "I wish I'd have thought of it, but it wasn't me. I'd own up to the brilliance of it."

"And now what am I supposed to do with the thing? If I toss it out, all the men here will think I'm an absolute idiot. If I keep it, all the women will think I'm an absolute pig."

"Is it just family there?" Jacob asked.

"Yes."

"Then you pick her up, hold your chin high, and carry your lady off to her new abode."

Stephanie snickered.

"And the more they laugh," Jacob went on to say, "the higher you hold your head up and play into it."

"Did you happen to tell your brothers about our cancelled date?" Stephanie asked.

"Well, yes, but their shock this morning was too real. Tony choked on his eggnog."

"Where do you even go to get a hold of one of those things, this close to Christmas?" Stephanie asked.

"You'd be surprised," Roger muttered.

"Did you tell anybody else?" Stephanie asked.

"No," Roger answered.

"Who could have overheard the conversation?" Jacob asked.

"You know what?" Stephanie asked. "Your father is a prankster. If he overheard you guys talking, he's the type that would think pissing off the women would totally be worth the laugh."

Roger sighed into the phone. "Are you two sleeping together, yet?"

"No," they both answered.

"Good." He hung up.

Stephanie pocketed her phone and turned to Jacob. "Joy wouldn't have, would she?"

"What? Offer him a consolation prize?" he asked with a grin. "After the last few weeks of getting to know her... I wouldn't put it past her."

She shook her head over the phone call one last time and started checking on all the dishes she was preparing for dinner that evening.

"Christmas movie marathon?" he asked.

"With wine?"

"Of course. Isn't that how adults, with nowhere to go today, all do it?"

"Absolutely."

Santa knocked on the same door of a Scandinavian large-animal veterinarian, that he'd knocked on many years before, but a different man opened to answer it.

The man took in the measure of the stranger at his door before his gaze settled on his face.

"Some years ago, I required some help. I knocked on this door, and a Dr. Lars Anders came to my aide," Santa said.

The silent man looking back at him opened his mouth a full two seconds before he was able to make any sound come out, so taken was he with the stranger on his doorstep. "That was my grandfather. He died some thirty years ago."

"But you are Dr. Frode Anders, yes?"

He nodded. "I am."

"And you treat domesticated reindeer, as well, yes?"

He nodded. "I do."

"I find myself in need of your services."

"For a reindeer?"

"Yes. I couldn't manage to bring her with me. But if you're willing to make a house call, I'll take you to her. I know it's Christmas, but her leg isn't doing well. She won't sleep, and she hasn't eaten. I don't want her in pain for any longer than necessary. I'm afraid she means a great deal to me."

"Are you... are you who I think you are?"

"Yes."

"You mean that story my grandfather used to tell all us kids is true?"

"Blitzen had a seizure. I didn't know what to do, and I showed up here on Christmas Eve, with her in my sleigh and begged for help. He didn't know me, he didn't have to believe in me, but he chose to help me. I left her with him and had to go finish my trip, down a reindeer. Afterwards, I came back with my smaller sleigh and two of the reindeer and stayed for three days as your grandfather nursed her back to health."

"A vitamin deficiency," Frode answered.

Santa nodded. "Yes. If your grandfather hadn't done the bloodwork and the research needed, and figured out what was wrong, it's something that would have eventually caught up with all the reindeer."

"Much like the news said your high blood pressure caught up with you."

"Yes, exactly."

"And you've come back here because it's familiar?"

"I've come back here because your grandfather trained your father, and he trained you. Which leads me to believe you'll be as thorough as he was. And, because you grew up with that story, it was my hope you'd get to the point of belief quicker than another veterinarian would, since I need you to trust me enough to come with me."

"Why can't you bring her here in your big sleigh?"

"The reindeer are exhausted and will take upwards of a week to recover. I couldn't ask them all to fly again. Vixen and Cupid volunteered, but I need to get them back to the comfort of their own barn so they can get the rest and care they need. That year I came here to wait for Blitzen, it set the recovery of the whole team back and it took them an extra week to recover."

Frode nodded his head and took in a breath. "How did the reindeer get hurt?"

"A misstep on a roof. The leg is swollen above the hoof. She was limping upon arrival home, but now she won't bear weight and the pain is keeping her awake. I'm told she refused her food mix, as well. When I left, they were looking for a way to move her and get her to our x-ray machine. The one in charge of her care fears there's something broken, and that will put him in over his head in knowing how to handle it. We have basic medical supplies and equipment, but that's about it."

"Give me a few moments to pack up some clothes and supplies."

"Of course."

The doctor left the door open and began stuffing supplies in a medical bag. "Come in and sit down," he called out.

Santa let out a grateful sigh. "I thank you. I'm still recovering, and this little trip has seemed to steal my energy."

Frode put a mug of tea down in front of Santa. "I was just making this when you knocked. Drink."

Santa nodded. "Imagine the story you'll have to tell your grandkids, next year."

Frode chuckled as he looked over the contents of his instrument kit, making sure it held all he thought he might need. "I don't have grandchildren, yet."

Santa took a sip of the still hot brew. "You will, come October."

There was rather loud gasp from the doorway in the back of the clinic area.

Frode smiled, "That would be my wife, Claudette." He turned to the doorway, "You might as well come on out and lay eyes on the proof of what you always called my grandfather's lies."

She stepped forward, trying not to sputter. "Well, you have to admit, for those of us… more normal people, it was a bit of a fantastical story."

"Of course," Santa said. "I hope you won't miss your husband too much, while I have him away."

"Oh, no, I understand. And I'm used to him disappearing. Our celebrations were done this morning, anyway."

Santa looked around. "You're still running the business from inside your home, I see."

"Well, we have added onto the home since my grandfather's days. But I get enough middle of the night emergencies that it saves time to have everything I need right here."

"I'll go pack up some clothes, for you," Claudette said, disappearing through the doorway.

"I guarantee she'll be on the phone with our daughter the whole time she's gathering a few outfits for me," Frode said under his breath.

Santa chuckled.

24 THE GIFT

Jacob had been following arrows on the floor since the moment he'd entered the cardiac wing. He knew they were meant for him, because they were headed straight for his office, and along the way, there were life-sized cut-outs of high-profile patients he'd either treated or dealt with while he'd treated their family members. Along the way, there were also a couple of men in black suits and shades taking up positions in the hallway corners.

He was so immune to the presence of security that he didn't even pause at the sight of them anymore. Since his security detail was reassigned after Santa went home, he just figured someone from the First Family was probably in for one reason or another.

The path led him straight to his office. And that's when he sighed. He saw that there were also arrows leading back out of his office and on down the hall. He had to remind himself of the spirit with which this had all been set up for him and stop worrying about how long this whole thing was going to take.

He did have to smile at the ridiculousness of all the cut-outs, wondering what it was they thought he was supposed to do with them after this. Shaking his head, he unlocked his office door, and opened it.

"Ho, ho, ho!" Santa said, from the computer monitor that had been turned towards the door. "It's about time you showed up!"

Jacob squinted at the monitor, "Are you in mid-flight?"

A man sitting on the bench next to Santa entered the frame, "Hello!"

"Did you kidnap that poor, innocent human?" Jacob asked.

Santa chuckled. "Sort of. His wife is giving me three days to return him, before she calls the authorities. I don't think she fully believed that I am who I am."

"You're supposed to be resting. You are not supposed to be flying through tunnels at warp-speed."

"I'm taking it as easy as life will allow. Besides, I'm taking it slow in comparison to my normal speed. I can't abuse Cupid and Vixen, after their long flight."

"What are you doing, then?"

"Comet was injured during the deliveries. Joy is still knocked out cold from exhaustion, and I needed to get a veterinarian."

"An elf could have handled the short ride."

"They don't know any vets, and I had an in with this one, sort of. Plus, I needed to feel useful. I'll rest once we land, and I get this guy to Comet."

"Is he the Easter Bunny's vet?"

The man appeared on the screen again, "Bunny? We don't have a bunny in my country. We do have an Easter Rooster, but I've never met it."

"Easter Rooster?" Jacob asked.

"Well, it certainly makes more sense to have a rooster delivering eggs than a bunny, does it not?"

"Where are you from?"

"Sweden."

"Look at it this way," Santa interrupted, "at least I'm closer to home than if I'd have gone elsewhere for help."

"Alright. So, what are you doing on my computer, this fine morning?" Jacob asked, refocusing.

"Stalling you while your colleagues finish gathering."

"Gathering, where?"

"Wherever the arrows end up leading you to."

"What the hell is going on?"

"They called it a congratulatory walk."

"For what?"

"Damned if I remember. I got side-tracked hunting down the grandson of a vet for domesticated reindeer that I had need of nearly eighty years ago, in the hopes he'd believe me enough to come to the North Pole with me."

Jacob looked around his office, which held three more cutouts, and looked back at the monitor. "Are you making this stuff up, just to stall me?"

"Nope. Just catching you up on the chaos that is my life."

He shook his head, but then focused on Santa's current problem. "A word to your vet?"

The man beside Santa re-entered the frame. "Yes?"

"If the reindeer age like Santa and his wife, then they age every time they leave the North Pole, but not while they are in there. And they've done eight hundred years of flights. They spend nearly every bit of their aging flying, landing, and taking off again."

"Really?"

"Yeah. And I think it's worth considering that Comet has not been one of the reindeer who have recently had downtime while aging, here in the States. Mrs. Claus mentioned Donner was having trouble with a hoof when Santa took ill, and she wasn't given downtime outside the bubble, either."

"Noted."

Santa grunted. "Stephanie just texted me. Everyone is in place. Put your stuff down and follow the next set of arrows."

Jacob set his stuff on his desk. "You get home and put your feet up," he told Santa.

Santa gave a nod. "That's my plan."

Jacob let out a sigh, turned, and headed back out into the hall. Though his face and demeanor didn't show it, he was intrigued. A congratulatory walk? Congratulatory for what?

He rounded the corner and was met with even more cut-outs of former patients smiling back at him. His anticipation went up yet another notch as he realized that he'd been alone in the halls for far too long in this building. Which, in his experience, could only mean that they were *all* gathered and waiting for him.

He was coming up on turning another corner, and he could feel the silence and anticipation hanging in the air, and he knew that they were all waiting for him there. He came to a stop in the hall, not quite having the nerve to be the center of a congratulatory spectacle when he didn't even know what it was that he had accomplished. It was the one thing that made him shy.

The guard standing in the corner ahead of him murmured something into a microphone attached to his wrist.

Footsteps walked in his direction, just before he looked up and saw Stephanie walking toward him. "I told them I was going to have to come and get you," she whispered.

"I don't like not knowing what I'm walking into," he whispered back.

"I know. All the fancy-smancy big-wigs of the hospital are waiting at the end of the hall, for you."

"Why?"

"You've been nominated for an award. And the hospital wants to capitalize on the publicity. But the people who work with you also wanted to make it special for you, hence all the cut-outs."

"Are there cameras?"

"Oh, yeah. Not only are they planning a couple videos for YouTube, but also a commercial for the hospital."

His hand moved to massage the back of his neck. "What award is it?"

"A big one."

He lifted an eyebrow.

"I'm just here to give you a heads up, not to give away the surprise completely."

He sighed, relaxed his shoulders, smoothed his clothes, and took a step forward, determined to get it done.

"The President is waiting with the hospital board," she warned.

He froze again.

"He's excited and genuinely pleased. Just go with it." She gave him a wink and headed back around the corner.

He took in a fortifying breath, lifted his chin, and walked to the corner and turned.

The millisecond he appeared, at least fifty people lining the hall began clapping and cheering for him. No fewer than three cameras were pointed in his direction, and all he could do was search for Stephanie in the crowd.

She caught his gaze, and raised her eyebrows at him, pointing to her frown. She then smiled as her hands moved to give him a double thumbs up.

He took the hint and plastered a smile on his face.

She made vertical circles with her thumbs still up and brightened her smile.

He forced his own smile wider, making sure his eyes appeared to light up, showing excitement for the unknown that was about to be revealed to him.

Looking towards the end of the hall, he spotted the awards case that had been brought up from the main hall, and now stood against the far wall. And standing in front of it was a woman with an official-looking certificate. Beside her stood the President of the hospital board, and next to him was the President of the United States.

His eyes moved back to Stephanie, wondering what the hell kind of award he'd been nominated for, a Nobel? As inconspicuously as he could, he drew in a deep breath. He then stepped forward, letting the energy of the applause propel him forward.

The cameras followed him on approach, and then settled around him as he came to a stop in front of the trio.

The woman stepped forward, "Doctor Jacob Hershey, it is my official duty to inform you that you have been nominated for the Cardiothoracic Surgery Foundation Award in Department Leadership. You are one in five to receive this annual nomination in recognition of not only your leadership approach, but in the results your team produces. Five recommendations are required for consideration. Leaders from three countries, and the North Pole have provided testimony to the quality of care they have received, along with testimony from the US President regarding your professionalism in negotiating through the politics involved in communications. In this light, it is my great pleasure to present to you this certificate of nomination. Further information and instructions will arrive in your hospital email momentarily. Congratulations!" She handed him the certificate and shook his hand as flashes from cellphone cameras lit up around him.

The woman stepped to the side and the President of the hospital board came forward. "Doctor Hershey, as you know, an award nomination of this magnitude speaks well not only of you, but your team, the support staff, and the very hospital itself. In addition to your patients' lives, you've done yourself and the hospital a great service. We take immense pride in your accomplishments and hope that you will accept our offer to display your certificate in our awards case, as a placeholder, in hopes of displaying your award, should you win." With that, he pointed to the case where room had been made for an empty frame, right in the center.

Jacob turned to stare at the certificate frame, lights bouncing off the glass, and nodded.

"Excellent," the board president said, and took the certificate from Jacob's hands, as flashes surrounded them once again, and stepped back.

Jacob looked down at his hand, as the memory of the feel of the parchment against his fingertips quickly faded.

The President of the United States stepped forward. "As you know, this prestigious, international award is quite an honor. It was my honor to gather the necessary testimonials and nominate you, personally. On behalf of your patients, thank you for always being there when they need your expertise. The treatment of the high-profile patients that come here seeking help has a global impact. You and your team never cease to amaze. You have the appreciation of numerous nations. Thank you for your service." He held his hand out.

Jacob reached out and shook it as flashes lit up around them.

Taking a breath, Jacob turned to the audience, shrugging his shoulders and shaking his head. "I don't know how to respond to any of what just happened."

The people in the hall teetered with quiet laughter.

"What I do know is that it's more than a little rude to have the certificate taken from me, the moment I received it. I didn't even get to read the thing."

People smiled with their laughter this time.

The board president tried to hand the paper back.

Jacob waived it away, "Nah, it's too late now."

The board president smiled with the laughter and stepped back with the paper.

"What I do know is that both Presidents up here are right. I don't get a nomination like this, without all of you. I treat and heal no one on my own. It takes a strong department, working well with other strong departments to do what we do, here. So, I don't mind sharing the certificate, and hopefully the award, with everyone at the hospital. Put it in our case. Because we've all helped to earn it. And if it's my name that gets placed on it, then I'm damn proud to represent the efforts each of us put into our jobs, every day.

"And thank you to those who put in the efforts of all the cut-outs. I'll admit to being too wary and confused to appreciate them as I walked here. But on my way back to my office, I'll be sure to take my time and appreciate the memories they evoke. Thank you all."

Applause and congratulations went around the hall as final photo ops were taken advantage of. Then everyone took their time dispersing, as they and Jacob took their time looking at the cut-outs and discussing the past cases they'd all had some hand in caring for.

Jacob finally made it back to his office, to find Stephanie there. His monitor had been put back in its place, and a small giftbox now sat center-stage on his desk. He paused long enough to give her a quick kiss before he picked up the box and smiled at her, "What's this?"

She smiled. "I maybe made a last-minute gift request on your behalf, during my last session with Santa."

"Is this the gift you were talking about?"

She nodded. "I didn't know of any other place that could make a custom gift so quickly. So, I asked Santa, and he handed the assignment over to the elves. It was delivered here because we thought it would be more fitting for today."

Jacob, not knowing what could possibly be in the box, took his seat at his desk and began to unwrap it. Inside, laying on a bed of tissue paper, was a small sculpture made in the same fashion of the Santa and Mrs. Claus holding a baby figurine he had from Erin. But his was different.

Jacob held it up to the light, looking at it from every angle. It was Santa lying on an OR table, covered by a surgical drape. And leaning over him was a doctor in scrubs, holding a heart in his hands. "This is both exquisite and disturbing."

She chuckled. "But perfect for you."

He nodded agreement, then shook his head as he looked up at her.

"It's not perfect for you?" she asked.

"No. But I think you are."

She beamed a smile. "You think I'm perfect for you? That's high praise to have to live up to."

"You already have. You knew exactly how to help me handle the spectacle they made of the nomination, on top of having the perfect gift made for me."

"Yeah, well, right back at you," she whispered. "You always know how to bring a smile to my face. Your every action towards me makes me feel heard. And no one has ever been more respectful to me than you."

He stood to pull her into his arms. "I think we need a joint New Year's Resolution."

She looked into his eyes. "We vow to let go of the past and its hurts."

"And embrace our future and all the joys there are to come with it."

She nodded and he leaned down to kiss her. Her arms encircled his neck as she rose on tiptoe to seal their vow.

EPILOGUE
TWO YEARS, MINUS A DAY AND A HALF, LATER...

"Oh, my goodness," Joy breathed as she peered at the sleeping baby in the crib.

"Am I nuts, or does she have my nose?" Santa whispered.

"How mad do you think Jacob and Stephanie will be, if I pick her up and she wakes?"

"How much do you care?"

"Not a whole lot."

Santa caught Joy's eye and winked at her, just before he leaned over and gently scooped up the newborn.

"Oh, you're so naughty," Joy admonished.

He shot her a look, "You know you love it."

She quietly chuckled as she took a seat in the nearby rocking chair. "Hug her up then hand her over."

Tiny blue eyes fluttered open in the dim lighting of the nursery, then widened as they looked up and were met with eyes just two shades bluer.

"Merry Christmas, little one," Santa whispered. "It's a privilege to be here to meet you, tonight. That's something you can thank your daddy for, someday." He glanced at Joy, "I think she's smiling at me."

"She's too young to smile."

A tiny, wavering hand reached out to bat at his whiskers.

Joy chuckled, "They're never too young to try and pull at your beard, are they?"

He smiled down at the baby, "No, they're not." He let out a happy, contented sigh and handed the baby over to Joy.

Joy took the baby into her arms and got teary-eyed staring down at the bundle. "Welcome to the world, little Nicolette Joyanne Hershey. It's my sincerest Christmas wish that you have a happy life."

"Because it's more or less your fault that she exists?" Santa asked.

Joy rolled her eyes. "Don't you listen to him," she told the baby. "Your parents would have found their way to each other, eventually. Maybe not soon enough for you to exist yet, but eventually."

Santa could only smile as Joy lifted the baby to her shoulder and started working her magic to lull the baby back to sleep. He turned and reached into his pocket. He pulled out the traditional figurine and moved to place it on the back rail of the crib, against the wall, right in the center, right where little Nicolette's parents would be sure to find it.

Santa glanced out the window and yawned. "Sun's coming up. We need to get going."

"We made this our last stop, what's the hurry?"

"I promised Frode we'd drop off half the reindeer for recovery, before his grandchildren leave to go home. It's well past noon, there already."

Joy made a face.

"Blame Jacob. He's the one that gave the vet enough information to put together that the reindeer occasionally need periodic recovery time outside the North Pole."

"I would love to blame him, but the reindeer seem to benefit from it so much that I can't."

She stood and gently laid Nicolette in her crib.

With a smile from Santa, and a happy sigh of contentment from Joy, they both laid a finger aside their nose.

CURRENT AND UPCOMING TITLES

By O. L. Gregory

Daughter of the Bering Sea (February 2013)
Gift of the Bering Sea (May 2013)
Bering Sea Retribution (October 2016)
The Complete Bering Sea Trilogy (October 2016)

~~~~~~~~~~

Lulling the Kidnapper (July 2013)

~~~~~~~~~~

The Daddy Secret (August 2014)

~~~~~~~~~~

Madam President (November 2014)

~~~~~~~~~~

Walk of Shame (December 2015)

~~~~~~~~~~

The Island Cottage (November 2016)

~~~~~~~~~~

She Waves (September 2017)

~~~~~~~~~~

I Used to Be (October 2017)

~~~~~~~~~~

If It's the Last Thing I Do (December 2017)

~~~~~~~~~~

Come What May (July 2018)

~~~~~~~~~~

The Possibility of Me (December 2018)

~~~~~~~~~~

We're All Broken (December 2019)

~~~~~~~~~~

The Hitch (December 2020)

~~~~~~~~~~

The Miracle of Mrs. Claus (November 2022)

~~~~~~~~~~

Dear Ruthie (November 2023)

By Judy Kay and O. L. Gregory

Looking to the West (December 2013)
Rusty's Beautiful Skye (December 2014)
Teddy's Drive-In (November 2015)
Sweet on Coco (December 2018)
Luke Has Faith (December 2018)
Embracing Dawn (December 2018)
Green Valley: The Complete Harper Family Series (December 2018)
~~~~~~~~~~~
The Morgan Brothers (December 2020)

Find me here:

www.facebook.com/beringseatrilogy

A SPECIAL THANK YOU TO A SPECIAL READER

When this author ran out of creative elf names and started using David and Carl as placeholders, I put out the call for help on Facebook.

Vicki Wannop answered that call and threw several names at me. Chip and Figgy thank you for their new monikers, and I thank you for the helping hand.

ABOUT THE AUTHOR

O. L. Gregory is a prolific author, passionate wordsmith, and hardcore night owl who spends her days dreaming of stories and her nights furiously typing. With a collection of over 20 published titles in genres including thrillers, adventure, and romance, she loves to provide her readers with a delightful source of escapism featuring larger-than-life characters and thought-provoking themes.

O. L. Gregory currently resides in southeastern PA with her supportive husband, teenage children, and their three cats. When not dreaming up her next story idea, you can find her indulging her addictions to crochet, travel, Post-It Notes, Mountain Dew slushies, and bath bombs.